The Mystery 101 Series

Missing Persons 101

Heath P. Boice

Book 1

Windstorm Creative
Port Orchard, Washington

Missing Persons 101 (The Mystery 101 Series) Book 1
copyright 2007 by Heath P. Boice
published by Windstorm Creative

ISBN 978-1-59092-655-0
First edition September 2006
9 8 7 6 5 4 3 2

Cover concept by Heath P. Boice
Cover design by Buster Blue of Blue Artisans Design.

This is a work of fiction. Unless otherwise noted, the example companies, organizations, products, people, and events depicted herein are fictitious and no association with any real company, organization, product, person, or event is intended or should be inferred.

All rights reserved, including the right to reproduce this book or portions thereof in any form whatsoever, except in the case of short excerpts for use in reviews of the book.

Printed in the United States of America.

For information about film, reprint or other subsidiary rights, please contact legal@windstormcreative.com

Windstorm Creative is a multiple division, international organization involved in publishing books in all genres, including electronic publications; producing games, videos and audio cassettes as well as producing theatre, film and visual arts events. The wind with the flame center was designed by Buster Blue of Blue Artisans Design and is a trademark of Windstorm Creative.

Windstorm Creative
7419 Ebbert Dr SE
Port Orchard, WA 98367
www.windstormcreative.com
360-769-7174 ph

Windstorm Creative is a member of Orchard Creative Group, Ltd.

Library of Congress Cataloging-in-Publication data available.

To Katie, who started it all.

Acknowledgements

Thank you to the student affairs profession for providing such great material; for those of you who have ever said, "I could write a book!", now you know it's possible.

I'd also like to thank Leah W., Lainie and Chris P., Nan & Larry P., Tony P., Natalie D., Teri W., Susan P., Christine P., Kim O., Katie H., Jane P., Colette S., & MaryAnne N for useful feedback and edits; my work is better for it!

Special thanks goes to Judy, Blanche, Sharon, Franca, and Jim.

Most importantly, I'd like to thank Katie, who prompted me to begin my professional writing career, and Natalie for supporting it.

I also want to acknowledge the support of Kelly C. for her counsel and advice, as well as David K. for consistently asking me, "So, what's new with the book?"

Likewise, many thanks to my friends and mentors at CCS and The College of Saint Rose... you planted a seed... I have done my best to nurture it.

And to the staff at Windstorm—thank you for making my dream come true.

Finally, thanks to mom and dad for encouraging my imagination.

The Mystery 101 Series

Missing Persons 101

Heath P. Boice

Book 1

1

In retrospect, I think that being missing is worse than being dead. Although I don't relish either, death at least, has a distinct end. A missing person on the other hand becomes an ambiguous figure who inspires fear, doubt, and breeds anticipation. Anticipation for anyone who knows the missing person, lives in the same community as the missing person, and for those looking for the missing person. In my case, I fit into all three categories.

I'm Douglas H. Carter-Connors, Dean of Students at Westmire College in the tiny New Jersey shore town of Westmire Shores. I doubt that anyone as a child aspires to be a dean of students. In fact, I'm not sure that anyone under the age of eighteen or who didn't go to college even has a chance to know one. It's not a very glamorous job. Most of the time, deans of students spend their time mediating disputes between students, faculty, or staff, serving as an unofficial counselor to students, faculty or staff, or finding better ways to work with students, faculty or staff. As I said, not very glamorous; although last year I did get to have dinner with Danny Glover before a campus speaking engagement. I got clear through dessert before I realized that my fly was open.

Until the disappearance of Jessica Philmore, I never considered ever having a role in detective work. After all, as a college administrator, the career combination is not a likely partnership. However I seemed to fall into it out of necessity. There were just too many questions that I couldn't leave to others to find the answers. Where was she? What happened to her? Was she dead? Were the disturbing events that happened on campus and in town after her disappearance linked in some way? Thus began my unintentional foray into amateur sleuthing.

As far as being a dean, I love my job. I get to work with the young people that most of society calls, "our future". Contrary to popular opinion, I think we're in pretty capable hands. My students are bright, dedicated, and have an affinity for good conversation and fast food; as I said, pretty capable hands. I'm forty, seven years married to Barbara (formerly just Connors) with a five-year-old son, Ethan. I'm the type of man who hyphenates his name out of respect for his wife and marriage, begrudgingly listens to NPR because I should, and loves red wine. Actually, I love wine of any $5.00 bottle or higher. But, I digress.

I remember the day that I got the disturbing news about Jessica Philmore like it was yesterday. I strolled into the office at exactly 9:35 a.m., as usual. The Dean of Students Office (DOSO) suite is located on the second floor of the Student Center. It's the perfect location for high levels of student interaction, which I love; and a couple of buildings and multiple layers of brick away from the president's office, which I also love. The President of the College is my boss and we have had a new one each year for the last four. They just seem to keep dying—but that's a story for another time. Since I report directly to the president, I've had my fill of the eccentricities of each president du jour. I try to keep my distance by keeping the president happy.

The Dean of Students Office, is a suite of three private offices circled around a large reception area that is governed by Mrs. Judy Wessler, my Administrative Assistant. Judy is fifty-something, ample breasted with a frame to match, with jet-black hair that casts a slightly purple tinge under the fluorescent lights of the office. Judy is extremely competent, overprotective of me, and quintessentially New Jersey. She has long nails, a gravelly voice and a Brooklynesque accent that can easily scrape paint off any wall. Don't even try messing with her.

Judy greeted me at the door as I entered DOSO,

pushing me directly into my office with her hefty bosom in my back and a file folder in my rear. She moved me so quickly, I barely noticed the middle aged woman sitting nervously in one of the easy chairs in the reception area.

"Mrs. Philmore is here to see you. She doesn't have an appointment, but in this case, I don't think she needs one. Her daughter is missing." By this time, I had at least had an opportunity to put my briefcase down.

"Mrs. Philmore," I wondered for a moment, "Jessica Philmore's mother?"

"Yes, do you know Jessica?"

"No, but I know the name." I answered. When you work at a college with only about fifteen hundred students, you pretty much know everyone's name, even if you don't know the face. Judy continued, "Her mother says that she hasn't heard from her in over a week."

"Well, that doesn't exactly mean that she's missing; maybe she's just ignoring her mother."

"You just wait until Ethan goes off to college and say that," Judy responded immediately. I stood corrected, and rightly so. Judy has a way about cutting to the quick-quickly.

I sat down at my desk and asked, "Do we have a file for Jessica?" I knew we did because Judy had prodded me with it all the way into my office.

"Right here," she said as she handed it to me, "not much in it... a couple of alcohol violations last year, but nothing since." Judy's voice turned into a hush as she placed one hand on her hip and moved the other as if she was conducting an orchestra, "...but you know the Philmores... they're part of the Brooklyn Philmores." She winked and nodded as if I was in the know.

"Who are *they*?" I asked.

"Oh my *Gawd*," Judy whispered without moving her lips, "The Brooklyn Philmores own most of the amusements up and down the shore... been doing it for years... very well to do, *very* old money." I didn't know that running ring tosses, tilt-o-whirls, and cotton candy stands were much money at all. What I did know is that these boardwalk amusement areas are sprinkled from Coney Island to Cape May, into Maryland, and beyond.

Judy's face turned grim, "I bet someone took her for ransom... or she was on drugs, or she left the country." Since Judy seemed to have all to possibilities covered, she shook her head, pursed her lips, and folded her arms all-knowingly. "Hmm," was all I could manage without offending Judy's know-it-all sensibilities. "Why don't you send Mrs. Philmore in?"

Judy turned with a, "You got it," and walked out of my office as I examined Jessica Philmore's file. Judy was right... nothing out of the ordinary. It's not unusual for a student to get written-up for minor college violations like underage drinking, being too loud after quiet hours, or even smoking the occasional joint. It seemed as though Jessica had been busted for possessing a twelve-pack of Budweiser and a bottle of Popov Vodka respectively, both within the first month of her first year at Westmire. She was sanctioned appropriately in accordance with the Westmire College code of conduct, completed all of the required sanctions in a timely manner and had not been heard of since. In the Dean of Students Office we don't typically keep academic records on file, which I'd have Judy look up later, but all in all, Jessica seemed like an average Westmire junior.

Mrs. Philmore entered my office under Judy's custodial direction, holding a Westmire College mug brimming with tea. I'm sure that in Judy's past life, she was a greasy spoon waitress or fairy godmother. I stood up, greeted Mrs. Philmore and asked her to have a seat adjacent to my desk. She was a tall woman with flowing blond hair, wearing something from Ann Taylor, Talbots, Jones New York or one of those names that my wife only buys at the outlets. Her heels were burgundy to match her perfectly pruned nails and artfully crafted lips. She clutched a designer handbag close to her silk blouse as if to guard it from thieves. I didn't mention the coordinating pearl necklace, earrings and bracelet... I thought that would be a given.

After Judy's introduction, I wasn't sure how to begin the conversation, so I opened with, "Tell me about Jessica." Mrs. Philmore took a sip of her tea, pursing her lips and keeping her lipstick perfectly intact.

"I spoke with her last week... Monday. She had an exam on Wednesday, so I called her that evening to see how she did. Sarah said that Jessica wasn't there... oh, Sarah's her roommate. Sarah Borden. I've called everyday since and left messages on her cell phone and the voice mail in her room... finally, just this morning, I called her room again and got Sarah. She told me that Jessica left early this morning... something about an early lecture. Now, it's been a while since I was in college, but I know that there aren't lectures at 7:00am. When I pressed Sarah, she became quiet, and said that she had to go. I pressured her further and Sarah said that she hasn't seen Jessica for several days. When I heard this, I came right here; I only live in Manhattan. I went to Jessica's room first, but no one was there... I thought that Sarah would wait for me... but she wasn't there. That's why I came to your office. Your secretary was very nice to me... gave me some tea while I waited for you... I just assumed that you would be here by 9am." It was a jab, said out of either superiority or panic, and I didn't take it personally. I'm never in the office before 9:30am and don't make any excuses for it. Given the number of campus programs, lectures, student meetings, and emergency calls during the night, my job is hardly 9-5.

I knew that my next question was touchy, but I asked it anyway, "So are you sure that Jessica's missing?" I was right. Mrs. Philmore slammed her mug on my desk, hugged her handbag closer, and stood upright, "I haven't spoken to my daughter in a week; her roommate keeps making excuses," her tone was reserved but sharp, "what am I supposed to think?" I was waiting for another slam, and it came right on cue. "You're the Dean," she glared, "Aren't you supposed to watch these students?"

"I try," I responded, accustomed to this question, "Let's see what we can find out." As the Dean of Students, or any college administrator for that matter, we're used to this kind of parental challenge. In the sixties, students fought against being parented by college officials and won. The courts ruled that "in loco parentis" (school's acting in the place of parents) was unconstitutional for adults over the age of 18. However, given the number of calls I get from moms and dads, the courts never shared their opinion with parents themselves.

I stood up from my desk next to Mrs. Philmore. She had a good 5 or 6 inches on me. So, I looked up at her and asked her to walk with me to the outer office where I deposited her next to Judy. "Judy," I said, "Is Jerry in?" Jerry Ricardo is my Assistant Dean of Students and coordinates residence life and housing. I needed to know if he had gotten wind of Jessica's absence. With the grace and agility of a Lawrence Welk dancer, Judy simultaneously escorted Mrs. Philmore to one of the reception area's easy chairs and answered my question, "Yes, he's in his office."

The Office of Residence Life, and Jerry's office, is not in the DOSO suite, but right next door. I turned toward Mrs. Philmore, whom Judy had already planted in the easy chair as if she were potting a delicate orchid, "Mrs. Philmore, I'm going to check with Residence Life to see if they have any information. I'll be right back." Before I turned to leave the office, Mrs. Philmore had already bounced up and moved into my wake, "I'll go with you," she said matter-of-factly. I stopped abruptly, and turned to face her, looking upward to meet her eyes.

"I'd rather you didn't," I said politely. Mrs. Philmore looked at me as if she didn't understand what I was saying. "Excuse me?" she uttered.

"Let me see what I can find out and I'll be right back." I was prepared to explain my logic further, but I think that she was so stunned by the fact that I had denied her her way, she stopped arguing; like a puppy that you cuff across the nose when they pee on the carpet. As I turned again to leave the office, Judy had already given her another mug full of tea and was extolling my virtues, "Please sit down Mrs. Philmore, I'm sure this is very difficult for you, I'm a mother of five myself. But the Dean is *wunduhful...* if anyone here can help you find out what's happened to your daughter, it's him." I smiled to myself, and walked next door to Jerry's office.

The Office of Residence Life consists of an outer office and the private office of the Assistant Dean. The outer office is staffed by Mrs. Ronnie Branch, secretary to the Assistant Dean. Ronnie is a tall, stately woman vaguely reminiscent of June Cleaver. Her very presence adds comfort and professionalism to the threadbare office filled with worn tweed chairs and mismatched end tables cluttered with brochures on topics ranging from "The Real Dope on Drugs" to "How to Live with Herpes". I'm confident that some of this propaganda has been in the office since 1974; maybe it came with the furniture. I could see Jerry, through his office doorway, talking on the phone as Ronnie greeted me with her motherly smile.

"Good morning, Doug," she said, "Did you have a nice weekend?" I had, but my post-weekend daze was quickly diminishing.

"I did, Ronnie, thanks... I'm going to break in on Jerry," I said moving toward his door. Ronnie nodded, understanding that I was on a mission, "He's on the phone with a salesperson trying to sell him new bunk beds for the residence halls... I'm sure he'll appreciate the excuse to get off the phone."

I walked into Jerry's office and sat in one of the chairs across from his desk. He made a hand motion indicating that he was wrapping-up his phone call. His tall frame towered over his desk, his torso elongated by his navy pinstripe suit. He looked like a giant in his tiny office; I on the other hand, looked like an average human being given my 5'6" frame. Jerry wrapped-up his call with a 'don't call us, we'll call you' sort of closing line and turned toward me.

"What's up, boss?" he asked in his usual congenial tone.

Jerry is a competent, eager professional about ten years my junior.

"Hey," I began, "Have you heard anything about Jessica Philmore?" Jerry leaned back in his chair.

"The other day Sarah, her roommate, called about getting a single, why?" As the name implies, a "single" is a coveted room on-campus for one.

"Her mother's here... she hasn't heard from Jessica in a week and thinks she's missing." I explained, "Did Sarah say anything about that?"

"No," Jerry recalled, "In fact she didn't give much information at all, she just asked about singles on campus. Although you know what? She didn't seem interested in being put on the singles waiting list. She said that she was calling for a friend, whose roommate was considering leaving Westmire, and asked if in that case we would assign another roommate, or leave the room a single. I told her that it depended on the time during the semester, and whether or not we had anyone waiting for a room on-campus. I did mention that we *always* have a waiting list. On that note, she hung-up."

"Hmm," I wondered, "Sounds somewhat coincidental, don't you think?"

"Yeah, I would say so... do you want me to call Sarah in?"

"Yes... I think we should talk to her as soon as possible."

"Ronnie," Jerry called from his desk, "Can you pull Sarah Borden's class schedule, please? We need to get her into the office as soon as possible."

"Wait," I interrupted, "I mean, get her schedule, but I don't want to call her in... if something's up she may get suspicious and run... Jerry can you have one of your staff go to her room, pick her up, and bring her here?"

"Sure, Doug... do you think something's really wrong?"

"I don't know yet," I replied, "But I have a mom in my office who's worried sick... enough to come directly here from Manhattan this morning. *She* thinks something's wrong, and until we find out differently, I think we need to proceed carefully."

"Only at Westmire," said Jerry, "Just when you don't think this place can get any weirder, it does." What Jerry didn't realize yet, was that this wasn't the half of it. In fact, on that sunny day just after the start of another school year, Westmire College and the town of Westmire Shores would be turned upside down when we learned that one of our own had disappeared. This is what provided me an introduction into the world of the lost; a course in life that I call, "Missing Persons 101."

2

I have a doctorate in education. Over the years I've discovered that in most situations, I might as well have a doctorate in shit. Especially when dealing with distraught parents. It occurred to me that as we looked into the disappearance of Jessica Philmore, we couldn't do it under the hawk like watch of Mrs. Philmore hovering around the office. Now, tell me how a doctorate in education prepares you to tell a mother of a missing child that she needs to leave campus and wait somewhere else? Regardless of training, it was my job to break the news to her nonetheless; just call me Dr. Shit-head.

I found myself sitting across my desk again from an impatient Mrs. Philmore, and as I suspected, she didn't take well to the idea. "What do you mean, wait somewhere else?" she asked craning down her neck to look me in the eye, "How could you even suggest such a thing? I'm not leaving here until you find out where my daughter is... she was last seen on *your* campus." I didn't want to break it to her that until we did some investigating, we weren't sure where she was last seen.

"Mrs. Philmore," I began, as if reasoning with a mama grizzly, "This is a difficult time for you..." It was natural to add, 'I understand how you feel', but I really didn't and was trying to be careful not to come off as contrite. As a parent, a missing child is one of the greatest fears we can experience. Situations like these require the skill of a police officer easing down a suicidal jumper; I played it as safely as I could.

"Let us talk to a few people in the next few hours, get some information, and I'll call you with an update. In fact, if you don't want to go back to Manhattan, we'll get you a room in town. You can stay there as long as necessary..."

Her eyes grew wider and I realized that I had stepped into a potential hot zone. Time to tip-toe around the reality again, so, without skipping a beat I quickly added, "which I'm sure won't be long." I held my breath, hoping that she didn't notice the sweat beads on my forehead.

She sat down next to my desk and inhaled deeply, "She's all I have... and until I know where she is, I'm not leaving. I'll wait in your reception area... out of the way." With that, she began to cry. In one of the few counseling classes that I took in graduate school I was taught that a person in a counseling role should never offer a client a tissue. The fear is that this act takes away the permission to cry. I always thought this was odd, because permission or no permission, a nose leaking snot like a runny faucet is never attractive and *has* to be embarrassing. Once again, I threw my training to the wind and handed her a box of tissues that I always keep on my credenza.

"Thank you." She said, wiping her nose. "Jessica's father and I are divorced, I'm all alone." I wondered when dad would enter the picture and this saved me an awkward question.

"Does he know that you've not been able to speak with Jessica?" I asked, wondering if maybe Jessica was actually with him.

"No," she sniffed, "They don't get along... and he's too busy to even notice. I usually speak with him every month or so just to update him on Jessica's life. I'm not going to call him about this unless I have to." At least it seemed as if the parents communicated from time to time which could prove to be helpful later. Now, since we were getting along so well, I wanted to get Mrs. Philmore off campus before Sarah Borden was escorted into my office. Mrs. Philmore must have detected my sense of urgency to get her out of my office in anticipation of Sarah and said, as if on cue, "I'm not leaving here until I find my daughter." All I could do was argue my point over again. I wanted to avoid throwing the distraught mother out of my office on her pretty little camel hair skirt. Now *that* would be ugly.

"Mrs. Philmore," I fibbed, "I'm sure that we'll find Jessica." I actually had a feeling, a nagging feeling, that it would take a while to figure out what happened to Jessica Philmore, "But it may take some time." Somehow she had stopped her flow of tears, and stared at me with an unyielding gaze, prompting me to utter a solution. I emphasized again, "Let me and my staff do some fact-finding."

She continued her piercing stare without saying a word and I fought against squirming in my chair. It felt as if her eyes were boring through my head. Her insistence actually struck me as condescending, which perturbed me. Although Mrs. Philmore was clearly used to getting her own way, I couldn't be bullied into finding her missing daughter any faster.

I met her gaze and raised my chin, "Mrs. Philmore, as the Dean of Students at Westmire and as a father, I am concerned about Jessica. However, my staff and I can't investigate her disappearance properly with you camped out in my office. Since I know that you live a distance away and want to be close, let me find you a place to stay where you'll be more comfortable." She continued her stare, obviously too stunned to respond, but the tremble in her lip and her silence gave me permission to continue. Without hesitation, I leafed through my Rolodex, found the number for the "Misty Dorm by the Sea", a local bed and breakfast, and dialed. Co-owner Peter Gaines picked up on the second ring. "Thank you for calling Misty Dorm by the Sea," he sung, "How can I help you this morning?"

"Hi, Peter." I said, "This is Doug Carter-Connors." Peter and his partner Patrick Sheen are eager businessmen who clearly want to catch both tourists who like the beach, and Westmire College alumni who visit the town regularly. Peter and Patrick don't know that deans like myself abhor the word "dorm" since a dormitory implies an antiseptic living space where people merely sleep and don't build community. We like the term "residence hall". I don't labor the point with Peter and Patrick, however, because they're amiable guys and the term "dorm" probably suits their establishment better than a campus residence hall anyway.

"Well good morning, Dean Doug, what can I do for you?" Dean Doug is the title that I ask my students to use since "Doug" is too informal and "Dean Carter-Connors" is closer to a haiku than a name. "Dean Doug" caught on pretty quickly around campus, and became so popular that it is used all over town.

"Do you have a room available for the next few days..." I was entering touchy territory again and Mrs. Philmore once again caught my gaze, however, the fact was that we had no idea how long it would take to locate Jessica or where this mystery was going to take us. I back-tracked as best I could, "We'll probably only need the room for tonight, but I just want to see what you have available." Mrs. Philmore looked away again, her silence affirming my intent to continue.

"Well yes, you caught us at a good time... it's just past Labor Day and the leaf peakers haven't come to town yet. Will you be needing a single or double?" Peter and Patrick were used to Westmire College booking rooms throughout the year for visiting faculty, guest speakers, and special others.

"A single will be fine."

"Private or shared bath?"

"Private, and put it in the name of, uh, Mrs. Philmore but send the bill to me." It wasn't until that moment that I realized that Mrs. Philmore had never offered me her first name.

I could hear Peter scribbling before saying, "All set, Dean Doug, she can check-in any time and the room is free until Friday... anything else I can help you with? Want to reserve the honeymoon suite for you and that lovely wife of yours again sometime soon?" Peter's intent was friendly, even innocent, but what he accomplished was my face turning a bright shade of crimson. On our last anniversary, Barbara and I got a sitter and spent the night in the Honeymoon suite, or should I say in the "jacuzzi for two" in the Honeymoon suite. I ended up so shriveled that I thought I had lost parts of myself down the drain. But, even though I thought we kept our intimate moments quiet, I wasn't so sure now. Ordinarily I wouldn't care, but frankly, I was mortified at the thought of the town gossiping about the fact that the Dean of Students at Westmire, or his wife, acted like howler monkeys in bed. In fact, I didn't relish the idea of anyone in town thinking about us in bed at all. Luckily for me *and* Mrs. Philmore, I hadn't used my office speakerphone.

"Maybe next year, Peter." I offered, "This will do it for now." I ended with Peter, wishing that Barbara and I had spent our anniversary in the Poconos, and escorted Mrs. Philmore out to Judy's desk where I was relieved to hand her off. "Judy, will you see that Mrs. Philmore gets to the Misty Dorm? We got her a room there until we can reunite her with Jessica." It sounded a little dramatic, but limited the need to discuss length of stay. With that, I told Mrs. Philmore that I would call her later in the afternoon at the latest and retreated to Jerry's office.

"Doug," Jerry said when he caught sight of me, "You alright? You look flushed." I wasn't sure if it was the pressure, or the images conjured-up by Peter in our telephone conversation.

"I'm fine. Um, I put Mrs. Philmore up at the Misty Dorm, so we have some time to try to figure this out. What's up with Sarah Borden?"

"I called Jenny Robins, the RA on her floor," said Jerry. An RA is a Resident Assistant, student leaders in each residence hall hired by us to support and supervise resident students. "Jenny said that she just saw Sarah go to her room a few minutes ago. She said that she would get her and bring her right here. They should be here any minute."

Jerry had no sooner said this when we heard the sound of jingle bells slide into the outer office quickly followed by the pungent odor of patchouli oil and sandalwood. I looked out of Jerry's doorway and saw Jenny Robins and Sarah Borden standing next to Ronnie's desk. Jenny was exchanging pleasantries with Ronnie while Sarah stood uneasily beside her.

Sarah looked like an evil biker-smurf. She had dyed her hair royal blue (the last time I saw her a week ago her hair was a boring chartreuse), which was in sharp contrast to her ghostly pale skin and all-black clothing. Her eyes were lined in thick black liner that had the appearance of permanent marker and was complemented by blue eye shadow that matched her hair perfectly. Although Sarah's deathly black garb was monochromatic, it was full of a variety of textures including denim, polyester mesh, and some sort of burlap-looking material. She was fiddling with a hefty length of silver chain that surrounded her neck and snaked down her torso into her left pants' pocket. The chain was secured at her larynx with a combination padlock. This young woman sure did know how to accessorize.

Since I didn't want Sarah to think this was an ambush, even though it was, I backed-up behind Jerry's door, and took a seat out of her line of view. I looked over at Jerry who was already walking out to meet them. I heard Jenny's bubbly high-pitched voice greet Jerry and then hand-off Sarah, "Hi, Dean Ricardo! I found Sarah and brought her over, I told her that you just wanted to talk to her, that she wasn't in trouble. I told her that you were cool." Although I couldn't see Sarah's face, I was sure that if she knew that she was about to be double-teamed by both of us, she would unleash her dog chain necklace and wrap it around Jenny's neck.

"That's right, Jenny, thanks for your help." Jerry replied, "Sarah, thanks for coming, will you come into my office please?"

As Jenny began to chatter to Ronnie, I heard the familiar jingling coming closer to Jerry's office like some ghost of Christmas Nightmare. Sarah walked in and nearly gasped when she saw me as Jerry closed the door and moved behind his desk. Behind her dark and brooding appearance, she looked like a little girl caught with her hand in the cookie jar. I stood up and offered her a seat next to mine, "Hi, Sarah." I began, "Have a seat, Dean Ricardo and I want to ask you about Jessica. Have you seen her lately?" I knew that it sounded harsh to dive right in, but if Sarah was as off-guard as she looked, I wanted to take advantage of the moment.

Sarah's eyes shuffled back and forth connecting first with my face and then with Jerry's. She turned back to me and said in a trembling voice, "Um, a few days ago, I guess."

"When exactly, Sarah?" I responded.

"I don't know," She sounded scared and the pace of her speech quickened, "Last week, Thursday or Friday, maybe? Jessica's always going somewhere so I didn't really notice."

"Are you sure you saw her last Thursday or Friday?"

"Um, yeah. Well, no. It could have been a week ago or so, I just thought that she was with her boyfriend."

"Does she spend a lot of time with her boyfriend?"

"Pretty much. She spends the nights with him a lot of times... and the weekends too."

Jerry jumped in to give me a chance to think of my next question, "Sarah," he began, "Who is Jessica's boyfriend?"

"Chris Fagan... he's a senior. He lives in the campus townhouses... number 4." I knew Chris Fagan well... he had a disciplinary file an inch thick. If I had a fan club on campus, I'm sure that he wasn't the president.

"Have you seen Chris in the past week?" I started again.

"Probably, but I don't really talk to him. He's not very nice to Jessica." A look of panic intensified on her face, "What's wrong? Did something happen to Jessica?"

Jerry looked over at me for the answer, and as the Dean, I guess it was my responsibility to carry his pass.

"We don't know anything, Sarah." I said as reassuringly as I could, "Jessica's mom called today and said that she hasn't heard from Jessica for a while. We're trying to figure out who saw her last, and when."

Despite my attempt at tact, I had clearly floored the little black and blue smurf. Her eyes welled-up with tears and she brought her hand up to her mouth, "Yeah, I talked her mom this morning. Jessica's my best friend at Westmire. She's my *best* friend." Her tears began to overflow onto her cheeks, leaving heavy black tracks. Now it appeared as though Sarah had drawn spider webs on her face with marker. I must say, the look suited her. Jerry, who had the same counseling philosophy as me, offered Sarah a tissue, which she grabbed numbly.

"Where do you think she is?" she asked, "What do you think happened to her?"

"Sarah, we're not sure that anything *happened* to her." I offered, leaning toward her, "We don't want to jump to conclusions. Did she mention going somewhere? On a trip, maybe? With Chris or some other friends?"

"No. She didn't say anything. And her suitcase is still in our room... Sarah has a lot of clothes and shoes. She didn't have room in her closet, so she asked if she could put her suitcase in my closet. I don't have a ton of clothes, so I said yes. Her suitcase is still sitting in my closet."

I didn't like the sound of that. If Jessica had gone somewhere on her own volition, wouldn't she have packed a few unmentionables? And wouldn't she tell her friend Sarah?

"You should talk to Dirt," Sarah continued. I knew that "Dirt" was Chris Fagan's pet name. I'm not sure if it was meant to explain his character or his appearance. He always looked worn, unkempt, and as if he smelled of B.O.

"I bet he did something to her," Sarah speculated, "They're always fighting, he's mean to her. Treats her like dirt." Her speech faded off, understanding the irony of what she had just said.

"You've seen them fight?" Jerry asked.

"It's not too hard to come across... they fight all the time. I don't know why they're together."

"Sarah," I asked cautiously, "Have you ever seen their fights become physical?"

Sarah immediately looked down and began picking at the black nail polish that adorned her fingertips. She responded by silently nodding her head.

"Sarah," I asked, "Can you tell us about that?"

She continued to dig at her cuticles and answered without looking up. "I never saw him hit her, but he pushes her around a lot. A couple of weeks ago he pushed her down right in our room. She hit her head on her desk so hard that I thought maybe she was knocked unconscious. But when I went over to her, he stood between us and told me to mind my own business. I thought he was going to hit me too. I was really scared, the way he looked at me, he's crazy."

"Was Jessica alright?" I asked.

"Yeah, she had a bump on the back of her head, but she said she was okay. I wanted her to go to the health center, but she wouldn't. Dirt practically dragged her out of the room and told me that I better not tell anyone at school..."

"When did this happen?" Jerry asked.

Sarah looked up with an expression of both shock and excitement.

"About a week ago!" she blurted, "That might have been the last time I *saw* Jessica."

Sarah might have remembered more, but our meeting was interrupted by a piercing scream beyond the walls of the Residence Life Office. I immediately jumped out of my seat speeding past Sarah and Jerry as I pulled open the door. Loud voices were coming from a herd of people standing out in the lounge just outside of the entrance to Residence Life.

Suddenly, I saw Ronnie cut through the crowd and run into the office, one hand on her stomach, the other at her mouth. Her pallor was a sort of iridescent green, like the strand of pearls that graced her neck.

"Doug, you've got to come quick." She exclaimed with a breathy uncharacteristic loudness, "It's the most horrible thing I've ever seen!"

3

Westmire College is not exactly what I would consider the epicenter of academia, but we hold our own. We are a small, private, liberal arts college located on the New Jersey seashore. We sit in Westmire Shores, a small town packed with an eclectic mix of artists, senior citizens, and business types who make the 1:05 minute train ride into New York City every day. The town is something that Norman Rockwell might have painted after a few drinks and a very late night of raving in the city. At first glance, the Shores (as locals and regular tourists call our town) is a picture postcard of Americana... tree-lined streets, baby strollers, people flying kites, served up with a sprinkling of tasteful gift shops and restaurants. However, spend some more time here and the Shores shows a different flavor. Kind of like a puppy that licks you one minute and then overcomes you with hot, dog breath. You're still infatuated, but struck by reality.

Like last year, on a perfect July day, a man discovered a putrid stench emanating from a pricey candy-apple-red BMW on one of our tree-lined streets. The stench turned out to be the body of a local lawyer who had been suffocated and then literally wrapped in piles of his own legal briefs with clear packing tape. Or Mrs. Johnson, the woman who always loved to sit on her porch rocker through each and every season; one day in February, the paper delivery girl who had waved to the ill-tempered Mrs. Johnson each day for a week without even a wink, discovered that the poor old woman was frozen solid. The girl stopped delivering papers after that, which I'm sure was just fine with Mrs. Johnson. As I said, Westmire Shores is cute, but odd.

But not all of our oddities involve murder or death; most involve queer events and community members. For example, every July we have the Ladies' Auxiliary Vegetarian and Pig Roast. As you may have guessed, it began as the 'Ladies' Auxiliary Pig Roast', managed by blue-haired ladies in white gloves with paper flowers pinned to their polyester blouses. However, around 1986 after a particularly compelling episode of the "Sally Jesse Raphael" show on the topic of 'political correctness', the ladies determined that they should be more inclusive of those who do not eat roasted pork on a spit. Hence, the name change, meant to include all non-meat eaters everywhere. I'm sure they don't realize that the name, "Ladies' Auxiliary Vegetarian and Pig Roast" implies that they're roasting not only pigs, but vegetarians too, which is perhaps why not one vegetarian has attended the event before or since the name change. As such, at almost any time of year, you can hear members of the Ladies' Auxiliary badmouthing those "inconsiderate," "ungrateful" vegetarians for not even bothering to be social and thank them for their gracious hospitality. Clearly the meaning of the whole thing is lost on them.

Like the town that is our namesake, Westmire College is also somewhat accustomed to odd events happening on-campus; but none as odd as the one that Ronnie was yelling about the day that we discovered that Jessica Philmore had disappeared. Although Ronnie is normally poised to a fault, she ushered me toward the Student Center lounge with quivering hands to match her voice. As I made my way to the area, I was struck by the shock on people's faces. A couple of young women were crying; most were simply standing in silence. The din that abounded a few moments ago had lapsed into an eerie quiet. There were only eight or so students there, all standing in a semi-circle next to a grouping of couches. They were facing the north wall of the lounge, which was flanked by two soda machines, a photocopier and a snack machine.

At first I didn't notice any visible reason that would incite such a visceral reaction from Ronnie or the crowd of students. But then came an odor that met my nostrils like hot, rancid candy. If smells had an appearance, this one would be dark, wet and filmy. It was an icky sweet profusion that seemed like formaldehyde-laced cotton candy. Instinctively, I put my hand to my nose as the crowd parted to let me see what they were fixed on. Ronnie was right, the sight was pretty horrible.

Everyone was staring at the snack vending machine. However instead of the usual mixture of Twinkies, milky-way bars, chips and gum, it was evident that a few new items had been added. Woven between the metal spiral coils that usually held snack items, were bloody fetal pigs, dead rats and one bloody kitten. All of the animals (about seven or so total) were interspersed among the other snacks and smeared with blood, which had splattered the ding-dongs and candy like scarlet rain. The heads of the pigs, rats, and kitten were facing the plastic window of the machine in unearthly positions looking out at the crowd with black, half-opened eyes. The limbs of the animals had been distorted, some reaching up, others dangling down, some reaching straight out as if for help. The kitten, especially, looked like a bloody beanie-baby with matted fur hanging limply on a skewer. Some of the animals looked as if they were either half-eaten, or half-dissected, showing ripped open bellies dripping with dangling entrails. Adding more drama to the already grisly sight was the word, "MURDER", written in blood (of course) on the outside of the vending machine window.

I joined the crowd, staring blankly at the gruesome snacks. I couldn't help but wonder if a bag of chips was one dollar, how much would a bloody pig go for? I was startled by Ronnie's voice coming from behind me, "I came out here to fill the photocopier with paper... the lounge was empty until I screamed. I'm sorry to have caused such a scene, but I was so shocked! Doug, who could have done this?" It was a question that was expected, one that I was even wondering myself, and a question that turned everyone's attention to me. I'm sure that the skittish crowd was reassured when I responded with a resounding expertise, saying, "I don't know." What I did know was that we needed to clear the lounge before it teamed with anxious, hysterical students trying to get a peek at the bloody exhibit. My thought was affirmed when a camera flash began clicking in the front of the crowd. It was a reporter from our weekly school newspaper, *The Westmire Word*.

I raised my hands like a politician and turned to face the crowd, showered with camera flashes. "Okay folks, that's enough. I'm sorry that you had to see this, but in order to figure out what has happened here, we need to clear the lounge." I started swaying my arms directing the students to the exit at left like an air traffic controller. My actions elicited mumbles from the crowd as they complied. "This is disgusting!", "Who did this?", "What's happening?", "I'm going to be sick!" and "What is that smell?" The only student who questioned me was the reporter, "Dean Doug, who do you think is responsible for this heinous act?" I find it endearing when eighteen-year-old, budding *New York Times* reporters use words like "heinous" and "scrupulous."

"Since I got here just before you did, Mike," I responded, "I'm not sure. But I'll keep you posted as soon as we learn something."

"But Dean Doug," Mike pressed, "Do you denounce these actions?"

"Mike I disagree with vandalism, and if you will excuse me, I'd like to focus on what has happened here instead of having this conversation with you." It was a little more than I wanted to say, but it was from the heart. With that, Mike picked up the rear of the crowd and exited the lounge, snapping my photo one more time as he left. I turned to Ronnie and was thankful to see Jerry standing by her side. "Jerry," I said, "Pretty sight, huh?"

Jerry simply stood frozen, staring at the vending

machine. "My God," he said, "That's hideous." It occurred to me that we had left Sarah in the office. "Where's Sarah?" I asked.

"Oh, I told her that she could leave for now, and that we'd be in touch later."

Although I was anxious to find Jessica, I hadn't expected that I would have two situations vying for my attention simultaneously. "That's fine." I responded, "Can you lock the lounge doors and put up some signs saying that it's closed? Ronnie, will you please call security?"

"Do you want me to call the police, too?" Ronnie asked.

"Not yet, I'd like to get security over here first and then we'll see what they suggest." Westmire College has its own security force composed of one retired police officer, two unemployed actors, and a pair of police rookie wanna-bes. In terms of protocol in situations like this, we work with our security officers first, and then make a determination of whether or not to involve the town police force. I knew that given the circumstances, we might need the Shores Police Department, but I didn't want to step on security's toes. Chief Tina Braggish, the head of our security department and the retired police officer on our force, treated Westmire Security with all the urgency of the NYPD and FBI combined. I was one of the few people on campus to know that in reality, Tina had only worked in a sleepy, small town in south-Jersey. Perhaps this is why she acted with such zeal at Westmire; she got more action here than anytime in her thirty-year career.

While I was waiting for security to arrive, I went closer and examined the contents of the snack machine. I was more perplexed over the smell that emanated from it than anything else. As I said, it didn't have the odor of rotting flesh, but of sickly sweet candy; like syrup. I looked at the machine and saw that a few drizzles of blood that had fallen on the carpet. I kneeled down, touched it with my forefinger and then tapped it against my thumb. It was sticky. Had the blood coagulated and become sticky? Is this even what happens to blood? I put my fingers closer to my nose like I had seen in crime shows. It smelled sweet, like corn syrup. I looked up and examined the inside of the vending machine again. Upon closer examination, something about the blood didn't look right. It was too red. This wasn't blood, it *was* corn syrup. Dyed corn syrup. Although I couldn't be certain, I must say that I was a bit relieved by the thought. Despite the presence of the dead animals, unless they once had red sugar-syrup coursing through their veins, the blood used in the vending machine wasn't real blood at all. The sweet syrup, mixed with the pigs that looked like they came from a biology lab, explained the smell of sugary formaldehyde too. If I remembered correctly, fetal pigs used in science classes come in a big bucket of liquid preservative that we always called formaldehyde. Whatever it was, *that* was the same smell.

About twenty minutes later, Chief Braggish lumbered into the lounge. "What've we got, Doug?" she asked, barging in like a juiced-up Oompa-Loompa. Like many of the people in our town, Tina Braggish is a caricature of a human being. She's about 5'3" tall, and nearly as wide. As she entered the lounge, I could see her uniform struggle to cover her rotund body and the buttons straining to do their rightful duty. She had bleached blonde hair cut into one-inch spikes that made her hat look as if it was resting on a pincushion. Tina didn't really walk, she waddled, which is probably why she had acquired the nickname, "Quacky." The other reason that the name fit is because she is absolutely nuts, which is probably why no one calls her "Quacky" to her face. In her wake, Tina left a scent reminiscent of Juicy Fruit gum and liniment.

Tina surveyed the crime scene and shook her head, "In all my years, I've never seen anything like this. What a waste." I couldn't tell if she was talking about the poor animals that had been sacrificed, or the poor Ding-Dongs that had been defiled. If I'm not mistaken, I think I saw her lick her lips.

"Ronnie found it about a half hour ago." I said. Tina

stepped closer to the vending machine and inspected its contents. She stood on her tiptoes, peering at the kitten that was at the top and then crouched down to inspect the pigs and the rats in between. Since Tina was silent, I felt the need to speak, "I don't think that's blood. I think it might be corn syrup."

"I think you're right," Tina responded not looking at me, "Blood's not nearly this vibrant. Who's the vending company?"

"Oceanside Vending."

"Do you know the delivery guy?"

"I don't," I responded, "But I'm sure that Judy does. Since my office manages the vending contract, Judy has regular interaction with the delivery guys and the company."

"Ok," Tina said as she pulled herself up, "I'll need to talk to her for my report."

"How'd they get in there?" I asked. It was a rhetorical question and I didn't expect an answer.

"Well, at first glance, the casing of the machine doesn't look like it was tampered with. And it doesn't appear as though they pulled the machine away from the wall and went in from the back." Tina said with an annoying air of expertise.

"How can you tell?" I asked.

"If you moved a machine of this size, you'd leave skid marks on the carpet." Both of us looked down. She was right, no marks at all. Tina began again, "So, someone must have had a key, unless the delivery guy did it himself, which I doubt. That's why I'll need to talk to him. I'll talk to the professors in the biology lab, too. The pigs look like the ones used in dissections, don't you think? And I bet the rats were also used in experiments of some kind."

"Right. But what about the kitten?" I asked.

"Not sure." Tina said taking off her hat and scratching her spiky locks, "Could be a stray that was found dead. Could be animal cruelty. We'll have to look into that."

"Should we call the police?" I asked.

"I don't think it's necessary, Doug," Tina responded sincerely, "Tampering with a vending machine on campus isn't exactly big time crime. Most likely, the animals were already dead and the blood is fake. Looks to me like we've got ourselves a messy, distasteful prank. And since the vending company contracts with the College, we're responsible for the vending machine and its contents under a contractual obligation. You double-check the contract to see if I'm right. So, until we find the perpetrators, we're responsible for the damages," Quacky scratched her head, "But, when we find them, I suggest we make them make restitution. It's an expensive machine... and a lot of wasted food." With that, Tina's eyes lowered and I could have sworn that I heard a little prayer.

Despite her quirkiness, I trusted Quacky. She was right. We didn't have much of a crime, just a big violation of the Student Code of Conduct, and that was my jurisdiction, not a job for the Westmire Shores PD. "What do you make of the 'murder' scrawl?" I asked, "Part of the prank?"

"That'd be my guess. Adds more drama. Might cause more fear."

"What do you think it means?"

"Well, it's probably referring to the dead animals."

"You don't think it's announcing things to come do you?" I asked. It was dramatic, but warranted discussion.

"I doubt it, Doug. If it was real blood, or body parts, human that is, this would be a different story. But right now, I think what you see is what you get." Tina began jotting notes on a steno pad, "I'm going to have one of my guys come over and take pictures and I'll write up the initial report. Once I find out from Judy who stocks this machine, I'll talk to him. We won't be able to clean up this mess until then."

I escorted Tina back to my office to find it buzzing like a hive. People who don't know might think of the Dean of Students Office at a college is a pristine sanctum. In my experience, this couldn't be further from the truth. It's more like a combination of Mission Control, a house of worship, and a pizza joint. People come from all over campus to connect, share news, get information, complain, and sometimes even eat their lunch. I must confess that I find great comfort in this. Even though I don't enjoy attention personally, it's nice to be responsible for the center of activity on-campus. It makes me feel like I'm doing a good job.

Judy was standing beside her desk, with both hands resting on her heaving chest; beside her stood Ronnie, Jerry, and a gaggle of students all discussing the morning's events. Given the din, I'm surprised that anyone could hear the phone ring. As I entered, all eyes once again turned to me. Judy stood still as if her feet were bolted to the floor, "Oh my God, Doug, what happened? Ronnie and Jerry just told me everything!" As Dean of Students, I'm very used to being asked questions when people already know the answers. I suppose it's the job of any figurehead.

"Well," I began, "We're looking into it. Although it's messy, it doesn't seem quite as bad as we initially thought..." Judy interrupted, "But what do you mean, they said that there is blood and dead animals everywhere!"

"Not really," I said patiently, "Like I said, it's shocking at first, but it doesn't look as if the blood is real, and Tina thinks that the animals were already dead; maybe from the biology lab." Tina nodded her head and smiled, reveling in her expertise. Judy interrupted again; she was like a pit bull when she had something on her mind. "But what about the dead puppies?" she blurted. Ah, the rumor mill was busily at work, and fast too. I had to chuckle, "There are no puppies. Like I said, we don't think that animals were sacrificed here, it seems to be a prank." I wanted to end the interrogation there, and I knew the only way to do this with Judy was to involve her in another aspect of the hysteria.

"Judy," I asked, "Tina wants to ask you about the vending company. Why don't you go into my office where you can have some privacy?" This time, Jerry butted in, "Ah, Doug? I need to talk to you in your office first."

Ronnie took control, "Judy, why don't you and Chief

Braggish go next door to my office. I'll stay here and cover the office. Doug, you and Jerry go and talk." I looked around the office, many of the students had left, and the few who remained were now talking intently with each other. Except for Jenny Robins, the RA who brought Sarah Borden to see us earlier in the morning. I hadn't noticed her before. She was standing uneasily, hands fiddling with her book bag, her eyes looking beseechingly at Jerry and me. She looked as if she was about to burst, I couldn't help but ask, "Jenny, is everything alright?" She took that as an invitation to run over to us. She moved as if she had some sort of propeller attached to her behind. She was clearly nervous and her eyes welled-up with tears. She didn't say anything, but stared at Jerry.

"That's what I want to talk to you about." Jerry said. "Can we go in your office?"

I walked into my office and moved toward my desk. Jenny and Jerry took seats across from me. "What's the matter?" I asked. Jenny looked at Jerry for an affirmation.

"Jenny may have some information relevant to Jessica Philmore. Go ahead, Jenny, tell Dean Doug what you told me." He looked both nervous and a little skeptical.

"I'm sorry that I didn't tell you earlier," Jenny started, eyes bouncing from mine to Jerry's, "But I didn't know about Jessica until after I brought Sarah here. I would have said something, but I didn't *know*."

"It's ok," I reassured her, "What's wrong?"

"Well, I just never thought it was important to tell anyone. Until now, I mean. I can't believe that Jessica's missing!"

Jerry was becoming impatient, "Jenny, just tell Dean Doug."

"Well, Sarah and Jessica don't get along. Jessica tries, but Sarah hates her. She barely even talks to Jessica. And last week, Jessica came to see me because she was upset."

"Why?" I asked.

"Well, Jessica was upset, and pretty scared. She tried to talk to Sarah to see if they could work things out, you know, like I tell all of my residents." Jenny's chatter became more high-pitched and quicker so, even though she was beginning to ramble, I knew that the punch line was coming quickly. "Like Dean Ricardo always tells us," she looked over to Jerry, "encourage our residents to work out their problems on their own, and then come to the residence life staff if there is a problem."

"But what happened?" I persisted.

"Well, Jessica tried to talk to Sarah, but Sarah wouldn't listen. She ignored Jessica, became very quiet, and then just started chanting!" With that, Jenny looked relieved to have finally said what she needed to say, but I still didn't understand.

"Chanting?" I repeated.

"Yes!" Jenny repeated, "Chanting! Jessica said that Sarah put a spell on her!"

"A spell?" I asked. I still didn't get it.

"Yes!" Jenny almost yelled, "A spell! Sarah Borden is a witch!"

4

I must say that I wasn't surprised to learn that Sarah Borden's personality matched her look. She had lied to us. Although Sarah cried that Jessica Philmore was her *best* friend, her Resident Assistant told a different side of the story. According to Jenny, the last time she saw Jessica was *over* a week ago when Jessica complained about Sarah casting a spell on her. I was more concerned about the lying than I was about the revelation that Sarah was a self-proclaimed witch. Perhaps just because I've had a lot of experience with students telling various forms the truth over the years, but I had never encountered a practicing witch that I could remember. Why hadn't Sarah told us the truth? Did she know more about Jessica's disappearance?

I was glad to have Chief Tina "Quacky" Braggish hot on the case of the carnage in the vending machine, so I could focus my attention back on Jessica Philmore. From what we knew, she had been missing for at least a week, and I was beginning to feel a real sense of grimness that I didn't like. Although we needed to speak with Sarah again soon, I also wanted to talk with Jessica's boyfriend, "Dirt" Fagan (I never before realized that Westmire was infamous for nicknames). Now that Sarah's credibility was shaken, perhaps Dirt didn't throw Jessica around as Sarah had accused. Maybe Jessica was hiding out with him trying to flee from the wicked witch of Westmire? I waited patiently at my desk, shuffling papers around from one spot to another and leafing through Dirt's substantial disciplinary file while Jerry went to pull him out of class. We don't pull someone out of the middle of a class often, but given the circumstances, it seemed warranted.

The file on my desk was bright red, and as thick as a

small novel. A while back, Judy had taken the initiative to make all disciplinary files red so they could be easily found on my desk. I'm sure that subconsciously there was another reason for her color choice, the Scarlet Letter, perhaps, or "code red". Nonetheless, the system worked and everyone in the office knew that it was not a good thing to have a "red folder". Even Miss Bettie, the building's head custodian often quipped about the stack of "red folders" on my desk.

As I flipped through the pages, I felt like a superhero looking at the dark past of my arch nemesis, "Dirt". He had a rich history both on and off-campus, and I had a paper trail of residence life incident reports and off-campus police reports to prove it. It often comes as a shock to students at Westmire that their off-campus conduct is subject to on-campus disciplinary action. It was a deal that was struck with the local community several years ago, before I arrived, when there was an outpouring of cries from the community that Westmire students were creating havoc off-campus. As a dean, it is a concept that makes perfect sense. The idea is that Westmire students don't stop being Westmire students when they leave campus. So, whenever a student gets into trouble off-campus for illegal drinking, possession of drugs, assault or similar actions, the local police forward a copy of the police report to me. In turn, I treat the incident as if it occurred on-campus and file appropriate charges under the student code of conduct.

Dirt was no stranger to my office. I had met with him throughout his college career to discuss a few alcohol violations here, some vandalism there, sprinkled with some verbal harassment, and minor theft. Although Dirt had multiple violations, there was nothing so substantial that ever warranted a suspension or expulsion from the College. Although the local police had once mentioned Dirt as a suspect in a rash of small time convenience store robberies, they never had any evidence to move the case forward. Whenever he was called in to meet with me, Dirt was always mildly belligerent, defensive, and gritty; but was he the kind of guy who would actually do something horrible to Jessica Philmore?

I looked up with a start to find Judy standing in the doorway.

"Mrs. Philmore just called. Any word?"

"No," I said gravely, "nothing yet. We're waiting for Chris Fagan now, and then we have to talk to Sarah Borden again by the end of the day. What'd you tell Mrs. Philmore?"

"I said that you were in meetings about Jessica all day and that you were giving this top priority. I told her that either you or I would call her by the end of the day with an update." It was times like this that reminded me how great Judy was. She always had my back.

"Thank you for that." I said, "I will call her by the end of the day, I'm just hoping that I have something to tell her." Judy turned around to leave, and I stopped her.

"Judy?"

She turned on her heel and looked at me, "Do you need something else?"

"No, I don't need anything, I just want to say thank you. You're the best."

Judy tipped her head, and looked at me over the top of her glasses, smiling, "Flattery will get you *everywhay-uh*." She exited the doorway, but quickly put her head back in.

"Jerry and Chris are here." She said, "And Chris doesn't look happy."

"Oh, great. Send them in, please."

"You got it."

Judy was right, Chris did not look happy. He also looked like he hadn't seen a shower in days. Although he always had a grungy look, he had moved from grunge to garbage pail. He was a slender almost frail kid who seemed a bit taller than he actually was. He wore skin-tight jeans that had once been blue, but were now a worn sandy color dappled with grease stains. They were ripped and torn beyond fashionable and sat atop dusty black cowboy boots. He had an untucked flannel shirt creeping out from beneath a denim jacket that was adorned with at least 50 safety pins. The collar of the jacket was flipped up to protect his delicate neck. Dirt's face was chiseled, pale, patched with dark stubble and framed by dark, greasy shoulder-length hair. Today, Dirt also sported quite a shiner on his left eye. He swaggered into my office and took his customary seat. Jerry, who had a look of exasperation, followed.

Dirt started the conversation, so I didn't have to, "I'm barely passing that class," he said without making eye contact, "If I fail, I'm blaming you." There were no pleasantries necessary here, and I was happy to jump right in.

"Chris," I began, not giving him the satisfaction of using his nickname, "we don't usually call people out of class, but this is important. When was the last time that you saw Jessica Philmore?" He looked up at me through a veil of hair, "Why?" he asked quickly. I could actually sense fear in his voice, which was not usual for Dirt.

I had to play this one rough, "I asked you a question," I responded. Dirt looked me right in the eye and swallowed hard, "About a week." he said grimly. I could tell that he was scared, but I wasn't yet sure why.

I started again, "It seems that no one has seen Jessica for about a week. It also seems as though you were the last person to see her." I was shocked to see Dirt's lower lip begin to tremble. He threw a hand up to cover it, and began feasting on the tip of a finger. Jerry and I stayed still, staring at him. Clearly, Dirt knew something.

Suddenly, he shot up from his chair and began pacing around the office. Next, he began banging his forehead against his closed fist, "I knew it, I knew it, I knew it," he repeated through clenched teeth. He grabbed the back of the chair he had been sitting in, and leaned closer to my desk, "I love Jessica." He said, "I *love* her. I didn't do anything to her!"

"Chris," I replied, "I didn't suggest that you did anything to her."

"But you were thinking it." He turned to Jerry, "And so were you!" Jerry looked stunned, not knowing what to say. Chris began again, "I knew this was going to happen. From the minute she was missing, I knew that you'd blame me."

"Blame you for what?" I asked.

"For her disappearance. Don't you think I've been worried? Don't you think I've been looking for her? I've looked everywhere. She's gone... just gone." I was happy that Dirt cracked quickly, but stunned by the reality that he was confirming Jessica's disappearance.

"Chris," I said, "When did you see Jessica last? Tell us what you know."

"It was a week yesterday. Last Tuesday we had a fight. She was upset and took off in her car. I didn't think anything of it because Wednesday morning I saw her car back in the usual lot. I knew that she was mad at me, so I didn't worry when I didn't hear from her. But by last Sunday, when I hadn't seen her on-campus, I went by her room. That's when her crazy roommate said that she was gone. No one's seen her. She hasn't answered her cell phone. She hasn't even e-mailed anyone. I was hoping that she went home or something."

"No, her mother was here today. That's how we knew. Chris, why didn't you let us know?"

"I was going to. At first I just thought that Jess was avoiding me... but as time passed, I got scared. I don't have a great history on this campus; I was worried that I'd be blamed. I really didn't get worried until a day or so ago... like I said, I thought she was just ignoring me. Then I thought that maybe she went home. I couldn't exactly call there... her mother hates me."

"Would she have gone anywhere else?" I asked, "Her father's house maybe?"

"No. Jess hasn't talked to her father since the divorce.

That was almost five years ago. My God, she's gone. She's gone. I bet that crazy bitch roommate had something to do with it! Why are you bothering me? She's the crazy one! She thinks she's a friggin' witch! Did you know that?" Chris had begun pacing around the office.

"Chris, have a seat." Jerry said.

"No, I'm fine." Chris responded.

"No," I interjected, "Chris, have a seat, we can't talk with you walking around the room." He looked at me defiantly, but slowly moved to the chair and sank. "Did you talk to her roommate?" he asked.

"Yes," I said, pensively, "She blames you. She said that you and Jessica had a volatile relationship." Chris leaned over my desk, "See what I mean? I knew I'd be blamed. Jess and I fought a little bit, I already admitted that, but I would never hurt her. I didn't do anything." Dirt was beginning to panic and I wanted to take advantage of it, "That's not what Sarah told us," I responded, "Sarah said that the last time she saw you and Jessica, you had thrown her across the room."

"That's a lie!" Chris jumped up from his chair, "I never hit Jessica. Yeah we argue, but I've never laid a hand on her. That crazy bitch is trying to blame me!"

"How did Jessica and Sarah get along?" I asked.

"Sarah wouldn't talk to Jessica. Jess tried, but Sarah ignored her. Whenever Sarah was in their room she'd read books on witchcraft and black magic and chant." Chris looked at me and then at Jerry, "She'd actually practice spells. She said that she needed to be alone for her magic to grow stronger. She wanted Jessica to move. A week ago Jessica was freaked out, she said that Sarah had cast a spell on her. Sarah told Jessica that it was a spell to make her disappear. I guess it worked! I'm telling you, Sarah wanted Jessica *gone*."

Although Sarah threw the initial blame toward Chris, his story had been at least partially corroborated by Jenny the RA. Funny that Dirt Fagan now seemed to be an upstanding citizen. This changed the entire face of my investigation. If Jessica Philmore was missing, I had to contact the Westmire Shores P.D., but I wanted to be sure that no one had seen Jessica before I called. When I did contact the police, I knew that they'd want to take a statement from Dirt. I was afraid that if I let Dirt leave my office now, he might run. I excused myself and left Jerry with Dirt. Judy, who was typing furiously at her computer, turned to me, fingers still clicking at the keys, "How's it going?" she asked.

"Ok, I sighed. I need you to do something for me right now. Can you check with Jessica's professors and see if they've seen her in class within the last week?" Judy stopped typing and grabbed her steno pad. "Already done," she said.

"What?" I asked surprised.

"Well, I knew that you'd want Jessica's class schedule, so I pulled it up. She has twelve credits. Since we were worried that she was missing, I checked with her professors to see if she has been in class, I knew that you'd want to know. I've heard from all but one, and so far, she's been absent."

I shook my head, "You amaze me."

"You ain't seen the half of it." Judy winked.

"Ok, I need you to call the police; make sure you get Chief Morreale. Have him come over here and take a statement from Chris while he's still in my office. I'll be back shortly with Sarah Borden, don't let the chief leave." I had already begun to move toward the office doorway.

"You're leaving the office?" Judy asked, "Where are you going."

"I'm going to Sarah's room. The chief's going to want to talk to her, and I want to get to her now." I said as I walked, "Call Quacky and have her meet me at Cambridge Hall!"

When I got to Cambridge Hall, Quacky was outside waiting for me. Cambridge is a two-story brick building with four white pillars marking the entrance. Quacky was standing at attention, arms behind her back, feet eighteen inches apart. She looked like an oversized lawn gnome. As soon as she saw me approach, she moved from her hyper-vigilant pose toward me, "Hi, Doug. I just got Judy's call; she didn't give me many details. What's going on, it has to be pretty serious for you to come to the residence halls?" Tina was right; typically I would have sent an RA or Jerry to get a student. But Jerry was busy babysitting Chris and this was too important.

"I need to go to Sarah Borden's room and bring her back to my office." I said. A lot had happened in the last hour or so and the reality of Jessica's disappearance was making me feel a real sense of urgency. Even so, I felt that I had to fill Quacky in on some of the recent details, "Tina, Jessica Philmore is missing, and it looks as though she's been gone for about a week. Sarah is Jessica's roommate. I'm having Chief Morreale come to my office so that we can file a report and to take statements from Sarah and Jessica's boyfriend, Chris Fagan." I began to walk toward the entrance of Cambridge Hall with Tina waddling closely behind grabbing at a hefty ring of keys strapped to her belt. Since residence halls are locked at all times for safety reasons, Tina unlocked the front door and we entered the lobby which smelled like a mixture of bubble gum, perfume, and disinfectant.

We went to the stairwell and began climbing one flight to the second floor. Tina was breathing heavily behind me as she lumbered up the stairs, struggling to keep up. I was glad that this wasn't an actual life or death emergency or we might really have been in trouble with Tina as my back up. I was waiting for her to keel over with each passing step. I reached Sarah's (and Jessica's) room and took a deep breath. For some reason, I was nervous. As I waited for Quacky to catch-up, I examined the closed door. The names, "Sarah" and "Jessica" were written in curly script on cutesy construction paper cut outs of puppies. This was a common duty of an RA to welcome residents and build community. Clearly, perky Jenny Robins had been hard at work. On Sarah's puppy nametag, someone had drawn devil horns.

Oftentimes, a student's residence hall room door acts as part bulletin board, part personal propaganda place, and part message center. This door had the definite appearance of two distinct personalities and was almost equally divided down the middle. On Jessica's half were the magazine cutouts revered by college students: Pictures of the beach, Absolut vodka, a few "hot" guys, as well as a Green Peace sticker and an erasable memo board. On the board, someone had written, "Jess, where are you? Love, me".

Sarah's side of the door had been covered with black construction paper. A few magazine cutouts also adorned this side of the door, but I was scared to know from which magazines. There was a picture of a decapitated squirrel, a bloody dragon with swords sticking from its neck, a crystal ball and a bumper sticker that read, "Resident of Salem lives Here." There was no memo board. Apparently Sarah didn't care to receive communications from mortals.

Quacky approached from behind and caught sight of the door, "It's like night and day. Do they get along?"

"Apparently not." I said, "But I didn't know that until today. Are you ready to go in?"

Tina clutched her keys, "Just say the word."

"We'll try knocking first." Although I hadn't been an RA since college, and residence life procedures were managed by Jerry, I remembered that Residence Life etiquette dictated that one must always knock and identify oneself before keying into a room. I knocked, "Sarah? This is Dean Doug, may I speak with you please?" There was no response. After thirty seconds or so, I knocked again, "Sarah? This is Dean Doug, open the door, please." Again, no response. Some other doors began to open up and down the hallway and I could see many chattering heads taking a peak. I supposed that Quacky was right; it wasn't very often that the Dean comes knocking at your door.

I turned to Quacky, "I think we're going to have to key in." Tina already had her master key ready. "Sarah," I announced as I knocked again, "This is Dean Doug and Chief Braggish, we're going to key into your room now." With that, Tina put the key into the lock and turned the handle. For some odd reason, my heart was racing. Did I expect to find Sarah Borden crouching over the gruesome dead body of Jessica Philmore? I'm not sure what I expected, and perhaps it was the uncertainty that was getting to me.

As we entered the room, the first thing that struck me was the darkness. The windows had been shrouded in heavy black material so dark that it shielded the room from all daylight. I reached for the light switch and turned it on, but nothing happened. The bulbs must have been unscrewed or removed. While my eyes were adjusting to the light, or lack thereof, I could smell the scent of sandalwood and newly extinguished candles. I made a mental note since the use of both candles and incense in the residence halls is strictly prohibited for safety reasons. Would you want twenty nineteen year olds jazzed on a mixture of cheap vodka and Kool-Aid playing with burning objects? Not a wise idea.

As Quacky and I tried to get our bearings in the room, we both kicked something over on the floor, almost simultaneously. As I strained to see what the objects were, Quacky had already pulled out her trusty flashlight. The beam of light seemed so bright, I had to shut my eyes for a second. What we saw, as Quacky moved the light around the floor, was a group of five smoldering white pillar candles strategically placed in what could have been a three-foot wide radius. Quacky and I had knocked over two of them. A black ribbon had been placed on the floor connecting each of the candles and creating a design on the carpet.

"Looks like a star." Stated Quacky, flashing her light over the symbol.

"It's not a star," I said recognizing the design, "It's a pentagram. Symbol of witches."

"Witches? You mean like, real witches?"

"I think so. And it looks as if Sarah has been performing some sort of ritual or spell."

Immediately from the corner of the room came the curt voice of Sarah Borden lashing out at us, "I was praying!" she said through clenched teeth. My heart was racing; she had really startled me. Tina immediately pointed the light in the direction of the voice and the illuminated sight was frightening. Huddled in the corner, covered in a black robe, was Sarah. Her eyes flashed in the light and her shadowed face looked vaguely like that old Halloween gimmick when you put a flashlight under your chin to scare people. Her face was still streaked with black from earlier in the day, and her blue hair looked shocking, sticking up wildly around her head. She sat on her bed, hugging her legs up to her chest. Her voice quivered slightly and it appeared as though she was shaking.

"Sarah," I began, speaking with a dry mouth and throat, "Didn't you hear us knock?" Sarah's pupils were the size of pinholes in the light of the flashlight, and she squinted through her black eyes, "I thought that you'd go away. I was in the middle of prayer and didn't want to be bothered." I was annoyed with Sarah for not opening her door, I was annoyed with Sarah for scaring me, and now, I was annoyed with Sarah because there wasn't any light.

"Sarah," I asked, "Is there a light in this room that works?"

"On the desk." She stated quietly, like a pouting child. Quacky quickly turned the flashlight around the room until it landed on a desk and a lamp. When she turned the lamp on, I had never been so happy to see the product of a forty-watt bulb. Other than the pentagram on the carpet and the black material over the windows, the room looked fairly normal. Clearly, Sarah had taken the room over. There were clothes scattered all around. Sitting opposite the bed on which Sarah was crouched, was the bed I assumed to be Jessica's. Although it was neatly made, covered in a yellow bedspread, it had been littered with black garments.

"Sarah, I need you to come to my office." I said sternly.

"The spirits are with me always." Sarah said, almost sweetly through her darkened lips.

I said, "I need you to get up and come with me. Now."

"The spirits have rallied around me through my prayer. I've been growing stronger. Jessica's disappearance is a sign of that strength." If I had any saliva left, I would have swallowed hard. I must admit that I had chills running up my spine. Quacky must have had the same reaction, because although she stood at attention, she had forgotten to turn off the flashlight that she was still shining limply in Sarah's direction.

"So you do know about Jessica's disappearance? Were you involved?" I asked.

"I'm glad she's gone. It's my first reward, a sign that the spirits are with me. I wanted her gone, and now she is."

"Sarah, you were involved with Jessica's disappearance?" I asked again. She considered this question carefully, and then a smile crossed her face, "Yes," she stated and then rose from the bed. A wave of fear rolled through my body; I felt numb.

"Sarah," I asked, "Are you saying that you had something to do with Jessica's disappearance?"

"Yes," she smiled widely. "I had everything to do with it."

5

This was turning out to be a very long day indeed. I started the day learning that one of my students might be missing. Then I discovered that someone had defiled all of my Twizzlers and Ding-Dongs with bloody squirrel meat, and now I had a practicing witch in my office being questioned by the Westmire Shores Chief of Police. By the time I brought Sarah to my office, the Chief had already questioned Dirt. Since my office was being occupied, I ended up sitting in Jerry's office. He sat at his desk, playing the role of reassuring Dean to a beleaguered student. After I relayed my account of what had happened in Sarah's room, I was downright sulking.

"Doug, it will all work out," began Jerry's attempt at encouragement. However the shocking string of events quickly turned the Dean as counselor, to Dean as National Enquirer reporter, "You really saw a pentagram on the floor?"

"Yes, Jerry." I responded, taking off my glasses and squeezing the bridge of my nose with my fingers, "In fact I knocked part of it over. That can't be good."

"Holy shit." Was all the response that Jerry could muster, and it seemed pretty appropriate since I now faced calling Mrs. Philmore. I reached across Jerry's desk and moved his phone closer to me. "Jerry," I said as I picked up the receiver, "can you give me the number for the Dorm by the Sea?" Jerry flipped through his Rolodex and dialed the number for me. Innkeeper and owner, Peter Gaines, picked up on the second ring, "Thank you for calling Misty Dorm by the Sea, how may I help you?"

"Hi, Peter, this is Doug Carter-Connors, may I speak with Mrs. Philmore, please?"

"Oh, Dean Doug," cooed Peter, "It's just dreadful about her daughter. Poor thing has been pacing around the Inn all day. I just sent her up to her room with some chamomile tea, I thought that might help sooth her nerves, let me get her straight away." Peter put me on hold and forced me to listen to a new age rendition of "Moon River". Amazing what they can do with wind chimes and dolphin clicks. Although I wasn't soothed, I was certainly mesmerized by the mystical arrangement. A few moments later, Mrs. Philmore picked up her extension, "Dr. Carter-Connors, any word?" Her voice was hopeful and desperate which made the call worse.

"Hello, Mrs. Philmore," I responded gravely, choosing my words carefully. If I began with, 'I'm sorry to say...', Mrs. Philmore would think that Jessica was dead. If I started off with, 'Jessica's missing', I would sound insensitive. I chose a response somewhere in the middle. "We have spoken with students close to Jessica all day. We've also contacted all of her professors. Unfortunately, no one has seen her. We've gone ahead and contacted the Westmire Shores Police Department and they are here now gathering some information." I thought that "gathering information," sounded less ominous than, "taking statements."

I could hear gentle sobbing on the other end of the line, and then some sniffles, before she said anything, "When will the police know something?"

"I'm sorry to say that I don't know. I'm sure that Police Chief Morreale will want to speak with you and he'll give you a better idea. I suspect he'll be calling on you later today or early tomorrow, I told him that we put you up in the Misty Dorm for a few days."

"Should I contact Jessica's father?"

"Well, Mrs. Philmore, I recognize that that may put you in a difficult situation, but it may be a good idea." I refrained from saying things like, 'he has a right to know', but as a father myself, I felt that he did.

"I'll call him." She said flatly.

While we were on the subject of contacting parents, something else came to mind, "One other thing, Mrs. Philmore, is there anyone at your home in case Jessica tries to reach you there?"

"My housekeeper, Mildred, is there and is relaying messages." She replied. Of course the Brooklyn Philmores had a housekeeper, probably live-in. And of course the housekeeper had a name like "Mildred". I should have expected nothing less.

"Good," I responded, "Then I'll be in touch, please do the same."

"Of course, Dr. Carter-Connors." Mrs. Philmore replied, her haughty air returning. The impersonal nature of her approach had annoyed me ever since this morning.

"Please," I offered, "Call me Doug, or if you prefer, Dean Doug. In this situation, formality seems futile." She hesitated, and then quickly said, "Thank you." I knew that she was ready to end the conversation without any invitation for me to call her anything but "Mrs. Philmore". Annoyed once again, I pressed. "And what shall I call you?" She hesitated again, and then said, "Susan. My name is Susan." Perhaps I had broken some ice, or maybe I was just being a nudge; after the day I had had, I wasn't sure which.

"Thank you, Susan." I replied, "Take care." We hung up and I smiled just a little bit.

Jerry had left his office but I still sat there. The Chief had been speaking with Sarah Borden in my office for a while now. It occurred to me that I wanted to have her meet with one of the counselors in our Counseling Center just to be sure that being a witch didn't equal being crazy. If she was under some sort of psychological distress, I didn't want her harming herself or others (if it wasn't too late already). I was afraid to even consider the possibility that she had already hurt one other person, namely Jessica Philmore. I picked up the phone, and dialed the Counseling Center, which was actually right downstairs from my office in the Student Center.

The Counseling Center is staffed by two full-time psychologists and several part-time counselors. The two full-time staffers are kind and talented women for whom I have a great deal of respect. Both fifty-something, Dr. Francesca Marconi and Dr. Donna Reynolds-Ranier were skilled, compassionate, and always willing to assist at a moments notice. Since Francesca was free, I asked to speak with her and her secretary obliged.

"Hi, Doug, what's up?" Francesca asked getting right to the point.

"What do you know about witches?" I asked, playing with her a bit.

"The green kind, the good kind, or are people just being mean to you?" she responded. Francesca has a great sense of humor.

"All of them." I stated, ready to get to the point, "Sarah Borden, junior, lives in Cambridge Hall says that she's a witch and apparently has been casting spells all over campus."

"How is she presenting?" she asked in psychologist-speak. I had just enough experience to know that she wanted to know how she appeared.

"Well, she seems to be presenting like a witch. I mean, as much as I know about how a witch presents. Chief Braggish and I caught her in the middle of some sort of ceremony in her room that involved candles in the shape of a pentagram."

"What caused you to go to her room?"

"That makes the story more complicated," I began as I shared with Francesca what we knew about Jessica Philmore.

"And Sarah says she had something to do with Jessica's disappearance?"

"Absolutely, she takes full responsibility. I called the police and Chief Morreale is questioning her right now. Would you be free to chat with her a bit? I really want your opinion before I send her back into the residence halls."

"Sure, Doug, I'll be right up. But you know, Wicca is a religion. We may have some freedom of religion issues here. There can be a very fine line between religion, cult and, well, psychoses."

"I'm Catholic, Francesca, I'm well aware of that." I stated dryly. She laughed and said, "I'm coming up now."

I got up and headed back to my office to see if Chief Morreale was finished using my space and to meet Francesca. As I made it to the outer office, the Chief was just exiting my office with Sarah. Sarah was still dour-looking, as if someone had just dropped a house on her sister. "Hello, folks." I stated cheerily. Sarah did not respond.

"Oh, Dean Doug, hello," said Chief Morreale. Chief Philip Morreale is a tall, lanky man with an ever-congenial presence. His white, buzzed hairline crowns his head enhancing the bald dome on top. He has a large nose that looks more like a toucan's beak, which rests on a small silvery mustache and usually present gleaming smile. Of Italian descent, he can be heard muttering under his breath in Italian on the rare occasion that he is found to be out of sorts. Usually, however, he speaks in a cheerful Brooklynese.

"Hi, Chief." I said, offering my hand that he gladly took and pumped up and down vigorously.

"Do you have a minute, Doug?" he asked.

"Of course." I responded, just as Francesca entered the office. I greeted her, and then turned my attention to Sarah.

"Sarah," I said, "I know that you've had quite a day, but

do you know Dr. Marconi? I'd like to have you meet with her now."

"She's from the counseling center." Sarah uttered, still not making eye contact.

"That's right," I said, "She'd like to sit down with you for a few minutes."

"Do I have a choice?" Sarah finally looked at me through her veil of stringy black locks.

"No, I'm sorry, you don't."

"Why? Do you think I'm crazy? I'm only trying to be myself. I haven't done anything wrong... and I *didn't* hurt Jessica!" Her voice was rising slightly with every sentence.

"Sarah, I just want you to speak with her. If you are trying to 'be yourself' as you put it, Dr. Marconi can help you with that." I turned my body to bridge the distance between Sarah and Francesca. Francesca took the invitation. "Hi, Sarah," she said, putting a hand around Sarah's shoulder, "My office is downstairs." I was surprised to see that Sarah didn't cower from Francesca's touch as she was being led out of the office and down the stairs. I turned to the Chief and asked him to come into my office. Judy, who had been taking it all in like a court stenographer, followed behind and shut the door behind us. In the past two hours, Chief Morreale had questioned both Dirt Fagan and Sarah and I was anxious to get his take on the affairs at hand.

"So, Chief," I began, "what do you think about Chris Fagan and Sarah Borden?" The Chief took a seat, rested his hat on his knee and began sharing information from the last couple of hours. His conversation with Dirt Fagan was a duplicate of the one that I had earlier in the day. For that matter, so was Sarah's, although hers was a bit more juicy.

"So where does this leave us?" I asked.

"With a missing kid," The Chief responded sadly. "Does she have a car on campus?"

"Yeah." I offered glumly.

"I'll get the registration information and alert the State Police."

"Don't bother, the car's still in the parking lot."

"Are you sure?"

I paused, "Well, that's what Chris said earlier today, but no, I haven't checked."

The Chief looked worried and I knew what he was thinking. If Jessica's car was gone, then maybe she went off on a road trip. If her car was still parked on-campus, then chances were she left against her will. "I'll have security check right now," I said.

I called Quacky Braggish and asked her to check the car registration that we had on file for Jessica Philmore. In order to obtain a parking permit, any student or staff must submit this information. Quacky said that she would check and then see if she could locate the car. Since there is very little on-campus parking, it wouldn't take too much time to check the two major parking lots. A mere fifteen minutes later, Judy buzzed me to say that Chief Braggish was on the line.

I picked up the phone with Chief Morreale still waiting intently across from me. "Hi, Chief Braggish. What's up?"

"Her car's here all right." I looked at the Chief and nodded.

"You're sure?"

"Yup. Can't miss her car. Not many red BMW convertibles on-campus. And she's got a Jensen's Boardwalk bumper sticker. I remember talking to Jessica last year about going to the boardwalk. Nice kid. It's definitely her car." Jensen's Boardwalk is located about twenty miles down the shore in Prospect Point Beach. It was a summertime haven right on the Atlantic hosting rides and amusements along the boardwalk, an aquarium, restaurants, shops and all the cotton candy you can eat. My wife and I visited several times throughout the summer.

"All right. Thanks, Tina. Can you just keep an eye on

the car, and make sure it doesn't move?"

"Will do, Dean."

Chief Morreale got up from his seat, "I'll go by the Misty Dorm and speak with Mrs. Philmore. We'll have to file a missing person's report and get the word out across the tri-state area."

I thanked the Chief, and he left. It was almost 6:30pm and I was ready to go home. It had been quite a day. I packed up my briefcase, grabbed my sport coat, and turned out my office lights. I walked out into the outer office and shut and locked my door. For the first time today, the office was quiet. Judy had dutifully turned off half of the lights, straightened the furniture and locked up. Her desk sat perfectly tidied, with three number two pencils sharpened like mini spears, lined-up next to her steno pad ready for tomorrow. I was a little apprehensive about what tomorrow would bring; I struggled to be optimistic about finding Jessica alive. What I was certain of, was that I would go home and hug Ethan extra tight. God, what a day.

6

The college is a mere four blocks from my house and I pride myself on walking to work. It's just far enough away from the everyday travels of my students, but close enough if I have to run to campus in case of an emergency. Although I was eager to get home, I walked slowly. The late summer evening air was warm, salty, and snuggled me like my favorite security blanket. As I crossed Mt. Tabor Way, I glanced down the street toward the ocean and saw Chief Morreale's police cruiser parked next to the Misty Dorm by the sea. I was heartened to know that innkeepers Peter and Patrick would take good care of Mrs. Philmore tonight. I was off the hook.

I reached my house and unconsciously let out a sight of relief. Our house is a four-bedroom cape nestled in the back of a deep lot surrounded by a white picket fence. It's homey, cliché, and very me. There are rose bushes in the front, cuttings from my grandmother's lilacs in the back, and a brick walkway leading to the front door that I laid myself. Martha Stewart and Better Homes have nothing over on our house, and I wouldn't have it any other way.

I walked in the door and put my jacket and briefcase down in the hall. I stood for a brief moment, relishing the scent of home. I think that there are only a few times in your life when this familiar scent never fades from memory. For me, I remember the smell of the home I grew up in, and this one. I found Barbara cooking dinner in the kitchen. Ethan sat at the kitchen table coloring; a heaping pile of broken Crayolas beside him. He waved to me nonchalantly as I entered the room and I walked over and immediately kissed him on the top of his sandy-colored head.

Barbara and I share many of the household chores, but cooking happens to be her forte. Mine is gardening. Laundry, cleaning, and bill paying fall somewhere in the middle and the purveyors of such usually depends on scheduling. Barbara is a freelance writer who also works as a part time writer/reporter for our hometown paper, *The Shores' Sentinel*. She has a Masters in journalism from Columbia and she moved to Westmire Shores right out of graduate school to take the position of Director of Public Information/Community Affairs at Westmire College. Although I can't honestly say that it was love at first sight, it was certainly a whole lotta like. The first time I met Barbara on-campus I was immediately taken by her warm eyes, beautiful smile and infectious laugh. Although it sounds sappy, her warmth and personality seeped into my heart and has never left.

When Barbara and I met nearly ten years ago, I was the Asst. Dean in charge of Residence Life (the job now held by Jerry). Since it's a small campus, we sat on several committees together and became friends. At the time, Barbara was commuting to Westmire from the city. Our dating life began our foundation of collaboration and sharing of responsibilities. Throughout our courtship, we spent equal amounts of time between her tiny NYC apartment and my one-bedroom apartment in Westmire Shores. Between dinners in Manhattan and lazy Saturday afternoons at the beach, it's no wonder that we fell in love.

When we married seven years ago, we decided that it made the most sense to buy a house in Westmire Shores. I had just been promoted to Dean of Students after the untimely demise of my predecessor. It's a common occurrence at the College, but I'll share the details at another time. A couple of years later, we were blessed with Ethan. Barbara decided that she would rather change her career focus, go back to writing and journalism, work part time and not put Ethan in daycare. For us, this was not a haughty judgment about daycare, but a lifestyle choice that we made. Now, Barbara works primarily out of a home office writing local stories for the *Sentinel,* as well as freelance articles of national interest in magazines such as *Better Homes and Gardens, Islands* and *Parenting* to name just a few. Not only is she a beautiful wife and wonderful mother, she's an intelligent businesswoman who makes quite a nice living.

I walked over to her and gave her a peck on the cheek, "Hi" I said.

"Hi, honey." She said, stirring a pot of sauce, "How was your day?" I sighed, moving close enough to whisper so that Ethan wouldn't hear, "Do you mean the part about the missing student, the bloody vending machine or the witch?" Barbara stopped mid-stir, "What happened?"

"All in all, it was just another regular day at Westmire." I replied. I sat down next to Ethan, began offering him crayon choices and relaying the events of the day in a code that wouldn't upset a five year old. Barbara opened a bottle of red wine and handed me a glass; in retrospect, I'm pretty sure that I made gulping noises.

After reliving my day, eating dinner, and putting Ethan to bed, Barbara and I went to bed and made love. It was the sort of lovemaking that was less about sex, and more about human contact. The day had sucked all of the life out of me, and the connection with my soul mate made me feel normal again. I wasn't a Dean, a leader, or a witch hunter... I was a partner with a beautiful friend who loved me dearly. I slept peacefully that night, revived and ready for the day to come.

I got up a little early the next morning, threw on my running clothes before I lost my nerve, and headed toward the boardwalk. Although I consider myself to be a runner, I don't profess that it's easy or that I'm good at it. If I can pull out a mile or so by 7am I consider myself a triathlete, pat myself on the back, and reward myself with some lunchtime french fries. The cold mist in the air hit my warm body like a thousand needles, and it felt great.

I hit the boards longer than usual, pulling out nearly three miles. I'd like to think that it was due to my stalwart physical condition, but in reality, I knew it was simply procrastination. I wasn't sure what I would face when I got into the office. Dead rats in the soda machine? Aliens in the President's office? Or worse. Would we find Jessica Philmore alive? The mere thought of the contrary forced me to turn on me heels and head for the shower.

On my way home I ran by Cruiser, our native cross-dressing homeless person. He's 6'4", muscular, with shaggy brown hair usually peeking from a platinum blond wig. Cruiser can be found making daily rounds parading through town, pushing a wheelbarrow full of treasures, and often wearing some bright gingham or taffeta dress, and wide-brimmed chapeau. Given his size, he must shop at the plus-size shoppe. Someone once tried to replace the wheelbarrow with a shopping cart, but Cruiser protested that no self-respecting gardener would push a shopping cart. The fact that no one has ever seen Cruiser even touch a flower is beside the point. Cruiser's face is worn with a chin like a pincushion filled with whiskers. Gardener or no gardener, Cruiser sheds bulky gardening gloves for the pristinely white gloves of a debutante. Although a man of few words, he is cordial and a good man to have around. Cruiser vaguely reminds me of my old Aunt Lill.

That morning he was looking lovely in blue chiffon, light blue gloves, and white high-tops. His wheelbarrow was filled with various garage sale-type items including a birdcage and a red step-stool. "Good morning, Cruiser," I panted as I passed by. "Mornin', Dean," he replied in a husky voice. Although Cruiser is a vagrant whose origin is unknown, he isn't actually homeless. He lives in an efficiency apartment in the basement of the Unitarian

Church. In return for the room, he provides the church with a variety of services including delivering "meals on wheels" in his wheelbarrow, odd jobs around the church, and collecting donations at the weekly meetings.

I got home, used the house key that I keep under a red piece of slate near the front door (I hate to carry keys when I run) and trudged upstairs. I showered, got dressed, ate breakfast with Barbara and Ethan, and began my walk to campus. The late summer air was filled with warm moisture and the breeze off the ocean was filled with a delicious salty fragrance. My normal route to work takes me from my house on Walnut Lane, a left onto Asbury Avenue, a quick cross over Main Avenue and straight to University Place and campus. This morning I fought a dull sense of panic. I knew that the clock was ticking. Every minute that Jessica was missing was another strike against us... as the clock ticked away, our chances of finding her became dimmer and dimmer.

As I approached Main Avenue, I could see someone waving furiously in my direction. I squinted and saw that it was the Reverend Malificent Brown of the Shores Unitarian church. It's the biggest church in town, right on Main Avenue, that serves cappuccino after Sunday morning services and hosts monthly sushi suppers. Much like Wal-Mart, it has effectively knocked-out all competition for bible-clutching parishioners in a ten mile radius. Malificent is a gregarious, painfully thin woman who moves effortlessly through the pews like a ballet dancer. I might have thought that she actually was a ballet dancer if it wasn't for the fact that she chain-smokes and wears nothing but size 10 Birkenstocks.

She was dutifully clutching her Bible in her waving hand, her guitar in the other and balancing a cigarette devotedly between her lips. Malificent is at least six feet tall and willowy. She moves with the grace of a giraffe-- tall, oversized yet surprisingly elegant. A middle-aged woman, she keeps her pageboy haircut jet black to match her wire-framed glasses and daily outfit. She could just as easily pass for a beatnik if she wasn't a woman of the cloth. Malificent bent her lengthy legs enough to set her guitar down on the sidewalk while grabbing for her cigarette, "Dean Doug, I'm so glad I saw you," she began in an eloquent, soothing smoker's voice.

"Good morning, Reverend." I responded.

"Is the news true?"

"Which news?" I answered. Given the odd events of the day before, it was a legitimate question.

"The news about one of your students being missing?"

"Well, yes, it seems so, but we're still investigating." In a small town that's only a mile square, news travels fast as a rule, but sometimes I'm still stunned by swiftness of the Shore's very own information super highway. Malificent's piercing eyes bored into mine and she lowered her voice, "They're saying it's a cult? Do you need my help?" Malificent is an expert on everything spiritual, pseudo-spiritual, and even doubtfully spiritual; cults are her specialty.

"Cult, huh? I hadn't heard that, Malificent." I was reluctant to offer too much information, even though I trusted the good Reverend and thought that she may be able to provide some Wiccan insight if necessary at some point.

"Doug, I know this is delicate, but I'm here to help," her voice lowered to a whisper as she leaned down even closer to me, "And as the spiritual leader of this community, if there is any cult activity, people may become unsettled and look to me for answers." The Reverend Jim Jones couldn't have said it better.

"Malificent, I appreciate your concern and promise you that as soon as we know something more concrete, we'll let you know. But anything at this stage is premature." Malificent and I had developed a decent relationship over the years that she respected enough to stop pressing. "Well, this must be very difficult for you. Please keep me posted. I'll keep you and Jessica in my prayers." Well, at least Malificent's sources weren't totally wrong. Someone had told her that Jessica was the missing student, since I certainly had not. This part of the conversation made me even more anxious, and I wanted to get to the office. I didn't feel like pressing Malificent for her source. "Thank you, Reverend," I said and quickly continued on my way.

I made my way to the College now wondering what other rumors were spreading around town... and the Westmire campus. As I walked under the wrought iron gates of the main campus entrance, I got my answer. People began looking my way, staring and whispering. A few of them approached me quickly, and asked if the news was true, 'was Jessica Philmore really missing?' Others acted with more caution, simply asking me, 'is everything alright?' I could tell that some members of the campus were simply curious; others were totally freaked out.

I walked into the Student Center and up the stairs to my office. As I neared the plate glass windows looking into the outer office it looked as if Judy was hosting a cocktail party at 9:15 in the morning. She stood in the middle of the room, juggling a coffee pot, several mugs, spoons, cream and sugar on a plastic silver tray. She was surrounded by at least a dozen people. There were students, a couple of administrators, and a faculty member apparently all seeking information on the latest unusual event to occur at Westmire. Several teary-eyed young women were holding each other and fistfuls of tissues. The administrators present were Dr. Marconi from the counseling center and Keesha Cribbs, a member of my staff who serves as the Director for Student Activities. They were surrounding the distraught students offering support. The faculty member in the room was Dr. Reginald I. Preston, or as he is often called, R.I.P. He is old, the head of the faculty council, and unconditionally mean.

As I entered the office, all activity stopped and the focus was turned to me. Although my first reaction was to say something off-color about this impromptu party, I refrained. Instead, I looked around the room as said, "Good morning everyone." Judy put the tray down and came to my aid immediately. She grabbed a stack of yellow papers from her desk, which I knew were telephone messages, moved behind me, put her hand on the small of my back and whisked me directly into my office. She even closed the door behind her before anyone could follow.

"You're good," I said, "You may have a career in the secret service."

"It's all those years being a bouncer and a groupie at the Stone Pony. Move 'em in fast, move 'em out fast," Judy replied. The Stone Pony was a famous (or infamous depending on your social circle) bar and nightclub the next town over in Asbury Park where Bruce Springsteen began his career. I looked at her and smiled, "A groupie I knew, but you were a bouncer?" Judy winked at me, "I ain't just a pretty face you know." Upon that, she began briefing me for my day.

"You're a popular fella today, as you can see. P.S., I'm afraid you're in for one hell of a day."

"What's up?" I asked, sitting down at my desk.

"Well, the word is obviously out." Judy waved the messages in her hand, "Twenty messages... some left on the voice mail last night. Concerned parents, upset students, and even the President's office wanting an update."

"And what about the people waiting in the office?"

Judy then provided me both the details and her own personal commentary, "Girls from Jessica's floor, very upset. Dr. Marconi wants to give you the latest on the blue haired girl that you saw yesterday, who between you and me is a couple sandwiches short of a picnic, she's got *the look*. And then Dr. R.I.P. who demands to speak with you, as if you're scared. I told Julie in the president's office that you were dealing with a mob of people here and that you would be in touch soon, I cancelled all of your meetings for today, I told the few parents that I spoke to that you were in meetings all day long and that either you or one of your staff would call them back this afternoon, and I told R.I.P. to go jump off of the pier." I gave her a puzzled look to which she responded, "Just checking to see if you were listening."

"Let's start with Francesca, then I'll talk to Jessica's floor mates. We'll save R.I.P. for last."

"You got it," Judy sung as she opened the door, "Oh, and Keesha would like to speak with you when you have a minute... she says that it's related to Jessica."

"Is it important?"

"Doug, everyone out there seems to have something to do with the disappearance of Jessica... how can you judge which one is most important until you hear them all? Don't worry, I'll check in with Keesha again. If it's urgent, I'll bump her up to the top of your list." As usual, Judy was right. With such a large group of people vying for my ear, I just had to hear them one by one and hope that I got the most important bits of information sooner.

Judy sent Francesca into my office and she took the usual seat in front of my desk, "How are *you* this morning?" she asked in a concerned tone no doubt related to the number of people waiting to hear from me.

"I'm fine," I assured her, "How is our resident witch?"

"She's ok. I mean, Sarah is under some psychological distress and I would like to keep seeing her on a regular basis, but she's really ok. Without breaching her confidentiality, I'll confirm what you already know. Wicca is her religion, perhaps stemming from her rebellious relationship with her parents, but for now, it's what she does. I don't think she's delusional or psychotic. Weird maybe, but not a threat to herself or others." Of course I was happy to hear that Sarah's mental well-being was fine.

I trusted Dr. Marconi explicitly. However, I'm a bit ashamed to admit that I was somewhat disappointed. This news meant that the evil that we know wasn't really evil at all... which opened the door for a baneful unknown that terrified me. The internal clock that was ticking away somewhere near my heart began to tick harder.

I couldn't help but ask, "But do you think she *could* have had something to do with the disappearance, I mean, Jessica's disappearance?" I corrected myself because as soon as I began speaking of Jessica's disappearance without including her name, it felt as though my connection to her would fade even faster.

"Of course she *could* be, but Sarah contends that it is a balance in the earth... her Goddess and spirits are guiding her to wellness, and the same for Jessica... Sarah *feels* that Jessica is well too... they just were not good together, so the universe parted them."

"So she's a witch and a psychic." I said below my breath. Francesca remained silent, eliciting another outburst from me, "I'm scared, Francesca. Even though we've only known about Jessica's disappearance for 24 hours, she's really been gone for nearly a week. That's not good. You know that's not good."

"Doug, I know that you're feeling pressure and you *need* an answer... for the people out there as well as yourself. I know that. But I don't think that Sarah Borden *is* your answer. I'm pretty certain that she's not. What can I do to help?" Her question slapped me back into reality. Although I hadn't really verbalized it before, I was scared and sometimes fear makes people look for a scapegoat. Although Sarah Borden had some physical similarities to Frankenstein, I needed to extinguish the torch I was chasing her with. I took a breath and cracked a smile, "You're doing it," I said quietly, "Whenever I begin to get freaky, help me bring things into focus like you just did. Thank you." Francesca smiled, "Anytime. Shall I send in your next customer?"

"Customers. I'm going to talk with the young women from Jessica's floor... do you have a minute to stay?" I knew that in many cases like this, students sometimes needed the support of the counseling center as well as the dean.

"You're in luck," Francesca responded, "I am supposed to be at a committee meeting, but I didn't go so that I could give you the latest. I'm yours until 11:00am."

As I ushered the women, six of them in all, into my office, R.I.P. quickly stood up, "I hope you're not putting me off!" he called in his high-pitched, crackle, "This is important!" With that, he raised is hand in some sort of fist-shaking motion. I smiled, "Students first, professor. That's why we're here. Students first." And I shut the door. God, I hate him.

The six young women moved together en-masse as if they had their ankles tied together in a field day game. Their mood seemed two parts fearful, two parts misery and two parts melodrama. Francesca and I rearranged some chairs around the sofa that I have in my office including my desk chair and offered them a seat. Since all of the seating was taken, I propped myself on the edge of my desk, "Hello, everybody. I'm afraid I don't know all of you." One of the women who was somber, but not teary spoke up, "I'm Tara, and this is Sabrina, Sandy, Colleen, Christie and Beth."

"Thank you," I said, "And as you probably know, I'm Dean Doug, Dean of Students and this is my colleague Dr. Marconi who works in the counseling center. What can I do for you today?"

"We're here about Jessica," Tara began again, "We heard that she's gone... murdered. We heard that there is a cult on-campus, in our dorm, and they're killing people like they did those animals in the candy machine." With this, the other five broke down into tears, grabbing for the box of tissues that Colleen was holding. I shot a glance at Francesca, "Okay. Where did you hear all of this?"

"It's all over campus."

"Let me tell you that what you have heard does not match the information that we have," I began. I didn't want to give away too much information, but wanted to squelch the rumor mill at least a little bit, "All we know right now is that Jessica isn't at Westmire," I wanted to even avoid using "missing" with students, "That could mean a variety of things."

"What about the dead animals! 'MURDER' was written in blood!" one of the previously silent and sobbing blurted out.

"We have no reason to believe that the two are connected. In fact, the blood found in the vending machine wasn't even real." I wondered about sharing that detail, but figured it couldn't hurt. We really didn't have any reason to suspect that the two cases were related, in fact, until Malificent insinuated a connection earlier in the morning, I hadn't really considered it.

"What about the cult!" called out another formerly mute and melodramatic young woman.

"This is the first that I'm hearing of a cult." That wasn't totally true, Malificent had brought-up the subject earlier this morning, and I was intrigued to find out where this idea came from, "What have you heard about a cult?"

Tara spoke, "Mike from the newspaper was in our dorm last night, and he was talking about cults. He said that cults do a lot of animal sacrifices and stuff." Ahhhh, Mike Godfrey, our very own Geraldo Rivera right here on campus sensationalizing an already sensational story.

"We have no information about that, as I said, this is the first that I've heard of it." I was happy to hear that the idea of a cult came from sheer speculation and had nothing to do with Sarah Borden's witchdom.

"What about Jessica's roommate, Sarah, she's a witch!" sobber number one called out. Clearly I spoke too soon. I shot another glance at Francesca. Things were hard enough for Sarah right now, let alone, having the entire campus vilify her as the cause for Jessica's disappearance. I felt guilty enough that I had thought the same things myself. Although there were certain confidentiality issues that we had to maintain, I needed to dispel some of this myth flying around, "Sarah's religion is her prerogative, like yours. Wicca is a legitimate religion and I need to make something clear, this situation is not easy for Sarah either. She needs to be supported as much as you do."

"She's crazy," one of them said under their breath. It was time for me to stand-up for Sarah Borden, "One more time," I said, "Sarah is dealing with this situation as much as you are. If you can't support her, then I suggest you leave her alone. If I find that anyone on campus is making Sarah's life difficult, I will deal with that immediately under the Code of Conduct." This hung in the air like a fart. Although I rarely threatened students, I could see the potential for a whole floor of women, or an entire campus, ganging up on Sarah, just as I had done. Not to mention that these young women seemed most concerned about their own welfare, not Jessica's. I broke the pause in conversation with, "Do you have any other concerns?" Silence again as the group sniffed and looked at the floor.

I went back to my softer, supportive voice, "I know this is hard for you. If you have any more concerns, please let me know. Dr. Marconi is also here to help." Francesca chimed in, "My office is right downstairs in the Counseling Center, I'm here if any of you or your friends need to talk. In fact, I'll walk you out." With that, we ended the meeting and Francesca walked with them out of the office; she gave me a reassuring wink as she left. That left R.I.P. waiting. Although I dreaded even meeting with this confrontational old codger, I wanted to get rid of him as soon as possible so that I could talk to Keesha before I answered my stacks of messages. As my office door opened, I could hear R.I.P. shrieking. What was I in for now?

7

As I gave Judy the OK sign to calm her, R.I.P. barged past me and rushed into my office. I followed and shut the door, "Why Professor Preston," I began in a tone dripping with sarcasm, "Normally men of your stature wait to be invited in." "I'm not here to discuss etiquette, Connors," he barked. I wasn't either. I was actually referring to my suspicion that he was really a vampire. He screeched again, "When were you going to tell us, Connors?" R.I.P. was one of the many people in the world who either didn't care to realize that my name was actually Carter-Connors (the joining of my wife's maiden name and mine) or didn't believe in the concept and avoided it by protest.

"I'm not sure what you mean, Professor?" I asked.

"The walk out. THE WALK OUT!" he screamed in a tone that could shatter glass. Professor Reginald Ichabod Preston was about 5'8" but humped over at barely 5'4", 70 years old, and rail thin with a gaunt graying face and hair to match. He ambled around with a silver tipped wooden cane that he often shook during conversations for emphasis. This was no exception.

"Professor, please stop shaking that cane in my face and explain what you're talking about."

"This!" he yelled, as he pulled a folded up flier out of his jacket pocket. He unfolded it, and threw it my way. I reached down and picked it up off of the floor where it landed. It read, "Tired of poor teaching methods and unfair exams? REVOLT! THIS IS OUR SCHOOL! Walk out in support of better teaching practices and the rights of students everywhere. When? Tomorrow, 10am. Who? YOU! All classes... Where? Come and meet in the quad."

I moved behind my desk and sat down, thankful to have a big oak buffer between me and the length of R.I.P.'s cane.

"Please have a seat, professor," I said.

"I'm not here for a social call, Connors! I want answers! How long have you known about this?"

"About two minutes," I responded, "How about you?" With that, he squinted at me and moved closer to one of my guest chairs grabbing its back with his craggy hand.

"You mean to tell me that you didn't know about this?" he questioned.

"No, I didn't."

"I thought you were the Dean of Students?"

"Professor, that doesn't mean that I know what every student is doing." He was annoying me, so I pushed back a little, "As chair of the faculty council, do you know what happens in each and every classroom?" He continued to stand resolute behind the chair. "My responsibility is to my faculty," R.I.P. countered, "Your job is to handle students, which obviously you are not capable of doing. A walk out... ha! We've only been back in session for a week!" I replied with a blank stare. He continued with his best bitter scowl. I felt as though I was back in elementary school having a staring contest with my best friend David. Whoever blinked first, lost. I was certain that if we were anywhere near snow, old R.I. P. and I would have seen who could pee farther in the snow.

Since I had more important things to attend to and I wanted R.I.P. out of my office, I finally broke the silence. "Professor, what would you like from me?"

"Stop it!" he yelled, "Stop the protest!"

"Why? Don't students have the right to protest? Don't we, as an academic community, encourage all thought whether we agree with it or not?" I knew that'd get him where it hurt, and it did.

"But this is a bad time in the semester to set a precedent like this... students skipping classes."

"But isn't it a great beginning to the semester to see students so committed to thought and dedicated to academics?" All R.I.P. could manage was an exaggerated, "Hrrrumph!"

"Let them have their protest... if it even happens at all. Then, perhaps you and your faculty can take advantage of this teachable moment in class to engage students in a dialogue about their concerns as well as your concerns. Then, perhaps you'd like to arrange a time to go to the next Student Government meeting to discuss the issues at hand?" I must admit, pretty good advice.

"So that's it, Connors? Just let me deal with it? What are you supposed to do?"

"Offer you guidance." I said, doing my best to be smug.

"Well thanks for nothing. You can be sure that the faculty will know how unsupportive you've been. Not that they'll be surprised." And with that, R.I.P. creaked out of the chair, holding his cane like the staff of Moses, and righteously hobbled out of my office. And for once, I didn't care. I had much more important things to handle. I had a ton of messages to return, including one from the president's office. Although students came first, the Office of the President was a very close second. I picked up the phone and got Julie Diamond, the President's executive assistant.

"Hi, Julie, this is Doug." Julie and I have a pretty decent relationship. In fact, with the turnover in the President's office over the past few years, she was a constant contact who offered a sense of continuity. She was a grandmother of three, had platinum blond shoulder length hair and always looked as if she had just returned from Milan or a spa with a slightly haughty air to match. As my dad always says, 'she looks like she just came out of a band box'. Although I'm not exactly sure what that means, he's probably right.

In the past four years, Westmire has had four presidents. Oddly, they keep dying in office. Some attribute the deaths to coincidence. Others whisper about conspiracy. Still more just chalk it up to the odd nature of our town. I'm not sure where I stand on the subject except that the President is my boss and regardless of who they are, I'm accountable to them. After the last death, Dr.

Gwenyth Porter, Vice President for Academic Affairs and Provost was named "acting President." Since she and I sat on the President's Cabinet together, I knew her well and liked her a great deal. In fact, when she was given the "acting" title, I jokingly thanked her for being in line before me. If we lost another President, I would be the next "acting".

"Doug!" Julie said in a tone that was half whisper and half gossip, "What's happening?"

"Do you mean with Jessica Philmore?"

"We've just been *flooded* with calls, including Mr. Philmore himself. Gwenyth said that you should speak with him." It was always a toss-up whether a parent or concerned community member would call the Office of the President or the Dean of Students. Oftentimes, when they didn't get the answers they wanted from one, they called the other anyway. It is part of my job to first anticipate and then to keep President and her staff informed of everything relating to students that might evoke a flurry of calls. In this case, I had been so busy, Judy called Julie late yesterday but I hadn't had a chance to follow-up with a personal call.

"Is Gwenyth in?" I asked, knowing that it was rare to actually find the President in the President's office. She was normally on business calls meeting with donors or alumni trying to raise money for the College.

"No, she's in Atlanta meeting with some distinguished alumni there, but she's very concerned. She'll call you later from the road. So, when did you discover that Ms. Philmore was missing?"

"We discovered it yesterday, but she's been gone a week before we knew."

"What are the police saying?"

"That we've got a missing student. Other than that, we don't know much of anything yet."

"We're also concerned about the rumors. Parents and Trustees are very troubled. What's this we're hearing about a cult?" Julie's voice took the tone of a schoolteacher speaking to a pupil. When she said "we" or "we're" she meant she and the President even though it was language also appropriate for the Queen of England.

"Well, Julie," I began trying to defend the situation even though I was as powerless as everyone else, "I'm troubled about the rumors too, especially since they are unfounded. We have no evidence of any cultist activity on campus."

"But the dead animals in the candy machine? And is it true that there is a witch on campus? Doug, I don't need to tell you how disconcerting this is." She was right, she didn't and I wished that she hadn't.

"Julie, I've been telling people this all day and I hope that now you can help spread the truth." I was being defensive and now I was doing my best to stay polite, "We have no evidence of any cult on-campus. We did find a couple fetal pigs in the vending machine here in the student center, as well as a kitten." With this, Julie tried to interrupt with a, 'Well see!' sort of way, but I continued to talk over her and she stopped. "However," I continued, "According to Chief Braggish, the animals were dead long before they were placed in the machine... the pigs were probably from the biology lab. We're investigating to confirm that. Also, the blood that was found in the machine was just corn syrup dyed red. Now, in terms of a witch. We do have a student on campus that is Wiccan. This is a legitimate pagan religion and as an educated, academic community we need to support diversity. From what we know, she is not part of a cult and has nothing to do with Jessica Philmore's disappearance." Julie must have been able to tell that I was somewhat exasperated and although she seemed somewhat put off by my bullishness, she backed off, "Well thank you, Doug for the update. I know that it seems like everyone is looking to you to solve these mysteries. We will certainly do our best to put an end to the rumors. Now, while I've got you, what about the student walk out?" Clearly, R.I.P. had run to tattle to the Presidents' Office.

I started my next line of defense, "Professor Preston was in this morning and it was the first I had heard of it. I advised him to see what happens and offer to meet with Student Government to hear their concerns so that everyone could work out a solution. Julie, I have to admit that my priority these days is not to make Professor Preston's problems go away."

"Of course, Doug. I understand perfectly." Julie responded, either appeasing me or agreeing. I didn't care which. "Just keep us posted on all of these fronts, won't you? And please, if you need my assistance, just let me know."

"Thank you, Julie. I will. I appreciate your help. If you speak with Gwenyth before I do, please have her call me at her convenience." We hung up, but not before she gave me Mr. Philmore's office phone number. I called him directly and left a message with his secretary. He was the one connection to Jessica Philmore whom I hadn't spoken with and I was actually looking forward to gaining any insight that he might provide. While I had a moment, I decided to take a break from returning phone messages and find Keesha.

Keesha is twenty-five, been on my staff for two years and I trust her explicitly. She is a petite, striking African-American woman with big dark eyes that sparkle with both confidence and intelligence beyond her years. I knocked at her office door and found her busily typing at her computer.

"Hi, Keesha." I said, "Judy said that you wanted to speak with me?" Her eyes flashed, "Doug!" She wheeled her desk chair to face me anxiously, "Yes, when I found out about Jessica, I wondered if you knew about her history?"

"History?" I asked, "I checked her file but there's not much in it other than a couple of alcohol violations, what do you know?"

"Well, it's turning out to be something of a mystery. You know the student club, STOPP, Students Opposing Oppression?" Of our fifty or so student clubs and organizations on campus, STOPP was typically our most vocal, so I had more interaction with it than usual. "Yes," I responded, "That's the social activist group, right?"

"Right. Well, I just found out that Jessica Philmore is the president of STOPP." As Director of Student Activities, Keesha works with all of the student organizations in one way or another. She monitors organizations to make sure that they were abiding by the constitution set by the Westmire Student Government.

"Really," I remarked, surprised, "Jessica Philmore is an activist? That's odd, the president of STOPP is a student who we barely know?"

"That's the mystery. I had never even met Jessica until two weeks ago. It was at the student involvement fair during new student orientation." Each year, student groups promote their organizations to new students to drum-up membership. Keesha continued, "STOPP didn't list their officers for this academic year when they registered to attend the fair. They listed each officer as "anonymous". During the fair, I went up to the STOPP table and told them that in order to participate, they had to list their officers with our office. A couple of students challenged me, saying that anonymity was important for them as activists to avoid retribution from administration on campus. I let them stay at the fair, but told them that they needed to stop by my office to discuss it later that week."

"Was Jessica Philmore at the table?"

"Well, that was it. No, she wasn't, but she's the one who came to my office a few days later. It must have been just a couple of days before she disappeared."

"What'd she say?"

"She was really sweet. She introduced herself, explained that she was the president of STOPP, and then said how important anonymity was to their organization."

"Because of retribution of some sort?"

"She said that in the past, members have felt that they were treated differently by faculty and administration because of their political views. Some got lower grades;

some just got a hard time. So for the sake of the leadership, they felt that it was important to keep their leaders secret."

"How did she appear to you? Was she agitated or upset?"

"No, not at all. Like I said, she was very sweet... soft-spoken... I might even say mousy. I mean, stereotypically I think of activists as loud and proud. Jessica was the opposite, meek and mild."

"Sounds like the Gandhi or Rosa Parks variety activist."

"Exactly. Do you know Jessica, Doug?"

"No, I don't think I've ever met her, that's why I had to look in her file."

"Well now we know why. She works very hard at keeping a low profile. That's why she wasn't at the table at the involvement fair. She is a behind the scenes leader." Something about Keesha's insight struck me, but before I could consider it more fully, Judy stepped in. "Doug," she said, "Jessica Philmore's father is returning your call."

"OK, Judy, thank you. I'll be right there." I said, but Judy lingered in the doorway. I said nothing, but looked at her curiously. There was an uncomfortable silence left in the air.

"Doug," Judy began again, "I think you should take this right away. It sounds to me like Mr. Philmore is crying."

8

I walked into my office not quite knowing what to expect when I picked up the phone. Was Mr. Philmore upset over Jessica's status as a missing person, or did he know about a new development that I didn't? I hoped for the former. I sat behind my desk and took a deep breath, hesitating before I picked up the phone. If I had been a better Catholic, I'm sure that I would have crossed myself.

"Hello Mr. Philmore, this is Doug Carter-Connors," I said finally picking up the receiver. There was silence on the other end, which made my heart skip a beat. I heard a sniff, and then Mr. Philmore spoke, "Ah, hello, Dean Carter-Connors. Any news on my daughter?" Whew, he didn't know anything new. In fact, I knew more than him, which was sad.

"Hello, Mr. Philmore. I've been hoping to speak with you. You haven't heard from your daughter?" There was a brief silence at the other end, and then, "No." Another sniff, "I haven't spoken to Jessica in several months. She, uh, doesn't have much to do with me since the divorce."

"I'm sorry." I responded, it sounded trite, but I didn't know what else to say. His voice was gruff, yet refined, with only a hint of a Brooklyn accent. Clearly, through the culture of high society, money, or private school, he had modified his way of speaking to sound more like he hailed from the Hamptons.

"It's ok," he said, "It's been over five years since the divorce, and ever since Jess has been eighteen, I only see her one or two times a year. So Dean, any news?"

"I'm sorry to say, no. You've spoken to Mrs. Philmore?"

"Susan has been keeping me updated, reluctantly I'm sure. She said that the police contacted her last night as well."

"Yes, we've been working with the Westmire Shores Police Department."

"What about Jess's car?"

"It is still parked on campus. Of course, that doesn't mean anything, she could have taken public transportation." Perhaps it was my own fear as a parent that made me try to rationalize the possibilities. I knew full well that it was an equal possibility that Jessica was removed from campus by some other means... by force. Nevertheless, I continued, "The police are checking transportation records, credit card transactions, and things of that nature to try and locate her."

"Have you spoken to that dirt bag boyfriend?" Mr. Philmore's reserved weepiness had turned to anger, and his Brooklyn accent overtook his voice.

"Do you mean Chris Fagan?" I responded, hesitating to use the nickname "Dirt", which I was afraid would add insult to injury. No one ever wants their child to date a person whose name is synonymous with filth of any kind.

"Yeah. Tell me he doesn't know something!" Mr. Philmore called a bit louder.

"I've spoken with him and so have the police. At this point, Mr. Philmore, we are following every possibility. We are taking every step to find your daughter."

"Dean, I don't think you understand!" Mr. Philmore responded, venom rising in his voice, "I need some answers! How do I know that you're capable of finding my daughter?" For some reason, when Mrs. Philmore had challenged me, I became annoyed. But Mr. Philmore just seemed too desperate to elicit that response from me.

"Mr. Philmore," I began, "You don't know me. But I need to tell you that as the Dean of Students, and as a parent, I am doing everything I can to find your daughter. I can't imagine what this must feel like as a father, but as a Dean I can tell you that I will do everything possible to make sure that every "i" is dotted and every "t" is crossed. I can't promise you the outcome, but I can promise you that we are working with the police to do everything possible." On the other end, I could hear Mr. Philmore whimpering again, "Thank you." He said. I stayed silent, giving him a moment.

"This has been one hell of a couple months," he began again, "Do you know that, Dean?" I continued my silence, knowing that there was a story to come. I remembered that Judy told me that the Philmores were kings of a boardwalk shore amusement empire. Not that I really knew much about carnival workers. After he blew his nose, Mr. Philmore continued, "I've been negotiating with my employee's union for months now...they want a lot of perks that I can't offer, things have been tense all summer long." It became evident that whether I was a Dean, or a therapist, Mr. Philmore needed someone to talk to. He continued, "Seasonal workers aren't always the easiest to manage. Many of them are transients, gypsies really, moving from place to place all over the country during the year-- wherever the sun and the work are. How do I give health benefits to people I may only see for a few months a year? This is the kind of thing they're asking for. Don't misunderstand me, my workers are good people who work hard, but it's been tough."

Since I had never much thought about the carnival culture, I was intrigued and asked, "What's been the problem?"

"Their union wants better benefits, pay, retirement... the usual for any worker. But the problem is that at least 60% of my workforce never returns from month to month... people come and go all the time. From my perspective, it's hard to justify giving more to an unsteady workforce. But they're claiming unfair work practice. The situation has really heated up over the past couple of weeks, and now Jessica's missing." He let out a huge sigh, "I'm sorry to bore you with this."

"Not at all, Mr. Philmore."

"Oh, call me Jack, and thank you for your time, Dean."

"You can call me Doug, and I will keep you posted. If

you have any questions at all, give me a call."

"Thank you, I will. Oh, and I gave your secretary my cell phone number. With everything that's been going on at work, I'm often in the field. It's the quickest way to get me." With that, we ended the conversation. Jack Philmore had impressed me, mostly because his affect was in stark comparison to his icy cold ex-wife. A fleeting thought rushed through my mind that Jessica's disappearance was a contrived manipulation by Mrs. Philmore, and Jessica, to get back at Jack. Family wars can be very ugly.

Just then, Judy was knocking at my door, "Doug, the Mayor's on the phone for you." I hadn't yet heard from Mayor Theodore Carcass and wondered if any of his busybody constituents had pulled his ear. When you first hear it, Carcass is a funny name for the mayor and first lady of the Shores. When you learn that the couple moonlights as the owners and operators of our town's only funeral home, Carcass becomes a hilarious name. Perfectly fitting for a man named after a dead hunk of animal flesh, even though he assures us all that the emphasis is on the last syllable, "Car*cass*". This, I suppose, is perfectly fitting for a politician. I'm not sure that the pronunciation helps much, however, since children still snicker and sick people still cringe.

"I'll talk to him." I said, looking at the blinking button on my phone, "Mayor, this is Doug." Mayor Carcass is the perfect picture of a figurehead for our quirky little town: good looking at face value, but a little off. He's a perpetually tanned, strapping man of 6'2" with glimmering silver hair. Even though he's been a resident of New Jersey for at least 40 years, he speaks with somewhat of a southern drawl. Now, since small town politics are hardly a fulltime job, Mayor Carcass keeps himself busy with his duties as resident mortician and funeral home director.

On the other end of the line, the oddly southern gentleman jumped to life when he heard my voice, "Dean Doug," he called, the words coming out slowly like molasses, "What's this I hear going on down there? Is everybody alright?" Despite his sometimes saccharin manner, the Mayor is a good-hearted man whom I like.

"Well Mayor," I began, "Everyone's a bit shaken. We still don't have any word on the young woman who's missing."

"Oh! What a shame... and what's this I hear about voodoo and animal sacrifice?"

"So I see that Malificent has spoken to you." I could have let it go, but why not speak my mind? The statement clearly ruffled his southern sensibilities as he stammered, "Well, uh, a great many people have spoken to me... uh, they are all concerned. What kind of situation do we have, Doug? Murder? Religious sacrifice? Do you need help?" I was beginning to feel like a broken record, "We're working with Chief Morreale. He's working with other agencies to help find Jessica, and in terms of the other incidents, we have no reason to believe that voodoo or sacrifice is to blame."

"Then what is it? Doug, I'm not trying to challenge you, but when something like this happens in our sleepy little shore town, people get upset." This serious statement seemed humorous since there had been at least five unexplained or gruesome deaths in our "sleepy little shore town" in as many years.

"We're not sure what happened with the vending machine, exactly. Could be vandalism. May be a distasteful prank. But at this point we're confident that all the kittens and puppies in the Shores are safe and the only "voodoo" happening occurs when somebody dusts off their Ouija board." The Mayor breathed deeply and I could tell that he was relieved.

"Thank you Dean Doug, I appreciate that, and the town's folk will appreciate that information as well. That's all they want, some reassurance. I'll do my best to dispel any more rumors. You know how some of these people can get around here; sometimes it seems like everyone's a bit titched." Now that was the understatement of the Century, especially coming from Mayor Theodore Carcass from New

Jersey who speaks with a southern accent and embalms dead people. "I promise to keep you updated, Mayor," I responded and we disengaged.

I spent the rest of the morning returning phone calls. I spoke with concerned parents, Trustees, faculty and staff all worried about the incidents of late. One parent was alarmed because she had heard that there was a serial killer on the loose. I refrained from telling her that if there was, I hoped to be the next on the list so that I could be put out of my misery. By noontime I was starving, the fuel provided by my morning bowl of oatmeal long gone. With perfect timing, Jerry popped his head into my office, "Hey, Doug. Want to grab lunch?" I gladly accepted.

I normally bring my lunch. It's not because I'm particularly thrifty, but more for health reasons. If I bring a turkey sandwich and pretzels, I'm less tempted to grab a burger and fries. Today, however, I was happy that my lunch bag was resting peacefully on my kitchen counter at home, and I was ready to stuff my gut full of all the greasy comfort food my stomach could hold. We walked downstairs to the Student Center food court. Another reason for me to bring my lunch... constantly being tempted by the delicious aromas of boiling oil and pizza sitting right below my office, wafting up through the floor on a daily basis. Today, I embraced the scents of the food court like a cinnamon candle at Christmas.

We got our lunch (I selected the Big Burger Platter) and found a seat. The food court consists of a number of food stations-- sandwiches, pizza, grill, salad/vegetarian in a well-lit serving area that is adjacent to an expanse with tables and booths. At one time, probably 300 people can eat off of paper plates and plastic trays comfortably.

Today, the open space of the food court cast an odd sense of vulnerability over me. It suddenly made me wish that I had worn a disguise. Sunglasses or hat, Groucho nose, anything. I steered us toward a booth in the back corner of the room, hoping to avoid being accosted by anyone.

Fortunately, Jerry and I had a normal lunch with little conversation about Jessica Philmore. Once I filled Jerry in on the latest with the case, he filled me in on the latest trials and tribulations of his love life. Jerry is my closest friend at Westmire, so we often mix discussions of business with personal life. He has a social life that any extrovert would kill for. I, on the other hand, would rather be set on fire than to be cavorting around the bar scene on a regular basis. He talked about Jenny Benson the blond, Melanie Matakis from New York City and Beth from Bones pub who apparently did not have a last name. Perhaps if he met her somewhere beyond Bones pub, she would have. I grazed and listened with hearty fervor, conscious that I was not on the hot seat for the first time in several hours. Of course, all good things come to an end... sometimes abruptly.

As Jerry continued relaying his love life, I became aware of a buzz behind me. Some new stir had set people into motion, moving faster, with voices more manic than usual. Although Jerry was facing out toward the entrance of the food court, and I was facing the wall, he clearly was oblivious. I turned to look behind me, and saw people running into the seating area waving newspapers. Ah, the weekly *Westmire Word*, our campus newspaper, had arrived. Jerry suddenly tuned back into reality, perhaps because now he was speaking to the back of my head, and craned his neck out from the booth to look. "That can't be good," he said, deadpan.

We got up, dumped our trays in the garbage can and made our way toward the main corridor of the Student Center where the *Word* is delivered every week. As we approached, we saw students scurrying around the newspaper bin like ants on a sandwich. I made my way through the crowd, grabbed two copies and eagerly read the headline, "MURDER AT WESTMIRE?" was spelled in capital letters.

Now the *Westmire Word* is a weekly rag that serves up an even mix of sensationalism, slander and comics. Its current headline, a creative journalistic digression from the more common, *Murder at Westmire!*, was not uncommon on campus. In fact, the budding student journalists who produce the weekly drivel have used a variation of that very headline at least once a year since 1984. The result is always shocking, and the response always melodramatic, which is exactly why the editorial team keeps using it. It's sort of like having your favorite soap opera character die, and come back to life time and time again. Although it's ridiculous, you just can't wait for more.

I handed Jerry a copy, and we both headed toward the stairwell up to our offices. I had no intention of adding to the drama by standing in the hallway and reading the paper. After all, I assumed that I knew more than the writer of the article, so I probably already knew the details. As I stepped on the second or third stair, however, my plan to quietly go to the sanctum of my office was thwarted.

"Dean Doug!" I heard a voice behind me. Jerry and I both stopped and turned to look. Through the crowd, I could see the *Word* reporter, Mike Godfrey, waving a copy of the paper in his hand toward me. Wouldn't Jimmy Olsen be proud. He came closer to the stairs and the crowd began to huddle around him.

"Dean Doug, do you care to comment on the alleged murder?" he called, voice trembling with excitement. As I stood calmly on the third stair, I simply said, "No, Mike. I haven't read your article yet." I thought that was a fair, non-inflammatory statement, but apparently I was wrong, because then someone in the back of the huddle yelled, "He's the Dean and he doesn't even *know*?" This elicited a number of worried faces, outbursts and agitation among the masses, and I knew that I would have to explain myself, right there on the Student Center stairs for all to see. I felt like a dirty politician explaining an extramarital affair.

Instinctually, I raised both of my hands in the air to quiet the crowd, "I didn't say that," I responded. I wasn't angry, upset or shocked, so it was relatively easy to exhibit a sense of calm, at least that was my goal. I continued as the crowd *shushed* each other to listen, "What I said is that

I haven't read the *Word* article, so I can't comment on it."

"But Dean, don't you feel that these allegations are abominable?" Mike called. He was being obnoxious enough that I felt a little public flogging was warranted. This is student development at it's best, "Mike, although you have pieced together hearsay to render your article, I have no knowledge of any allegations. An allegation is an assertion without proof. If there are allegations, *you*, alone, have made them." My response generated some mocking, "Ooohs and Ahhhs" from the crowd toward Mike, but my attempt to diffuse the situation had worked. Attention shifted from me toward Mike, thus making my opportunity to exit.

"Now folks," I said, "Let me get back to my office. Among other things, I have a newspaper article to read. If any of you have questions, you know where to find me." I turned to Jerry who stood, frozen on the stairs behind me, looking faintly like a deer in headlights. As I passed him, I whispered, "They can smell fear. Move it buddy, or they'll follow." With that, he turned like an English guard and followed behind me to my office.

As we passed by Judy, she saw the paper in my hand and said, "I already put one on your desk. *Gaw-bage.*"

"Judy, the paper just came out?" She looked at me over her half glasses, "I've got connections. I got an advance copy." Jerry and I went into my office and shut the door, opening the paper at once. I hadn't felt like this since I sneaked a Playboy magazine into my room when I was twelve. The first few paragraphs of the article read:

MURDER AT WESTMIRE?
by Michael Godfrey

A shocking turn of events happened yesterday in the Student Center. The sound of screams could be heard all the way from the first floor as a second floor vending machine had been turned into a grisly spectacle. "It was awful," said Robin Tucker, WC sophomore, "There was blood everywhere. The stench was awful. Who could have done this?"

Sources say that Dean is worried for students' safety.

Apparently, perpetrators broke into the vending machine and replaced many of its snack items with dead animals, including fetal pigs and a kitten. Allegedly written in blood on the machine's glass was, "MURDER."

Ben Braddock, WC freshman commented, "What are they going to do about this? I pay a lot of money to be at this school... I should feel safe. This doesn't make me feel safe, it makes me nervous." Dean Douglas Carter-Connors, who was on the scene, would not comment on the case. However, in an exclusive anonymous interview, one WC staffer said, "Dean Doug is worried that there might be a killer on the loose. He's very worried."

"It looks like a cover-up to me," said Rhonda Parks, WC senior, "This isn't the first time. They cover things up so that other people, who don't live here, don't get upset. Well I'm upset and I live here. I want answers and I want them now!"

I looked at Jerry, "So.... Do *you* think I'm worried?" Jerry didn't respond, still engrossed in the rag. Other than the nervous state that I was allegedly in, as I suspected, there weren't any great revelations in the article. In true *Word* fashion, it argued for murder without any real evidence. In true Mike Godfrey fashion, it used too many sensational words like, "despicable" and "perilous". That kid is destined to work for the *National Enquirer* or the *New York Times*, I haven't figured out which. Of course, the article linked Jessica Philmore's disappearance with the candy machine murder mystery alleging that a probable sociopath was on the loose and also alleging that the administration (me) was covering it up to save the school's reputation. Little did Mike know that the reputation of his school's alma mater had been scarred long ago.

More disturbing to me were allegations of the connection between Jessica's disappearance and Sarah Borden's practicing witchcraft. Although Sarah's name wasn't specifically mentioned, the article indicated that, "according to sources, a student very close to Philmore, perhaps a roommate, is a known witch, practicing evil spells and incantations on a daily basis." I was now even more worried about what backlash this would have on Sarah.

Jerry and I closed our papers almost simultaneously. "What'd you think?" he asked.

"It's what I expected. Nothing new. I'm just concerned about Sarah Borden. Can you make sure that your staff keeps a close eye on her in the residence halls?"

"Already done."

Just as I was thanking Jerry for his help and he was walking out of my office, Judy stood in the doorway stopping him, hand on her hip, bow of her glasses held in her mouth, "Hold it there," she said, "Peter Gaines from the Misty Dorm is on the phone, Doug. He sounds upset." Jerry stopped and I picked up the phone.

"Hi, Peter, this is Doug. Everything ok?"

"Is Mrs. Philmore with you?"

"No, I haven't seen her today. Is she not at your place?"

"Well, I'm concerned. No one has seen her today. When our housekeeper went into her room to make it up early about thirty minutes ago, it was somewhat of a shambles."

"What do you mean?"

"The covers were torn off the bed, the closet door was wide open with hangers all over the floor, dresser drawers left half open: Shambles! I went to look, even the pot of tea that I brought her last night was on the floor, broken into a million pieces."

"Peter, did you call Chief Morreale?"

"No, not yet, I thought that she might be with you... I didn't want to call for alarm if there was an explanation."

"I'm sure that there's an explanation, but I don't know what it is. What about her personal items, are they in the room?"

"Well, she didn't have any. I guess when she came to see you in the morning she didn't pack a bag first, because when she was brought to the Misty Dorm, she was empty handed." Peter was right. I hadn't even thought that we put a person up in a hotel without any personal belongings. Peter continued, "I gave her a robe, a toothbrush and some other sundries to tide her over." As Peter spoke, another detail that I missed came to me: Did she have a car? How did she get to Westmire? In yesterday's confusion, I hadn't asked. I was going to have to check with Judy to see what she did with Mrs. Philmore when I handed her off yesterday.

"Peter," I said, "Hold on for a few minutes... let me check a few things and I'll get right back to you." I buzzed Judy and asked her to come to my office.

"What's up?" she asked.

"Judy, when you arranged for Mrs. Philmore to get to the Misty Dorm yesterday, how did you do it?"

"I called campus security and had them take her over there." This was not usual, but in this case, warranted and appropriate.

"Do you know if she had a car? Or how she *got* to campus yesterday?"

"No, and she never made mention of it. Is something wrong?"

"We can't find her."

"She's missing too?"

"I hope not. Can you do me a favor? Can you call her home and see if she's there or if anyone has heard from her? But be as discreet as you can, I don't want to alarm them."

"Them?" Judy inquired.

"Her staff. I believe that she lives in Manhattan and has a staff. She *is* part of the Brooklyn Philmores, after all, you told me that," I smirked.

Judy didn't even honor my humor with a reaction, "I'm on it!" she answered and turned out of the doorway, only to return five minutes later.

"Ok boss," she said, steno book and pencil in hand, "No luck. They haven't heard from her."

"Who'd you speak to?"

"Housekeeper, woman named Mildred who answered the phone. When I told her that I was from Westmire College, the woman said that Mrs. Philmore was here."

"Did you say that you were from my office?" I was afraid that we would cause alarm if Mrs. Philmore was thought to be here and we had no idea where.

"Oh ye of little faith, of course not. I said that I was Helen from the parent relations office updating our records."

"Judy, we don't have a parent relations office."

"And my name's not Helen, what's your point?" Leave it to Judy to unintentionally make a tense situation humorous. "At any rate, they think she's here."

"Thanks, Judy, great job. Now if you would, please give Chief Morreale a call and ask him to meet me at the Misty Dorm... and call Peter and tell him that I'm on my way." With that, I grabbed my jacket and headed off to the Misty Dorm by the Sea.

By the time I walked the few short blocks from campus to Mount Tabor Way, Chief Morreale's police cruiser was already parked outside of the Misty Dorm. In the tourist industry *that's* always good for business... I'm sure that Peter and Patrick were glad that it wasn't high season. The Misty Dorm is an old Victorian house complete with a widow's walk and gingerbread scrollwork that's one of the nicest in town. In my opinion, Peter Gaines and Patrick Sheen are the nicest innkeepers in town, too. The massive house is grey, trimmed in true historical fashion with multiple complementary colors: Cranberry, white, and dark grey. It's a beauty.

I opened the white wrought-iron gate that lines the circumference of the property and walked up to the front wrap around porch. Roses, geraniums, petunias and black-eyed-susans lined the walk, bursting in end-of-summer splendor. At the shore, gardens often last into November, until they die not of frost, but exhaustion. There was a middle-aged couple relaxing on the porch, one in the porch swing, and the other in a white wicker rocker. They held hands and gazed at the ocean, oblivious to my presence. I rang the doorbell and walked into the foyer, where I found Peter, Patrick, and Chief Morreale.

"Oh, Doug," exclaimed Peter, "I'm so happy that you're here. The Chief just arrived." Peter is a slight, white haired man in his early sixties who is almost never seen without a teapot in his hand, this moment being no exception. His partner in both business and life, Patrick, is a tall 6-foot something, with the same silver hair and the looks of a well preserved movie star. A devout Irishman, Patrick is never seen not wearing something green. Today, the green item of choice was his Bermuda shorts. I shook everyone's hand and then said to the Chief, "Have you been upstairs yet?"

"No, I literally just got here. Let's go up." Peter led the way up the stairs with the Chief, Patrick, and me trailing behind. Peter snaked us through the narrow halls, past many of the fifteen guestrooms, to #8. As Peter opened the door with a passkey, he said, "I wanted Mrs. Philmore to be comfortable, so I gave her a room with an ocean view." The room was big enough to be considered spacious, yet small enough to be cozy. It had light pink walls with white woodwork, frilly lace curtains covering a very large window, and a patchwork quilt on the white wrought-iron double bed. It was a dream for any little girl, or hardworking mother of three who needed to spend a weekend away. Although it may not be the taste of most husbands, it's aphrodisiac qualities seemed rich. The room's state of disarray was striking and in stark contrast to it's cutesy appeal.

Patrick and the Chief walked into the space, while Peter and I stood near the doorway to stay out of the way. Patrick pointed out the broken porcelain teapot that had shattered on the floor (he also mentioned that it had come from England and was one of his favorites), the empty dresser drawers pulled halfway out and the hangers resting on the floor of the wide-open closet. He also remarked that the beautiful quilt was in a ball at the foot of the bed, with the sheets half-clinging to the sides and the rest on the floor. Patrick put one hand on his mouth, the other on his heart and sighed deeply.

The Chief walked around the room inspecting it carefully. He looked under the bed, in the attached bathroom (most of the Misty Dorm's rooms have private baths), out the window and under the bed. "When did you last see her?" he asked finally, directing the question toward Peter or Patrick.

"Well, I brought her the chamomile tea at around seven, I guess," answered Patrick.

"And did you hear anything after that?"

"Not that I remember, but Peter and I were in the back having dinner. I made a lovely rack of lamb." The back quarter of the bed and breakfast is private living quarters for Peter and Patrick. Although I had never been back there, Peter once told me that it consisted of a bedroom, one and a half baths, living room, dining room, study, and well-equipped kitchen.

"And Doug, Patrick says that you're not sure if she drove here by herself?" the Chief asked.

"That's right," I said, "we don't know. Under the circumstances, I didn't even think of it. Mrs. Philmore arrived on our doorstep first thing yesterday morning. When we set her up here, Judy had Campus Security drop her off. Apparently there was never any mention of a car. Do you want me to check with Chief Braggish to see who dropped her off?"

"I'd appreciate that. And Patrick, depending on what we find out, I may want to talk to your guests."

"That's no problem," said Peter, "we only have a handful." As the Chief asked Peter and Patrick a few more questions, I went down to the porch to get better cell-phone reception and called Westmire Campus Security. As luck would have it, Security Chief Tina Braggish was available.

"Hi, Dean Doug. What can I do for you?" she asked in

the voice of an eager army recruit.

"Hi, Tina. Do you know who dropped Mrs. Philmore off at the Misty Dorm yesterday?"

"I did it myself," Tina said proudly, "Judy called, said that the woman was upset and asked if someone could escort her to the Dorm. This is an important case, so I wanted to make sure that we handled it professionally."

"Do you remember if she mentioned having a car?"

"She didn't, but I asked her, because if she was going to leave her car parked on campus, I wanted to make sure that we didn't ticket her. She said that she didn't have one."

"Did she say how she got to campus?"

"No, and I didn't ask. I'm sorry, Doug, should I have asked? Is something wrong?"

"No; I mean we don't know. We can't find Mrs. Philmore, but we're not sure of anything. But please, Tina, keep that confidential. We don't want any more panic on campus than we already have."

"Affirmative, Dean." Tina responded, "I'm sorry to hear about that. If you need anything else, please let me know."

"Will do." I said, and hung up the phone. What was going on with the Philmores? Was someone plotting against the family? I walked inside and back upstairs to share the latest twist. When I walked into room #8, I could tell that something had happened. Patrick was hugging himself around the middle and Peter's perpetually tanned face looked ashy. The Chief was standing near the room's telephone that was situated on one of the wicker night tables. He looked glum.

"What happened?" I asked suspiciously, "Why do I get the feeling that you have bad news that surpasses my bad news?"

"Will you excuse us?" the Chief asked politely.

"Of course," said Patrick, putting a coaxing hand around Peter's shoulder, "We'll be downstairs." As they left, Patrick shut the door behind them.

"It's Jessica Philmore," the Chief stated sullenly as soon as the door latched, "the station just tracked me down and told me to call Mayor Carcass. I just got off the phone with him. He's just gotten a call about a body, Doug. We think we've got your girl."

9

The body had been found on the beach. Apparently, a fisherman casting his line off the sand had grabbed onto it with his hook and reeled in a really big surprise. The Chief reluctantly let me jump into his police cruiser and accompany him the three short beach blocks. At first, Chief Morreale wasn't keen on me going to the scene, but acquiesced when he saw my demeanor. Since Jessica was my student, I wasn't taking no for an answer. The best I could do was to promise not to get in the way.

We parked on the boardwalk side next to the beach's Jersey Avenue entrance, which is on the south end, five blocks from the College. We got out of the car, and walked down the wooden plank steps onto the sandy walkway to the beach. The cool afternoon breeze gently moved the sea grass on the dunes flanking the path. I had never before felt such a mix of dread and excited anticipation.

As we cleared the dunes and entered the flat beach, Chief Morreale stopped in front of me and motioned for me to stay, "Doug," he said, "I know that this is important to you, but I need you to wait here for now." Peering past his shoulder as he was speaking, I could see the body lying awkwardly next to the water's edge about 50 yards away. Yellow police tape that I assumed said, "Police – Do not Cross", had been wrapped around stakes that circled the area.

One of the chief's officers, a lifeguard, and the fisherman stood near the perimeter of the tape. Presiding over all of them was Shirley "Mama" Porter, the Shore's beach manager. I could also see a couple of surfers, beachcombers and seagulls, all straining to get a look, standing on the beach a distance away. Dread got the most of me, and I didn't argue with the Chief to let me closer. Frankly, I wasn't sure if I was ready.

As I watched the Chief get closer, I found myself having to turn away. I looked up toward the sky, hoping to pull some comfort from its peaceful blue. Although not a religious man, I said a prayer. I prayed for Jessica, for her mother, and for myself. I took a breath, and turned back toward the scene. The Chief was bending down close to the body on his hands and knees. From what I could see, the corpse was stomach down in the sand, arms at the side. Long, dark blonde hair, wet and tangled covered the face. The Chief got up, spoke to the fisherman and Mama, and then to his officer. Mayor Carcass, now in his capacity as funeral home director, joined the scene from a south beach entrance north of Jersey Avenue, and immediately began inspecting the body.

After probably thirty minutes or so, Chief Morreale made his way back to me near the dunes. He took off his hat, and wiped his brow with a handkerchief, "We have a Caucasian, female. It's hard to say, but she appears to be 16-20 years old. Blonde hair. She's wearing a Westmire College sweatshirt." My heart sank to the pit of my stomach. "Doug," the Chief continued, "Can you identify the body?"

I began speaking slowly, as if on a sedative, "No, Chief, I can't..." Before I finished my sentence, the Chief broke in, "Now I understand that this is difficult, but we need to know..." I interrupted him this time.

"Chief," I said, "I've never met Jessica. I'm sure that I've seen her, but I can't be certain."

Chief Morreale thought, "Well, now since her mother's MIA, is there someone else from the College who can identify her? What about her roommate, the one with the dark hair or that boyfriend?" Although I wouldn't wish the task of identifying a body on anyone, I especially wouldn't wish it on a student.

"No," I said, "It will have to be Keesha Cribbs. She's on my staff and is one of the few who has actually spoken with

Jessica."

"Fine," the Chief responded, "We'll still be a while here. The guy fishing is pretty upset. So are Mama and her lifeguard. They were here closing up for the season when they heard the guy yelling. We need to take some pictures and collect some evidence before we transport the body to the funeral home... could be a couple of hours." In our town, the morgue and the funeral home are one in the same.

"I'll go back to the office and talk to Keesha. Call us when you need us." I said.

"Good. Thanks, Doug... and I'm sorry."

"Thank you," I said, "and thanks for your help." As I turned to make my way up the path to the boardwalk, the Chief called after me, "Doug, do you need a ride?" I waved him on, "No thanks, I'd rather walk." I responded without looking at him. If I had, I was afraid that he would have seen the tears in my eyes. I was already hoping that the sound of the surf covered the waver in my voice.

As I walked up the steps onto the boardwalk I could see the sandy imprints of feet on the planks moving toward the beach. Some were human, others were paw-prints, clearly outlined in the sand, like a less permanent version of the imprints on the Hollywood Walk of Fame. I wondered if any of the footprints were Jessica's; her final footsteps as a living human. I found myself stepping around the sandy images, being careful not to destroy them, just in case. It was the least I could do.

I ambled my way back to campus in what seemed like a dream state. This wasn't happening. Of all the odd and sometimes sinister things that had happened in this town, this was the worst. One of my students was dead, her mother was missing, and we had no idea why. I rehearsed what I would say to my staff, and just how I would tell Keesha that we needed *her* to identify Jessica. It was going to be rough. As I approached the campus, I vaguely noticed a faint buzzing at my hip. My cell phone was ringing. I keep it on vibrate for courtesy reasons, but mostly because I have no clue about how to make it ring.

I looked on the digital panel and saw that it was Barbara.

"Hi," I said.

"Hi, sweetie," She said, "I heard the news, are you all right?" I guess word spread especially quick.

"I'm ok," I said stopping short of the main gates on campus. This wasn't the sort of conversation to have in passing, "We'll have to go later to identify the body, and I have to ask Keesha to do it."

"Body?" Barbara said, clearly surprised, "She's dead? I just heard that she was missing?" I realized that we were talking about two different things.

"No, Barbara, they think they found Jessica Philmore's body on the beach... what news were you calling about?"

"Kate from the paper called me and said that now Mrs. Philmore was missing. She asked what I could find out," Kate Clark was the editor-in-chief of the *Shores' Sentinel,* our local newspaper for which Barbara freelanced. Although Barbara never wrote headline news (she mostly wrote features), Kate never could help herself from asking Barbara for the scoop on anything dealing with Westmire College. Of course, Barbara never capitulated, especially now. "Oh my God, Doug. They found Jessica on the beach?"

"They think so; they're pretty sure. The Chief and Mayor are there now. Apparently she was in the water and a fisherman dragged her to shore with his line."

"Oh, Doug." Barbara said in her kindly, consoling voice, "I'm so sorry."

"Thanks, honey." I said, "But you're right. Mrs. Philmore is missing too. What a mess."

"I wish you could come home right now so Ethan and I could be with you."

"Me too, but I've got bodies to see and missing people to find. I'll call you later, I have no idea how long I'll be."

We said that we loved each other and I walked onto campus. A few people stopped me along the way to ask if anything was new in the case, a few others asked non-related but welcomed questions about parking tickets and bad dining hall food. I did my best to remain cool and evasive on all fronts.

As I got to my office, the sense of dread was so large in my chest that it felt as if I would burst. I waved to Judy, who was in her usual position with the phone attached to her shoulder and ear, and the few students who were working in the office. Since Keesha's office was directly off the reception area, I had no reason not to stop there first, although I really wanted to retreat to my office and hide.

I looked into Keesha's office and was disappointed to find her sitting at her desk working on her computer. No procrastination for me. I went to her door and knocked quietly.

"Hi, Doug," Keesha said brightly, "What's up?" I moved into her office and shut the door behind me, precipitating a skeptical look from Keesha.

"That can't be good," she said.

"No. It's not." I took a seat adjacent to her and began. I hadn't been this nervous since I proposed marriage, "Keesha, I'm going to need your help this afternoon."

"Sure," Keesha said slowly, with a hint of reluctance, "Doug, what's going on?" Although she was young, Keesha was a wise woman with keen insight.

"Keesha, I'm sorry," I stammered a bit, "the best way to say this is to just say this... they found a body..." Keesha became rigid, and sat stoically in her seat. I continued, "... on the beach, this afternoon. We need you to identify it... the body." The word "it" seemed too disrespectful to me.

Keesha stared at me with disbelief but said nothing for a minute or two. I fought everything not to look away and continued to meet her gaze. Finally, she spoke, "They found her on the beach?"

"Yes."

"When do you need me?"

"Probably in a couple of hours. When I left the beach just now, the police were there investigating and Mayor Carcass just arrived. I assume that he'll take her to the funeral home and we'll meet there."

"I can't believe it." Keesha said distantly. She sat for another moment, and then rocked herself back into the present with a slight shake of her head, "Of course, Doug. I'll be here. You just tell me when."

"I wouldn't ask normally, but you seem to be one of the few staff members who knows what Jessica looks like... of course I'll go with you." With that, Keesha got out of her chair and hugged me. Although I care about my staff a great deal, I'm not particularly a "huggy" person. This time, however, I hugged her too.

As I was leaving the office, I said, "Just don't say anything yet... we don't want to panic people." Keesha agreed and the both of us pretended to work for the remainder of the afternoon. The paperwork on my desk became some sort of office solitaire. I would move one piece to the upper left corner and another from the middle to the bottom right, only to bring them back together in a neat stack and try again. It was futile. I couldn't concentrate on anything. Finally, at 5:15 or so, Judy buzzed me, "Doug, it's Mayor Carcass?" My heart began pumping furiously as I picked up the receiver, "Hi, Ted." All I heard on the other end was a deep sigh, "Hi, Doug," he drawled, "I think we're ready for you. She's here, and I've prettied her up as much as possible. Luckily, Dr. Geddes has already been here and completed the examination." Dr. Geddes was our town physician and when necessary, medical examiner.

"Well, one of my staff, Keesha Cribbs is going to identify her. We'll be right there," I said.

"Ok, that sounds fine. Why don't you come in through the back, so as not to raise attention? How long will you be, 15 minutes?"

"Yeah, probably."

"Good," said the Mayor, "That'll give me time to brush

her hair for you." I didn't know what to do with that comment. It both touched and repulsed me. We hung up, I got Keesha, and we headed out the door.

We walked slowly to the Lullaby Forever Memorial Home, on Jersey Avenue, which is only about 5 blocks away. Although the name was meant to offer a sense of serenity and comfort, it always struck me as creepy, in an ironic, laughable sort of way. Keesha and I made some small talk along the way, talking about family and TV shows, as if we were headed out for ice cream and not to identify a dead student. As we approached the funeral home, however, all conversation stopped in mental preparation. The Lullaby Forever is another of our town's Victorian houses. In New Jersey, Westmire Shores has the most Victorian structures next to Cape May. It is painted light pink with white and yellow trim, with bright yellow and white striped awnings over each window. It'd be a cheery little place if it weren't a house of death. I always thought that it looked more ice cream than funeral parlor.

We passed the home and went to the back door. The Mayor was right, if we had walked in through the front door, someone was bound to see us and begin speculation. We rang the bell and waited. Mayor Carcass answered a few moments later, wearing a light blue smock that made his hair even more shockingly white. He answered the door as if we had come for dinner, "Come in! Come in!" he said, "Can I get you anything?" Was he serious? What, a glass of Chardonnay maybe? I guess even funeral home directors don't know what to say. The back door entered into the home's office, which was covered in faded yet dark burgundy wallpaper. The vintage tin ceiling was painted white holding an ornate brass chandelier. Around the room were a few floor lamps, a large mahogany desk, and a couple of easy chairs.

Keesha and I both declined a beverage, and I introduced them to each other. Then, being as polite as possible, I said, "I think we'd just like to get this over with," hoping not to offend. "Of course, of course," the Mayor replied, and he led us down a dim hallway to a stairway that led to the basement. The Lullaby Forever Funeral Home was also the residence of the Carcasses. The top two floors of this three-story structure is their home. As I walked, I couldn't help but wonder how anyone could live over a funeral parlor? How do you put up your Christmas tree, watch C.S.I., or make love with dead people a floor or two below?

The foot of the stairs entered into what resembled a hospital's operating room. The walls were painted stark white, the floor institutional sea-foam green linoleum tile. There were stainless steel cabinets around the perimeter and a large, stainless steel overhead lamp that hung over a stainless steel table. On the table, laid a body draped in a white sheet. At the far end of the table, I could see strands of long, blonde hair peeking below the material.

The Mayor walked briskly to the head of the table, laying his hands gently on the shoulders of the body. Keesha and I approached much more slowly, practically shuffling our way, inch by inch, to the slab. I could only assume that Keesha was scared senseless because that's how I felt. As we reached within two feet of the body, Keesha stopped. She was now wrapping her arms around her slight middle, hugging herself. I moved next to her, put my arm around her shoulders, looked at the Mayor and then Keesha, "Are you ready for this?" I asked. Keesha simply nodded her head, eyes fearful, lips pursed. I tightened my grip around her shoulders and nodded to the Mayor.

"Please remember, the water causes some bloating," he said, "so her appearance is somewhat altered." Mayor Carcass gingerly pulled the sheet up and over, exposing the face and shoulders. The body's pale, green-tinted flesh made its blonde hair take on a golden hue. I could tell that the Mayor had tried his best to make her look as if she was sleeping by applying a touch of make-up around her face.

However, I could still see hints of ice-blue lips from beneath an application of a more natural rosy lipstick. I also noticed some abrasions on the face that had been touched up with a little powder. Despite his best efforts, this poor young woman still looked very dead, and through her stillness exuded a sense of anguish.

I turned my face away to look directly at Keesha. She had started to shiver a little, which I could feel from holding her. She stared, mesmerized at the person on the slab, eyes unblinking. The Mayor and I looked at each other and then back at Keesha. Although I didn't want to push her, the anticipation for her response bubbled up in me like bile. After sixty seconds of silence or so, I was shocked when Keesha took a small step closer, her eyes still fixed. Finally, she spoke, "Can I see her feet?" she said softly, with little air in her lungs to muster any volume.

I shot a worried glance at the Mayor and said, "Keesha, are you ok?" She did not break her steady gaze and replied, "May I please see her feet?" I looked again at the Mayor who nodded. He folded the sheet over the body's chest, and moved to the other end of the table to lift up the other end of the sheet. Again, he slowly lifted the sheet up and over the feet, and gently folded it over the shins. Clearly, the Mayor had not tried to make the feet look more alive. They were a yellowish green, covered with small cuts and scrapes. They turned in toward each other, big toes touching, as if comforting each other. Keesha breathed deeply, and then exhaled, shaking her head rapidly, "That's not her," she said.

I was stunned. I looked at the Mayor and then back at Keesha, "Are you sure?"

"Yes," she said, smiling now, "It's not Jessica." Keesha finally broke her gaze, and looked at me, "That's why I wanted to see her feet. Jessica has a tattoo on her right ankle." The Mayor and I immediately looked at the body's right ankle, seeing nothing.

"How did you know that?" I asked.

"When she was in my office that day, we talked about it.

She was wearing shorts and sandals, and I commented that I liked it. It was a leaf. She said that her parents didn't know about it, so she kept a band-aid over it at home." Keesha was speaking rapidly now, and took a breath to look up at the ceiling and clasp her hands, "It's not her!"

Unfortunately, I wasn't able to share in Keesha's jubilation. The young woman on the slab had been found wearing a Westmire College sweatshirt. If this wasn't Jessica Philmore, then who was it? As Keesha hugged me in celebration, fear rose within me and tightened its grip around my chest. Although I didn't recognize her, did I actually have two missing students and not know it? And now, was one of them actually dead?

10

It was almost six-thirty when Keesha and I walked back to campus. As we walked, Keesha chattered excitedly like a kid at Christmas. The shock of the experience had manifested itself through giddiness. Keesha didn't know that the body had been found wearing Westmire clothing, and I didn't tell her. She had been through enough. I wanted her to debrief and enjoy this sense of relief, no matter how brief.

I walked her to her car in the Student Center parking lot and watched her drive happily home. I stood for a moment, hesitating to run up to my office and grab my briefcase. I didn't want to know what I would find waiting for me. I took a breath, and took the plunge despite my trepidation. Besides, now that I was alone, I needed to call the Mayor and Chief Morreale to get some information on whom we had just visited at the Lullaby Forever Memorial Home. I would wait to call until I got to the privacy of my locked office.

The moment I walked into the Student Center, WC reality struck me. Flyers littered the bulletin boards reminding students, and me, of tomorrow morning's student walk out, which was the least of my worries. I put my head down, and walked briskly up the stairs to my office. As I reached to top stair, I saw a little old lady standing outside of the locked Dean of Students office suite peering in through the glass.

She was almost five feet tall, wearing powder blue polyester pants, which matched the hue in her tightly curled hair, white orthopedic shoes and a white cardigan. She was using one hand over her brow to peek through the glass better, and holding flyers of some sort in the other. Her hands were covered by white gloves, which was a dead give away. The dreaded Ladies Auxiliary. Where was Judy when I needed her? I fought the urge to turn back around, unseen, but knew if I had, she would probably still be waiting in the morning. These Ladies were persistent. Despite my desire to run, screaming down the stairs, I approached her like a good Dean should.

"May I help you, Ma'am?"

She quickly turned from the window and moved her peeking hand to her chest, "Oh!" she said, "You scared me to death! You shouldn't sneak up on people like that, you know." Perhaps if I didn't find her lurking around my office, I wouldn't have.

"I'm sorry, you looked like you needed something," I refrained to add, 'you looked like you needed something: Such as a life, a new hairdresser, or a new wardrobe.'

"I'm Helen from the Ladies Auxiliary," she said straightening her sweater, "I came by on Auxiliary business, but everything is all locked up."

"Yes, well, the office closes at 5:00pm." I replied. It was now nearly 7:00pm.

"Well I assumed that with everything that is going on around here, someone would be around," she said in her judgmental tone.

"Someone is around. You've found me," I said sweetly, "Let me unlock the door and I'll see what I can do for you."

I unlocked the door to the office suite and she followed right behind me. The only lights that were on came from the outside hallway and the copy room. I purposely didn't turn on the overhead lights, since I didn't want a stream of people running in to ask questions. I find that the fluorescent lights in the office after hours act like a big bug light attracting all sorts of creatures. Helen looked around in the dim surroundings, "Didn't pay your electric bill, hmmmm?" she asked curtly, "With tuition being so high, you must have the resources." I ignored her.

"Helen, what can I do for you?"

"I need to post these flyers," she said, waving them at me, "We're posting them all over town to help find that missing girl. You do know what I'm talking about, don't you?" I wanted to bust this cute little biddy in her very false teeth.

"Yes, ma'am," I said politely, "I've heard of the situation."

"Well, it's the least we can do. At the Ladies Auxiliary our mission is to serve. We even printed them in color! So, what do I need to do to post them on campus?" she asked. We have a posting policy on campus to limit cluttered bulletin boards that are so scattered with flyers that they become unreadable and end up looking more like art nouveau. We also don't post any flyer promoting events with alcohol, such as off-campus bar promotions. My office is the arbiter of the flyers and has to give a stamp of approval before posting. For this, I needed a doctorate.

"Let me see what you have, Helen," I said as she handed them to me. The top of the flyer read, "MISSING" in large red letters. The remainder of the text stated, "Jessica Philmore, Age: 20, Height: 5'5", Weight: thin, blonde hair, blue eyes, nice young woman. Westmire College student. If you have information, contact Westmire Shores Police Department at 555-9990. Reward." There were a few things that struck me about the flyer. First, these women had a better description of Jessica than I did, which made sense because posted largely in the middle of the page was a picture, which I had still been unable to find.

"This is Jessica?" I asked, embarrassed. Good thing I hadn't yet officially introduced myself to Helen.

"Yes, it is. Lovely young woman."

"How do you know her? Where did you get this picture?" I asked, thinking that if I dad it a few hours ago, I could have saved Keesha a trip to the morgue.

"Well, she's very interested in helping people. We met her last year at our annual Ladies Auxiliary Vegetarian and Pig Roast," her voice became quieter and she moved in closer to me, "We had to change the name a few years ago you know."

"Really..." I said, with barely a hint of sarcasm.

"So, Jessica came last fall and asked if she could help. We're not used to volunteers her age. That's where the picture came from - - last year's pig roast. Such a nice young girl... that's why we want to help. We're even posting the reward ourselves." She moved in closer again and lowered her voice, "Fifty dollars, cash money, but keep that one under your hat."

I took the remainder of her flyers, stamped them, and told Helen that we would post them for her first thing in the morning. I also confirmed that the Auxiliary had run them by Chief Morreale, which she assured me they had. Meeting Helen, although initially inconvenient, had proven useful since I now had a face to match Jessica's name. I walked Helen to the door, and thanked her for her help. As she left, she said, "You look familiar to me, young man... I don't think I got your name?"

"Jerry Ricardo." I replied. It had been a long day.

Even though I couldn't wait to get home, I still needed to talk to the Mayor and Chief. I went into my office and closed the door to make the phone calls. Since I had just left the Mayor's place, I called him first. Mrs. Carcass answered and indicated that he was working "in the basement", which I now knew first hand what that meant. When I explained that I had just been there, she immediately transferred my call downstairs. She must have announced my call somehow, because he answered out of breath, "Doug!" he panted, "I knew you'd call."

"Hell of an afternoon, huh?"

"Shocking's more like it, and in my line of work, we don't use that term lightly."

"So how do you go about identifying her body?" I asked.

"We're already on it. I just spoke to the Chief and he's checking records... missing persons databases and things of the like. Are you sure that you haven't gotten any reports of another missing student?"

A wave of panic coursed through my middle, "No," I responded, "Not yet, anyway. But we just found out about Jessica Philmore yesterday, and she's been gone a week."

"Well," said the Mayor as politely as he could, "Keep your ears open. I'm sure she's not yours." I knew that he wasn't sure at all, and neither was I.

"So you don't think that I have to call the Chief?" I asked.

"I don't think so, I'm sure that if he has questions, he'll call you. You should go home and spend some time with your family. That'll do you good." I agreed, thanked him for his help, and left my office and walked home. I was so preoccupied, I didn't even bother to sift through the stack of messages that Judy had left on my desk or peruse my e-mail inbox. In retrospect, I'm glad that I didn't, because I did enjoy my evening with Barbara and Ethan. If I had checked my messages before going home, I would have found one that would have haunted me all night.

11

As I walked to work the next morning, I saw that the town had been papered with the Ladies Auxiliary's "Missing" flyers. Although I had seen the flyers before, they evoked a renewed sense of urgency within me. I now had a face to match the name and it felt like Jessica was begging me for help each time I passed a telephone pole with her stapled to it. I was so taken with Jessica's beseeching stares that I totally forgot about the walkout that was scheduled for that morning... until I walked through the main campus gates.

On the main campus green in front of me, I could see about twenty students painting a large banner. I was glad to see that these activists procrastinated as much with social issues as they did with schoolwork. But, it was only 9:00am; they had a full hour before the revolt was to begin. Good thing Paul Revere wasn't a Westmire student.

I made my way to my office slowly, being stopped as usual by several students, staff and faculty members. One anxious secretary asked me if we had found "the murderer" yet. An excited assistant professor asked me whether the walkout would affect his 1:10pm class. An eager student asked me if classes would be cancelled tomorrow. Also as usual, I didn't have any answers for these folks, but made all of the appropriate facial expressions, head nods and lots of, "We're looking into it". It was nearly 9:30am before I actually made it to my office.

"Busy morning already?" Judy asked in greeting.

"More than usual," I responded, "Who's screaming the loudest for my attention this morning?"

"Surprisingly, no one. We've had a few calls about the walkout, but no one specifically calling on you." Judy stopped and just stared at me, searching for something.

"Are you sure?" I asked. Judy looked side to side and ushered me into my office. She immediately lowered her voice, "What happened yesterday, are you ok. How's Keesha?" Poor Judy, the suspense must have been killing her all night long.

"It wasn't Jessica," I said flatly. Judy looked bewildered, "Then who was it?"

"We don't know yet. But as for now, Jessica is still missing."

"Oh, thank God. I was so worried." While Judy asked a few follow-up questions before returning to her desk, I turned on my computer and began shuffling the messages on my desk from the previous afternoon. I knew that I only had a few minutes before I would have to run out to the quad to witness the dreaded walk out.

I was surprised that there wasn't anything too urgent in phone messages and turned quickly to my e-mail inbox. I glanced quickly, and again, didn't see anything that seemed too urgent. My daily inbox is usually host to at least 20 or so new messages, a mixture from students, staff and faculty, old friends, Barbara, and junk. This day was no exception. I took the message from "Anonymous99", without a subject, as junk, but I would find out later that it wasn't. Without anything seemingly pressing, I got up from my desk and headed to the quad to see what was happening.

By 10:10am, there was probably close to 300 students standing in the quad. As fire alarms rang from the adjacent academic buildings, many had begun chanting, "Westmire has no class! Westmire has no class!" The preppy leader standing on the bench had added a bullhorn to his arsenal of rabble-rousing paraphernalia, so he would alternate sounding the air horn with chanting to the crowd. I recognized him and walked up behind Keesha and Jerry. "Keesha," I asked, "Isn't that Josh Tucker?"

"Taylor." Keesha corrected, "Josh Taylor. He's a member of STOPP." As he continued chanting over the bullhorn as the crowd changed their tune, "Freedom, Yes! Class, No!", Chief Quacky Braggish stormed toward Jerry, Keesha, and me. She sniffed hard, in true Barney Fife fashion, and hiked up her pants around her extensive waist preparing for battle, "What do you think, Dean?" she asked, "Should I get the gas?" I chuckled and then realized that she was serious.

"I'm not sure that would be the best course of action right now, Chief," I replied with an almost straight face, "Is the fire department on its way?"

"Yes, but I'm sure that the fire alarms were pulled by someone in order to up the participation in the rally," she said, "If we find out who orchestrated this, they are in big trouble." In the distance, I could already hear the faint sound of sirens over the din in the quad, "Educate, don't retaliate! Educate, it's not too late!" was the latest cheer. Whatever that meant. I looked around the area for any signs of Professor Preston. I didn't see him. Since he wanted the burden to stop the walkout placed fully on my shoulders, he was probably hold up in his office, avoiding upset faculty members. Bastard.

By 1pm, there were still about 300 students protesting. Some had left, gotten lunch and returned, happy to have a sandwich and skip afternoon classes. Whether it was a protest, or a picnic, the nice warm, sunny afternoon was conducive to both. Jerry, Keesha and I had been joined by Francesca and many other faculty and staff, all of whom were looking for me to figure something out. Since the crowd wasn't unruly, there was no need to call in the town police, which made Quacky's sense of importance surge. The problem was that although the student organizers had planned the 10am start time, no one bothered to indicate a stop time. Therefore, as long as students were hanging out enjoying the park-like atmosphere, there was no sign of anyone leaving.

Josh continued his cheerleading on the bullhorn as students played Frisbee and rolled up their shirtsleeves to get a better tan. I was sure that their protesting parents from the sixties would be appalled. I knew that I had to do something to break-up this party and figured that the only way would be to try and talk to the organizer. I turned to my colleagues and said, "Ok, I'm going to talk to Josh."

"Do you need back-up?" Quacky blurted excitedly.

"No, I'm going in alone. But keep yoru eye on me in case things get ugly." I made my way through the crowd, stepping over beach towels and bodies, until I was in front of the bench that Josh had taken as his base. Although I knew that he saw me approach, he avoided my gaze and continued over the bullhorn, "Teach don't preach! Teach don't preach!"

"Josh!" I yelled. No response. "Josh!" On the second try, he looked down at me. "Can I talk with you for a minute?" I asked.

"Sure." He called down loudly from atop the bench, "What's the problem?"

"No, can I speak to you down here on the ground?" I asked. Not only was I not going to engage in a dialogue from atop the park bench, my acrophobia told me that the height of the bench was too high. Josh stepped down, "Hello, Dean Doug." He said nonchalantly, as if passing me in the hallway.

"Hi," I responded, "Josh, when do you plan on ending the walkout?" He looked at me with a blank stare, "Ending it?" he asked as though the thought hadn't occurred to him.

"Yes, what's the end time? We need to plan for additional staffing, if necessary, and want to anticipate when we'll need them. So, will you be done soon? Or do you plan on going all night?" I was lying of course, but this seemed like a decent conversation starter.

"We didn't really plan on an end time," he said, "We

want to make a statement and then force some dialogue with administration."

"Well," I responded, "It looks like you've accomplished that. Why don't we schedule a time for you to come into my office, we'll invite any others whom you request and we'll find some solutions." I was happy that this rational approach seemed to be working.

Josh looked at the ground, and then at the hundreds of students standing around looking at us. The intent stares of his peers must have been too much pressure, because his affect suddenly changed from innocent, to militant. I knew by the new look in his eye that it was going to turn ugly.

He looked around hurriedly to his fellow students one more time before jumping back up on the bench and responded, more to them than to me, "We're not ending it until we get what we want!" he yelled. This raised cheers from the immediate crowd who could hear him. I waited for the voices to calm down before calling up to him, "So then, Josh, what is it that you want?" He looked at me like a deer in headlights. Clearly, he had no idea. He looked around nervously and said, "A fair education!" This statement again raised cheers, and the crowd began chanting, "Fair education! Fair education!" Josh grabbed his bullhorn again, ignoring me, and began leading them once more in rousing gales of protest. So much for the rational approach, I needed to think up another plan or we'd be there all night.

I walked back to my colleagues, slightly embarrassed that I was overtaken by a nineteen year old, "Well that went well," Jerry kidded.

"Thank you," I replied, "Peer pressure will get you every time."

"What are we going to do?" asked Keesha, "We need one of those shore afternoon thunderstorms. That'd break 'em up quick!" Keesha was brilliant. We needed a thunderstorm, or a rain shower. And it suddenly occurred to me how to help Mother Nature make one. I walked over to Quacky and within seconds, she was wobbling off the quad set for her new-found mission. I headed back toward the Student Center, casually breezing by my colleagues one last time, "Looks like rain," I said in a low voice, "We'd better take some cover fast." Francesca looked at the sky and turned to me strangely, "Doug, there's not a cloud in the sky?"

"Who said anything about clouds?" I remarked, and walked off the quad. Despite their confusion, my colleagues followed. When I got to the steps of the Student Center facing the quad, I turned back toward the crowd. My peers did the same, clearly still unsure what was about to happen. What occurred within the next sixty seconds was quick, surprising, and wonderfully successful.

It came with some warning, a click followed by a hissing sound. Then, the lawn sprinklers in the quad jumped up and sparked to life showering the entire green with steady bursts of water. The reaction of the crowd resembled what would happen in an actual sudden rain shower at the beach. Students jumped as if hit with boiling water. Some covered their heads with their already soaking beach towels. A few tried to shield their textbooks by shoving them up their shirts. Shirts and shorts were clinging to skin, exposing far more than what should be considered decent. Young women tried to cover their faces with their hands to stop the torrent of black mascara from streaming down.

They ran from the quad, dispersing straight to the parking lots, keys already in hand, or to the residence halls, drenched in delicious sprinkler water. It was truly a sight to behold. Within minutes, everyone was gone, with the exception of Josh Taylor and a couple die-hard followers. Josh still stood on his bench, in all his drenched preppiness. His white button-down shirt and khakis were sticking to him like saran wrap. His brown wire framed glasses were spotted and fogged-up. He was still limply holding the bullhorn to his lips trying to regain control, "You guys!" he whined, "Wait! Stop! This is just another tactic to keep us quiet! Guys?"

After the mass exodus, Jerry turned to me, "I didn't know you had it in you," he said. I took this as a complement. Keesha smiled and said, "Wow, I don't want to get you on your bad side; you're mean." Francesca just gave me a pat on the shoulder. I must admit, I'm still proud of myself. Someday as I look back on my career in student affairs, spraying hundreds of students with the lawn sprinklers may just be one of my shining achievements. I'm sure it has to do with wanting to spray childhood bullies with a garden hose, but whatever. It worked and no one got hurt. I needed to get back to my desk and focus. It was only 2pm and I still had a missing student, a missing parent, and a dead stranger to deal with.

I walked into the office to the sound of applause. Judy and Ronnie were giving me a standing ovation in the otherwise empty office space. "We watched the entire thing from the window," said Judy coyly, "Very ingenious." I nodded deeply since taking a bow would seem showy, and continued to my desk, "Thank you, Thank you. Oh, and I expect that a dripping wet Josh Taylor will be by shortly. Please have him go back to his room, change into dry clothes and come back. I'll be happy to talk to him later this afternoon to process where he went wrong."

There were a few new messages on my desk, one from R.I.P. taken during the middle of the walkout. As I suspected, he was holed-up in his office while I took care of his dirty work. I had no intention of calling him. I turned my attention to my e-mail and once again, didn't see much of interest. So, I went to the bottom of my inbox and began working my way up. About halfway through, I ran across the message from "Anonymous99" which came without a subject. It had been sent at 5:04 yesterday afternoon. I clicked the message open lazily, with my finger already on the delete button. It grabbed my attention quickly, reading:

"I know something. Do you know if Jessica Philmore is ok? I'm not sure if I do anymore. If you give me some

details of the latest, I may help you. Do it soon. THIS IS VERY SERIOUS."

The message was not signed and came from one of those free e-mail services, leaving the sender totally incognito. Who was sending me anonymous e-mails? And what were they talking about? Did they know something about Jessica AFTER her disappearance but then lost touch? I picked up my phone and dialed Chief Morreale immediately.

12

Chief Morreale wasn't available to take my call, so I left a message. He called me about 90 minutes later, after I had spent about a half-hour meeting with a damp Josh Taylor. I tried to repair Josh's wounded ego by congratulating him on a successful protest. After some discussion, Josh and I agreed to schedule a meeting with the Student Government and Professor Preston in the next couple of weeks to address his concerns... once he figured out what they were.

"Good afternoon, Chief," I said after saying goodbye to Josh.

"Hello, Doug. I heard that you had some excitement on campus this afternoon?"

"News travels fast. Yes, it was an interesting afternoon, but we handled it just fine. I was actually calling you with a strange development with regard to Jessica Philmore."

"What've you got?" the Chief asked. I read him the e-mail.

"I'm not really good with the computer," he replied, "Any way you can trace it?"

"I don't think so. It's an anonymous message from a free online service. If it was from a Westmire computer account we could, but not this." The Chief paused, "Interesting. The Philmore girl's been gone for over a week; I wonder what sparked this new message?"

"Should I reply?" I asked.

"Couldn't hurt." the Chief responded.

"But what do I say?" For some reason, I was surprised by the Chief's response, "I don't want to jeopardize the investigation?"

"Doug," replied the Chief coolly, "You don't *know* anything, so what's to jeopardize? Obviously, this person either knows something or it's a hoax... let's see where it leads us. Let me come over there and I'll help you write the response. I have some updates that I want to discuss with you anyway."

"About the dead girl or the missing mom?"

"Both. I'll be right over."

Within fifteen minutes, Chief Morreale was sitting in my office. He always smelled of a mixture of aftershave and cigarette smoke that lingered long after he left. That, coupled with his grandfatherly or uncle-like way about him, always made me feel more secure. I was eager to hear what updates he had for me.

"So," I started right in, "You said you had updates?" The Chief smiled, "We got an ID on the missing girl. She's not one of yours." The news caused me to let out a huge sigh, "Who is she?"

"A runaway from north Jersey. Eighteen, only missing a day or so." It occurred to me that I had been so intent on identifying her, I hadn't stopped to wonder how she died, "What was the cause of death?" I asked.

"Looks like drowning due to intoxication. Dr. Geddes found ecstasy in her system. It's the water... always seems to lure children and people who are loaded."

"And the Westmire sweatshirt that she was wearing? Coincidence?"

"Well, maybe not. She could have been partying with some of your students... we may need your help on that later. But as of now, there doesn't seem to be any Philmore connection. And speaking of Philmores... Mrs. Philmore," the Chief continued, "It seems as though she's disappeared."

"You haven't found anything?"

"Nothing... but the strangest part is that no one seems to be *missing* her." I was ashamed to admit that this wasn't a surprise to me since Mrs. Philmore was such a cold fish. The Chief continued, "Her housekeeping staff doesn't seem worried, we even contacted her 84 year old mother in West Palm Beach, all she said was that she must be on vacation."

"Does she have a habit of disappearing?" I asked.

"We don't know. We contacted her ex-husband, who is the only one who showed any concern at all."

"So Chief, what does this mean? Two missing Philmores can't be a coincidence. They have to be connected somehow?"

"I agree, but as of this moment, we've got nothing. That's why it can't hurt to e-mail your computer 'deep throat'... it may give us something to work with."

"OK, let's do it." I said, turning to the computer. The Chief moved behind me over my shoulder. He read the e-mail and we discussed a reply. Actually, the Chief dictated a reply and I typed; this is what he came up with:

"Since we discovered that Jessica Philmore was missing this week, we haven't found any information about her. We are all extremely worried... any information that you could provide would be appreciated. If you would rather speak with me by phone, my # is: 732-555-3400. I hope to hear from you soon."

It was short and sweet, invited a response via telephone, and didn't discuss the investigation. These were all the criteria established by the Chief. Who knew who this crackpot was, but I was glad that we had him or her. It gave me a sense of hope... as the clock continued to tick away, at least we had something to investigate.

The Chief left and I used the remainder of my day returning messages. It was Friday and I couldn't be happier. Even though the semester had just begun, I needed a vacation. I wished for my lazy summer days at the beach with Barbara and Ethan. This is when I decided that the three of us should get away and go to the boardwalk on Saturday. I knew that this would meet both my needs to spend some quality time with my family and get away; little did I know that it would only make matters worse.

Saturday morning turned out to be a beautiful fall day at the Jersey shore. The temperature in the morning was already in the mid seventies, the sky was clear and the humidity was low. We were out of the house by 11:00am or so, which is pretty good when you have a five year old to coax into the car. Good thing that Ethan loves the boardwalk, possessing a particular penchant for cotton candy. As we headed south to on the Garden State Parkway, a mere twenty miles from the Shores, it felt as if the breeze was lulling me into a false sense of summer, conspicuously lacking dead bodies, bloody animals, missing people, or student protests. We were headed to our old stomping grounds: Jensen's Boardwalk at Prospect Point Beach.

At the Jersey shore, "the boardwalk" can mean many things. Of course, the boardwalk is always the wide planked walkway separating the beach with the street, perfect for strolling, jogging or gazing at the ocean. But some references to "the boardwalk" mean the location of a carnival type setting. This is exactly what Jensen's Boardwalk is. It is almost a half-mile of kitsch in Prospect Point Beach, a town not known for anything else. Thrill rides, kiddie rides, carnival games, shops, restaurants and even a large regional aquarium flank the boardwalk building a community fueled by games of chance and funnel cake sales. It's both a child's dream and a nostalgic getaway for adults where a few quarters can give you the opportunity to take home an oversized stuffed poodle or goldfish in a bowl. A place where the "locals" are seasonal carnival workers who only stay through October when the village is practically boarded up and disassembled for the season. Jensen's is open daily during the summer, then on weekends through October (although on a nice September weekday you may find some open games and rides).

We parked our car in a pay lot near the main entrance to Jensen's, setting the stage for a day of nickel and diming. Everything is a la carte, so it pays to have a cadre of dollar bills and quarters in your pocket at all times. I took a deep breath, savoring the scented air's comforting blend of salty and sweet: Ocean and cotton candy. The smell captivated both my senses and my soul and I was feeling more relaxed already.

We started out slowly with the ring-toss game, and then worked our way up to the kiddie rides before lunch. I knew that after lunch, which would be a sausage sandwich for my wife and me and a hot dog for Ethan, Barbara would urge us to go on the Ferris wheel in order to see the amazing ocean view. This was a plea that I would never honor in a million years due to the ridiculous height. As I told her time and time again, I don't do thrill rides. Instead, she and Ethan would strap themselves in as a duo while I strained my neck from beachside to keep my eye on them the entire length of the ride.

Although not Six Flags, a popular amusement park in central New Jersey, Jensen's was known around the shore for decent rides. In addition to a large kiddie ride section, there was a large merry-go-round, a roller coaster, a large ship-like thing that swung people to and fro, that dreaded Ferris wheel, as well as a Ferris mutation called a "Bomber". This evil Ferris wheel cousin locked people in fully enclosed cars before spinning them in the sky and then nearly crashing them back down again. Thank you very much, but I'll pass. Spraying water into a plastic clown's mouth is about as much thrill as I can handle.

We ran around the Boardwalk for a good part of the afternoon, finally taking a breather on the Merry-go-round. This is a ride that I can handle as long as I get the stationary seat on the edge that looks like an oversized, partially enclosed, park bench. We laughed as I sat still while Barbara and Ethan bounced up and down on an ostrich and a Palomino, respectively. Tired, full of junk food, and loaded up with a cache of plastic and plush trinkets, we decided that it was time to head back up the Parkway toward home. Our daylong junket to Jensen's Boardwalk had been a rousing success, leaving us all exhausted and relaxed.

We headed to our car, politely waving off the advances

of the carnies still hawking their games of chance. "Hey, Mister," one man called holding a dirty and poor rendition of Scooby-Doo, "Don't you want to win this for your kid?" Then, a woman who sounded as if she had just inhaled a carton of Camels, scoffed at our already won treasures as she croaked, "You can do better than that junk! I've got the real prizes." I couldn't help but wonder why this was legal, when prostitution wasn't. The tactics of picking up new clients seemed similar.

We had almost made it out, without spending another nickel, when we passed an enclosed shack that read, "Know your Future Today: Psychic-Tarot-Palm Reading." The shack was tiny; approximately 10' by 10', painted midnight blue and adorned with cutout yellow moons and stars. There were no windows, only a door on the front that was open. The doorway was concealed with strands of seashells hanging tightly together from top to bottom forming a curtain. A cardboard sign near the doorway announced that readings were five dollars. I was surprised when Barbara slowed down as we got to the shack, and then stopped.

"What are you doing?" I asked.

"I think I'll get my fortune told."

"You will?" I asked surprised, "Since when do you believe in this stuff?"

"It's not that I believe in this stuff, I've been thinking about writing an article on psychics and fortune tellers. Since we're here, this will be good research."

"OK," I replied, "But if she tells you that you're about to become rich, don't tell me. I don't want to get my hopes up."

Barbara disappeared through the shroud of seashells leaving them clinking softly in the breeze. While we waited, Ethan, who I was now carrying, seized the opportunity to get a deep-fried Oreo, a Jersey shore favorite. We found a bench almost opposite the shack and ate ourselves into a sugar stupor. Ethan and I enjoyed our greasy treats while we examined all of our prizes. I was particularly fond of the glow in the dark pen, while Ethan favored the stuffed green dinosaur before falling fast asleep in my lap. I held him, and the dinosaur, until suddenly, Barbara emerged from the shack, almost running. Her look was one of desperation as she scanned the boardwalk for Ethan and me. When she spotted us on the bench, she rushed over to us, plucking-up a still fast asleep Ethan into her arms, "Let's go," she said urgently.

"What's wrong?" I asked.

"Nothing," she said, beginning to walk, "I'm just ready to go." This is when I noticed that she had tears in her eyes. I gently put my arm around her shoulders, stopping her from walking, "Barbara?" I asked looking her in the eyes, "What happened?" Barbara held Ethan close to her, "She was awful, Doug. She said that something horrible is going to happen!"

13

So much for our relaxing day at the Boardwalk. Barbara was visibly shaken after her visit with the psychic, which upset me as well, "What did she say?" I asked.

"I don't want to talk about it," she replied hesitantly, "I don't want to repeat it." She was still clutching Ethan, stroking his hair. Ethan was still sound asleep in her arms.

"But Barbara, you're really upset. What could she have said?" I asked again, out of a mixture of empathy and curiosity. Barbara leaned into me, and whispered in my ear, to avoid waking Ethan, "She said that a dark cloud was looming for me... for my family." I didn't respond, thinking it best to just wait for her to finish. Barbara continued in choppy speech, "She said that the darkness was moving quickly. She said that she knew that I had a son. Then she said that my son would soon die." With this, she let out a whimper, trying not to wake Ethan up.

"My God, Barbara. Who was this woman? What kind of carnival psychic says that?"

"I don't know, Doug, I'm just ready to go." Of course, in typical male fashion, I felt the need to pursue it and fix her hurt feelings, "Barbara, you know that she's just some phony sitting in a shack, right? I mean, of course she knew you have a son... he was sitting 30 feet away... I'm sure she saw him before you went in."

"Doug, intellectually, I know. But she freaked me out. Let's just go," she said beginning toward the parking lot again. I understood Barbara's need to leave, but I couldn't stop my anger. What gave this charlatan the right to upset people like this? I couldn't fight the urge bubbling up inside me, "You go to the car, I'm going in there." I said.

"No, Doug, let's just go. I know I'm overreacting."

"No Barbara, this isn't right. You take Ethan to the car, I'll be right there." I handed her my keys, and walked to the shack before she could respond. I don't really have a temper, and I try to respect Barbara's feelings, but I just couldn't let this one go. Since I was still holding all of our prizes, I moved clumsily through the seashells making a great deal of noise. Once inside, it took my eyes a second to adjust to the lack of light and I squinted to find the psychic.

The inside of the shack was painted the same midnight blue color and had the same star and moon cut outs hanging on the walls and ceiling. On the inside, however, the celestial bodies were illuminated with a black light. The space was separated by a large, dark tapestry making two rooms. The first area I assumed to be the "reception" area and the second I assumed was where the readings took place. Since there was no one in the reception area, I popped my head behind the tapestry and found the "psychic".

She was a heavy woman adorned in multiple scarves and beads, sitting behind a small round table. She looked to be in her sixties, with dyed, jet-black wisps of hair sticking out of a purple turban. She reminded me of a heavier, more pensive Miss Piggy. In front of her was a crystal ball that reeked of plastic even in the dim light. Although I expected that she would be shocked that an intruder had barged into her private space, she looked at me calmly, "May I help you?" she asked in a quiet, raspy voice. Maybe she expected me, after all she was a psychic.

"Are you the person who just upset my wife?" I asked bluntly.

"I say many things," she said dramatically, raising her hands above the plastic ball, "I know many things... I speak the truth. It is not my fault if the news is upsetting." She was clearly feigning some eastern European accent.

"Ma'am," I responded, pointing the green dinosaur at her for emphasis, "You are no more a psychic than I am. I think it's unconscionable that you sit here and accept payment to upset people. You should be ashamed of yourself." She did not respond, but simply closed her eyes as though going into a trance. I waited, and she finally responded, "The spirits are dark. You have already seen great unrest recently... this will soon change to sorrow." She broke into some kind of chant and I had had enough. Barbara was right, fake or not, the woman was creepy. Having said what I needed to say, I took my dinosaur and returned to the car, only slightly unsettled. How did she know that the past week had been full of unrest? Although I knew that this was the ploy, say something vague that would be true for almost everyone, it still lingered in my mind.

We drove home, Ethan dozing in the backseat, Barbara and I trying to sort out the last 30 minutes. "Did you see her?" Barbara asked.

"Yes, nice turban."

"What did you say?"

"I told her that I thought she was a quack who shouldn't upset people."

"So what did she say?"

"Nothing." I didn't want to upset Barbara further, but she could detect my little white lie.

"Doug, she said something to you, didn't she?" I couldn't stand the hard-nosed interrogation, so I cracked, "She said that I had had an unsettling week, or something like that, and that it would get worse. Barbara, she's a fake who preys on vague facts and insecurities." Barbara and I continued to make small talk while Ethan dozed in the back. We put on the radio, trying to find a song to wash the latter half of our day away. Since it was almost 6:30pm by the time we got home and we were now both physically and mentally drained, we ordered a pizza and drank a bottle of wine to settle our nerves.

Although the psychic experience was beginning to relax a bit, we were both still a little preoccupied by it. We put Ethan to bed around 8:30pm or so, read him a story and gave him a dose of vitamin C as a precautionary measure to ward off evil spirits. Once Ethan was asleep for the night, Barbara and I went to our bedroom to get comfortable and watch some inane Saturday night TV. Although we rarely watch TV in bed, we needed the extra comfort that only the covers allowed.

I always think that the best test of true love is seeing your partner getting ready for bed long after the honeymoon. That night, I couldn't help but notice how sexy Barbara looked in her oversized, "Give me chocolate and nobody gets hurt" nightshirt. Gosh, I wanted her. She must have felt the same way about my worn-out, saggy boxers, because within minutes of getting into bed, we were naked. We made love being serenaded by voices from The Learning Channel. I had never enjoyed an episode of "Trading Spaces" more. As we melted into each other, I think that Barbara and I both felt better about our day. Our attempt to push the psychic a little farther from our minds had worked, even though she wasn't totally gone. That night I slept pretty well, only waking up to check on Ethan three times. Not too bad for me.

I woke up early on Sunday morning, and snuck out of the house for a run. It had rained during the night, leaving the streets glistening and steamy. The air still felt as if it was holding 100% humidity, leaving my sweatshirt and shorts immediately damp, without adding a beneficial cooling effect. It felt like running in a greenhouse. I ran hard that morning, which is unusual for me. Normally when I run on the boards, old ladies with walkers pass me. But this morning I ran as if someone was chasing me, an illusion fueled by the Ladies Auxiliary's flyers of Jessica that I passed on each and every telephone poll along my route. Each time I saw Jessica's face, I stepped up the pace. The calming effects of sex had worn off, leaving feelings of urgency only exacerbated by our previous day's visit with Madame Psychic.

I must have run three or four miles that Sunday, much more than my usual. When I finally decided to stop, I was drenched with salty air and sweat, and had to bend over with my hands on my knees to catch my breath. I was so exhausted that I actually walked down onto the beach and collapsed on the sand. I laid flat on my back, spread eagle, feeling the asynchronous beats of my heart and the surf. I stared with half-shut, glossy eyes at the light blue sky trying to poke through the lacey clouds. I must have laid there for at least fifteen minutes, trying to convince myself that my feelings of exhaustion were actually a sense of relaxation. For those few minutes, I didn't exist. No one knew me, or where I was. I had no responsibilities or anyone calling on me. I realized then how easy it would be to disappear.

Perhaps this is the same way that Jessica Philmore felt. Perhaps she wasn't a victim of foul play, but of environment. Maybe it wasn't murder after all. Maybe her life got so complicated that she left it. She made a conscious decision to vanish. I continued to consider this new theory as I languished on the pillow-like sand. In doing so, I immediately began to poke holes in my latest explanation of Jessica's disappearance. For one, although I had thought of a reason for Jessica to run away, what happened to her mother? The two cases had to be linked somehow, and it didn't seem feasible that both Jessica and her mom would be fed up with life enough to leave. Or did it? This is when I realized why I wasn't a law enforcement officer or investigator. This is also when I realized that I had been gone from my house for nearly two hours. If Barbara knew that I left at 6:00am, she would worry.

I pulled myself out of the sand, brushed off as much as I could, and headed back home. I was only four blocks away, so it didn't take me long. When I got to the house, I used the key that I had hidden outside to enter since my running shorts didn't have a pocket for keys. Barbara was sitting on the living room sofa immersed in the *Sunday Asbury Park Press*, "You've been gone a long time. I thought that maybe you ran to LA," she joked softly.

"I got stopped by an early snow in the Rockies, so I turned around," I replied, leaning over her shoulder to give her a kiss, "Anything new in the paper?"

"Not new to you, but front page news to everyone else," she said, holding up the front page for me to see. The headline read: VANISHED: 2 Missing, 1 dead in String of Local Disappearances.

"Well," I replied, "I was expecting this sooner or later. I'll need a cup of coffee before I read it." I went to the kitchen, made myself a cup, offered Barbara another cup, and joined her on the sofa. She handed me the paper, which I accepted with an eager reluctance. The article discussed Jessica and her mother, as well as the runaway found on the beach. For the most part, it was accurate, with the exception that at one point it stated, "Westmire College officials could not be reached for comment." When did they ever try to contact me? As of Friday afternoon, I was mostly caught-up on my messages, and Judy would never let me overlook a call from the press.

"Do you know this staff writer, Mark Clarity?" I asked Barbara since she was also a member of the press.

"Mark? Sure. He's a nice guy."

"Then why did he say that we couldn't be reached for comment, when I never got a call?"

"I don't know, honey, maybe he wrote the article yesterday? It said that you couldn't be reached, it didn't say that you didn't return calls." Spoken like a true reporter.

"It just doesn't make us look very good... like we're hiding something."

"I'm sure you'll get a call first thing tomorrow morning."

I spent the rest of the day at home, chatting with Barbara, playing with Ethan and catching-up on some of my gardening. My flowerbeds looked shaggy, long overdue for a trim. The day flew by and before I knew it, dinner was over and it was time for Ethan's bath. Giving Ethan his bath is my normal ritual when I'm not held up at work, and I had missed it everyday during the last week. Ever since he was a baby, I would get into the tub with him, since even if I didn't, I'd be soaked anyway. I looked forward to this time with my son, splashing each other, blowing handfuls of bubbles, and playing with rubber trucks in the tub.

As Ethan and I were sitting in the tub singing a rousing rendition of, "Rubber Ducky," Barbara came into the bathroom holding the cordless phone, "Doug, you have a call." I knew that it must have been important or she wouldn't have interrupted. I took the phone with a soapy hand, wondering briefly if I would electrocute us if I accidentally dropped the cordless into the water. I leaned myself over the edge of the tub to avoid this possibility and answered, "Hello?"

"Dean Doug? This is Security Officer Towers. We have a situation here at the college that I think you may want to see." Officer Al Towers was Quacky's right hand.

"What's the problem," I asked over the loud sound of Ethan's splashing.

"Oh, I'm sorry to bother you," he replied, "Are you at the beach?"

"No, officer, I'm in the tub."

"Taking a bath?"

"Yes, taking a bath." I didn't feel the need to qualify the statement, although it clearly seemed odd to Al. I wasn't ashamed to admit that real men eat quiche and take baths.

"Oh, well sorry. We've got a substantial group of students, at least 100, assembled on the front lawn." Oh great, I thought, another protest.

"What are they doing?"

"Singing songs."

"Singing songs?" I asked with my hair dripping onto the floor, "Are they doing anything else?"

"Well, they've all got candles and they're singing songs... I believe that it's about that missing girl, Ms. Philmore."

"Are they causing a disturbance?" I asked.

"Well no, not yet, but in light of the other day's protest, I thought that you should know." Although I was annoyed at the call, he was right.

"OK, Al," I replied with a sigh, "I'll be right there." I picked up Ethan, who was a prune anyway, toweled us off, and handed him off to Barbara. I then threw on some jeans and a polo shirt, and walked to campus in the cool evening air. Although I didn't grab a jacket, I wished that I had, as the cool breeze tussled my wet hair.

I arrived onto campus within fifteen minutes and as I walked through the main gates, saw the crowd immediately in front of me. Al was right, it appeared to be a group of 100 or so students, some sitting, others standing, most holding some sort of lit candle in their hands. There were two people serving as the focal point, a guy and a woman, sitting on the ground playing guitars and leading the current hymn, "Kumbaya". Some of the students held up copies of the Ladies' Auxiliary's flyers, swaying in rhythm to the music. A few others held up hand made messages on poster board that read, "Come home, Jessica. We love you." And, "We will not give up hope... Please God, guide her home." I have to say, it was a touching tribute to Jessica Philmore.

As I stood and watched from a distance, I saw security officer Al standing close to the group. Al Towers is young, probably 24 or 25, tall and thin, with buzz-cut hair. He has a boyish face and a wide smile that seems to make many young women on campus fall immediately in love. Once Al spotted me, he came right over to where I was standing, "Hi, Dean Doug, sorry to bother you tonight, and uh, to disturb, uh, your bath..." he looked away awkwardly, "but I thought that you might like to see this."

"No Al, I'm glad that you called, thank you. How long have they been here?"

"For about sixty minutes now. Did you know anything about this?"

"No, it's either impromptu or a well kept secret." I responded.

"Any word on Ms. Philmore?" Al asked.

"Not really, so far, there haven't been any leads." Al and I continued to make small talk until I felt so chilly that I couldn't take it anymore. I decided to run to my office and grab a sweatshirt. I walked briskly into the Student Center and straight upstairs to my office. As I went, I noticed someone in the cafeteria seating area that caught my attention. It was Dirt Fagan. Why wasn't he, Jessica's boyfriend, at the vigil for her? I grabbed the sweatshirt from my office, a nice grey one with "WC" written in big navy blue embroidered letters on the front, and decided to approach Chris.

He was sitting lazily in a booth, feet up, shoes off, reading a comic book. As usual, he looked unshowered, unshaven and unusual, "Hi, Chris," I said, as I approached. He barely looked up from his comic and simply nodded. Since he clearly wasn't in the mood for conversation, I initiated more, "What are you doing?" His eyes moved slowly from his reading material to meet my gaze, "Sitting here, reading. Is there a problem with that?" he asked.

"No. Not at all, I just wondered why you weren't out on the lawn with the others." He stared at me for a long time without saying a word, "Why would I?" he asked flatly.

"Well, it's for Jessica. I just thought that you'd be the first one out there." This made him immediately shift in the booth, in fact for a brief moment, he looked as if he was at a loss for words. He recouped by responding, "Well I'm not there, ok? Why don't you get off my back?" Before I could reply, he jumped out of the booth and slid past me, muttering, "I'm outta here." He was in such a hurry that he left his comic book on the table. I called after him, "Chris, you left your comic!" He did not miss a step or turn to look at me, he simply raised his arms high over his head and gave me the finger with both hands. Charming.

Since Dirt was a regular customer of mine, he must have known that this maneuver would automatically get him a personal invitation to visit my office. Although he always acted a bit odd, something about his behavior bothered me that evening. Why didn't he go to the vigil? Don't even dirty, moody, disheveled boyfriends want to light a candle of hope for their supposed love? Something was up. Tomorrow, I would send him an official letter charging him under the student code of conduct for flipping me off, and instructing him to come to my office. I needed another conversation with him just to see his reaction. Did he know something about Jessica?

It was now close to 10pm. I walked out of the Student Center and continued back to the front lawn. The number of students had dwindled to almost half of the original, leaving fifty or so participants peacefully humming and swaying. Since Al was still standing guard, I decided that it was clear for me to head back home.

I approached him and said, "Al, since the group is still peaceful and you're here standing watch, I think that I'm going home. Please call me if anything changes."

"Will do, Dean," he responded, "Thanks for coming out, have a good night."

I reached home by 10:15pm where I found Barbara curled-up on the couch watching television. Ethan was in bed. Since Barbara typically stays up much later than I do, I filled her in on my evening, kissed her goodnight and went upstairs. I dutifully performed all of my nighttime rituals of flossing, brushing, and taking my medication for high cholesterol, then I peeked in at Ethan, threw off my clothes and jumped in bed. I was asleep by 10:30pm and it was heaven. Luckily, I'm not one of those people who needs a long period of downtime before sleep.

I woke up before my alarm at 5:45am and decided that in honor of Monday morning, I would start the week off right and go running. I got out of bed and moved quietly out of the room, careful where I stepped to avoid some creaky hardwood floorboards. I checked on Ethan, who let out a huge sigh when I approached him. He was breathing. Good. I shut his door, went to the bathroom and brushed my teeth.

Still naked from my slumber, I walked downstairs tactfully, ready to cover myself with my hands if anyone was standing outside our windows. At this hour, it was still pretty dark and I wasn't too worried about anyone getting a look. Heck, I wasn't too worried anyway. I had seen each and every one of my next-door neighbors naked at least once, all trying to dodge the window on the way to the shower, ironing, or enjoying a late-night bowl of ice cream. I'm sure that they have witnessed the same.

Since I often get up before Barbara, I keep my running clothes and even some of my work clothes in one of the downstairs bedrooms that Barbara also uses as her office. This way I don't disturb her trying to fumble with shoes, suits, socks and underwear. I threw on my favorite royal blue running shorts, one of my million Westmire College tee-shirts and my sneakers, grabbed my mp3 player and ran out the door.

Although my run was uneventful that morning, the events that followed were not. I eked-out my usual mile in under ten minutes, pushed myself to do a quarter mile more, and then walked slowly toward home. As I left the boardwalk and proceeded onto Main Avenue, I saw Cruiser in the street pushing his wheelbarrow slowly and methodically in front of me. As I passed, I greeted him and waved, unable to resist peeking at this morning's treasures packed into the wheelbarrow. I saw the usual: Bottles and cans, discarded small appliances, some clothing, and a lobster trap. This is where I stopped. Something *inside* the lobster trap caught my attention and I couldn't resist taking a closer look.

I turned on my heels and approached Cruiser, who was now lumbering slowly toward me. He was looking lovely that morning in a pale pink taffeta gown, which he had tailored just for himself, by cutting it at the knee and ripping off the sleeves. His hairy legs and muscular arms bulged from underneath the fabric like oversized tarantula legs. His worn work boots were laced-up tight around his ankles, exposing knee-high white sweat socks. On his head, he had selected one of his many chapeaux, this time, a Westmire College baseball cap. He certainly was a man of taste.

Although I was now standing right in front of him, he didn't miss a beat or lose his pace. He simply nodded in my direction, highlighting his furrowed brow and stoic countenance and walked around me. As he did, I got a better view of the contents of the lobster trap, and was startled by what I saw. Stuffed inside, all crumpled and ripped, were the Jessica Philmore flyers. By the looks, Cruiser had gone to every telephone pole and bulletin board in town and took them all down. There must have been at least 50 of them. Jessica's warm eyes and innocent smile laid wrinkled and shredded, beseeching from the confines of the weathered wooden trap. *My God,* was all I could think, *What has Cruiser done?*

14

I once again moved in front of Cruiser, this time putting my left hand up to stop him, "Cruiser?" I asked as gently as I could, "Can I talk to you?"

"Can't now, Dean." Cruiser responded, attempting once again to move around me, "I've got work to finish."

"No, Cruiser, I need to talk to you." I replied sternly. This made him stop, although I could tell that he was hesitant. I seized the opportunity to continue, "I couldn't help but notice these flyers in your wheelbarrow?" I stopped, expecting a reply of some sort, but only got the same stoic stare from Cruiser. I continued, "Did you take the flyers down, Cruiser?" Cruiser looked away from me quickly and again tried to maneuver around me, "Gotta go, Dean." Since both Cruiser and his wheelbarrow are bigger than me, I decided that I should try and walk along side him rather than stand in his way.

"Cruiser," I continued, "Where did you get these flyers? Did you find them like this, or did you take them down?" For a brief moment, Cruiser stopped, shook his head, and then began pushing ahead. I was obviously making him uncomfortable. I continued again, "Cruiser, this is very serious. Do you know something about the woman in those flyers?"

"No," Cruiser replied quickly still keeping pace.

"Then why do you have these flyers?" I pressed, "I'm sorry to say that if you don't tell me, I'm going to have to call Chief Morreale." With this, Cruiser stopped, eyes darting in every direction. He dropped his wheelbarrow with a loud metal thud and put his hands to his forehead, "I CAN'T!" he yelled toward me, "I said that I wouldn't say anything and I won't. Dean Doug, please leave me alone! I have to get back to help the Reverend!" Cruiser then quickly picked up his wheelbarrow and began running down the street toward the church where he resided and worked.

I didn't chase after him. Although I had a good relationship with Cruiser and was not afraid of him, I wasn't sure why he was so agitated. Was it because he had removed all the flyers and I had caught him with them? Or worse, was Cruiser trying to cover-up something about Jessica's disappearance? Did Cruiser have something to do with it? I needed to call Chief Morreale but was afraid that if I waited until I got home, Cruiser would have time to dispose of the evidence. Not only was this troublesome, but when the Ladies Auxiliary found out about the defacement of their flyers, boy were they going to be pissed. I decided to go directly to the church where Cruiser was headed and call Chief Morreale from there.

The Westmire Shores Unitarian Church is located on the corner of Main Avenue and Pilgrim Parkway. In its heyday, the building used to be a brothel as well as a bar. Yes, even in tiny Westmire Shores. It is a three-story boxy, brick structure with airy wooden balconies painted white that surround each level. Inside, the main floor which used to be the bar area had been gutted and now served as the sanctuary. To preserve some of the historical integrity of the building, the twelve foot mahogany bar had been relocated to the head of the space in front of the seating area, and now served as the altar. My kind of church. During a service, it was hard to tell whether Malificent was offering a sermon or serving-up drinks.

On the second floor, the old "guest" rooms of the brothel had been dismantled, and I assume sanitized, and now served as a large community room. The "guest" rooms on the third floor had been converted into office space. From what I understood Cruiser lived in an apartment-type space constructed in the basement, although I had never seen it.

As I approached the front steps leading to the church's porch, I passed the narrow alley between the church and the neighboring building. As I walked by, I saw Cruiser's wheelbarrow ditched halfway down the ally next to some cement steps that led down to the basement. I assumed that this was the entrance to Cruiser's apartment. I tried to shield my eyes from the bright morning sunlight to get a better look at the contents of the wheelbarrow in the dim alley, but found that my eyes couldn't adjust to the differences between light and dark. So, I took a step into the alley, feeling like a stalker.

As my pupils widened, I saw that the wheelbarrow had been relieved of the lobster trap. Obviously, Cruiser had ditched it on his way home. Unless he was guilty of something, why would Cruiser do this? I walked around to the front porch, up the steps, and into the foyer of the church. The ample foyer is covered in dark wood and is flanked by two sets of stairs, one leading down, and the other leading up. In the middle, directly opposite the front door, is the entrance to the sanctuary. I took the stairs leading up and headed directly to Malificent's office. Since I often met Malificent on my way to work, I knew that she was in her office early.

As I approached her office, I could see her door ajar and could hear the soft sounds of a guitar. I knocked quietly on the door jam and the music stopped, "Come in?" I heard Malificent call from behind the door. I entered Malificent's office to find her not behind her desk, but sitting in one of her three easy chairs strumming her guitar. Her long, skinny arms and legs seemed to clutch the instrument like a praying mantis dressed all in black. She looked surprised to see me, "Doug?" she said looking me up and down, "You can't be on your way to work?" I realized that I was still in my nylon running shorts and sweaty tee shirt.

"Oh, sorry Malificent," I said, "I wasn't expecting to drop by."

"What's wrong, you look bothered by something? Is it Jessica?"

"It's Cruiser, do you know if he's here? We need to call

the police."

"The police? What would they have to do with Cruiser?" Malificent asked as she stood from her chair and put down her guitar.

"Have you seen Cruiser?" I asked.

"Well no, not yet this morning, we usually meet downstairs for coffee around 9:00am. Doug, what happened?" I could tell that Malificent was disturbed and she had a right to be. When I explained to her what I had seen, she seemed even more troubled and went to her desk to grab a cigarette. She inhaled deeply before speaking again, "Doug, what are you thinking? That Cruiser had something to do with the young woman's disappearance?" As Cruiser's unofficial caretaker, she was mildly defensive.

"I'm not sure, Malificent, but when I asked him where he got the flyers he became agitated. Clearly he knows something. I think that we should call the police and have them speak to him."

"But Doug, *I* can speak to him. Don't you think that would be less intimidating? If Cruiser does know something and we call the police, he'll only become more upset and uncooperative." Malificent stood behind her desk and took another long puff while waiting for me to respond. Although I knew that she was probably right, I was also trying to keep the fact in mind that there was a police investigation going on. I was torn between the possibility of getting to the truth more quickly and sacrificing the integrity of the investigation. Against my better judgment, I agreed to have Malificent talk with Cruiser under one condition, that I go with her. I also told her that we would have to call Chief Morreale regardless of the conversation. Reluctantly, she agreed.

As we made our way down the three flights of stairs to the basement, I could sense Malificent's growing angst. When we reached the bottom floor, she turned to me on the stairs, "Now I think it's best if I go in first and then call you in." It wasn't a question, it was a statement and I agreed. The basement of the church had been compartmentalized into four almost equal sections. There was an area of metal shelves holding dry goods and canned goods that served as the town's food pantry, a carpeted area with several toys that served as a children's daycare during church services, and an area for storage. The fourth, fully enclosed section was Cruiser's apartment.

From the outside, it looked like a regular apartment that you would find in a complex. Neatly painted dry wall enclosed a grey door complete with nameplate and gold knocker. The name typed on a piece of paper within the gold nameplate holder read, "Mr. Charles Cruz". After all this time of knowing him, I never knew that it wasn't "Cruiser", but actually, "Cruzer", a derivation of Cruz. I felt slightly disrespectful.

Malificent used the doorknocker and waited for a response. She motioned for me to move away from the doorway and moments later, Cruzer opened the door. "Good morning, Cruzer," Malificent said gently, "May I come in?" She entered the apartment while I waited outside, inspecting cans of green beans in the food pantry. After about ten minutes or so of scrutinizing canned veggies, instant potatoes, and boxes after boxes of cereal, Malificent opened Cruzer's door and called me in.

The apartment was a studio with not much light, as one would expect in a basement. To the right of the doorway was a kitchenette fully equipped with undersized refrigerator, microwave and hot plate as well as a 1960's brown Formica-top table and two bright orange padded metal chairs. In the back of the kitchenette was a sectioned-off room that I took to be the bathroom. To the left of the entrance was the living area complete with pull-out sofa, coffee table, a couple of floor lamps and a TV stand adequately appointed with a 13" television and radio/cassette player. The living space was painted a pale blue that reminded me of moldy Feta cheese and a royal blue shag carpet that vaguely matched my running shorts. Oddly, the place didn't look half-bad.

Cruzer was sitting on the unmade pullout sofa bed, half

wrapped in a pink quilt with his head in his hands. He had thrown his wide-brimmed hat on the floor lamp next to him. The moment I entered his apartment, Cruzer began shaking his head and apologizing, "I'm sorry Dean. I'm sorry. I didn't mean it, I didn't know it was bad." Malificent had a strange look on her face, which could have been read as either shock or hope. I couldn't tell which. I looked to her without saying anything, looking for some sort of clue.

Finally, Malificent interrupted Cruzer's apologetic pleas and said, "Cruzer, why don't you tell Dean Doug what you told me?"

"I'm sorry. I'm so sorry," was all that Cruzer managed and it was this moment that showed me the extent of his mental state. Although I had never been quite sure of the exact nature of Cruzer's mental abilities, I was seeing a new side now. He was nearly sobbing, like a child, so upset that his lower lip was wavering as he inhaled each breath. I was shocked at his fragile state and fearful of what put him there.

"Cruzer," I spoke gently as I moved toward him, "What's wrong? I'm your friend, remember? Why are you so upset?" He looked up at me, clutching the comforter tightly to his chest. Tears ambled their way down his cheeks through his dense whiskers. "I didn't mean it," he said again, "I'm just so sorry."

"Cruzer," Malificent interrupted, "Just tell Dean Doug the truth." He looked at her, then at me, and then spoke again, "You were right. I did it." I felt butterflies stir in my stomach, "What did you do, Cruzer?" I asked.

"I took down those flyers. Every one of 'em. I did. He gave me $20, so I did it."

"Who gave you $20?" I asked, more puzzled than before, "Why?"

"Didn't ask why. Don't know why. He gave me the twenty and I took them all down like he said. I tried to do it before the sun came up, but there were too many of them. Oh, he's gonna be mad at me. Maybe take the money back. He deserves it back, I didn't do a good job."

I looked curiously at Malificent and then turned back to Cruzer, "Cruzer, who is 'he'? Who's this man?"

"I never seen him before. He just came up to me yesterday and said that if I did this job for him, he'd give me $20."

"Did you ask his name?" I asked.

"Nope."

"What did this man look like?"

"Shorter than me, brown hair that was all spiked. I could see that he had tattoos sticking out of his shirt collar. He was about my age, I guessed." Although I wasn't sure, I took Cruzer to be about 45 or so.

"What did he say, exactly," I pursued, "How did he act?"

"He was real jittery. He said something about mittens, or camping or something like that, and then asked me to do the job. Said to take all the flyers down before sun-up. He trusted me to do the job, so he gave me the $20 right there."

"Mittens?" I asked, "Are you sure?"

"Yeah, mittens, or mitts or something like that. Said there were problems at the camp and this was an important job. I didn't know it was bad. I didn't!" Once again, Cruzer became upset and placed his head back in his hands.

"Cruzer," I said trying to console him, "It's ok. I'm not mad, I'm glad you told us." With this, Cruzer looked up with a stained face and wide eyes, "Really, you're not mad?" he asked. "No, Cruzer, I'm not mad. You've been a big help." I replied, to which he jumped out of his bed and shook my hand, "Thank you, Dean. Thank you." I wasn't lying, Cruzer had been a big help. In fact, this was the biggest lead that we had yet.

"Do you know how you can help even more?" I asked Cruzer.

"How?"

"You can tell exactly what you told me to Chief Morreale." Malificent shot me some sort of look, but I ignored her. Cruzer seemed eager to please, "Sure, I'll tell him everything. Take the flyers, $20, mitts and camping."

"Great," I replied, "Just let me give him a call and you can tell him." I quickly looked around the room and didn't see a phone so I turned to Malificent, "Reverend, may I use your phone?"

"Of course," she replied reluctantly, "I'll take you to my office. Cruzer, I'll be right back and we'll have our usual morning coffee, ok?" Cruzer nodded and we left the apartment, Malificent was silent. As we approached the third flight of stairs, I broke the silence, "Malificent, are you annoyed with me?" She turned on the stair and looked back at me, obviously surprised, "No, of course not, why would I be annoyed?"

"You haven't said a word since we left Cruzer's apartment, and you seemed reluctant when I mentioned calling the Chief." At that point, we had entered Malificent's office, and she quickly shut the door in response to my question.

"Doug," she said curtly, "I know that we have to call the Chief. In fact, before he speaks with Cruzer I need to speak with the Chief privately."

"Why, what's going on?" I asked, hinting at the beginnings of exasperation.

"I'd rather not get into it." Her response took me by surprise, and since I had a one-track mind, prompted me to ask, "Is this about Jessica Philmore?" Malificent unleashed another cigarette from her pack and replied, "I'm not sure, Doug. It's complicated. Please, here's the phone." She pushed the phone across her desk toward me.

"Malificent, is there anything that I should know before I call the Chief?" I asked. She inhaled deeply and held her breath for what seemed like five minutes. I was almost sure that I saw smoke seeping from the corners of her eyes.

"Doug," she said in a cool, breathy tone filled with smoke, "I'm just not sure what this all means. Cruiser is a good man who has had a difficult life. I worry that people take advantage of him. I worry that people are unaware of the rich tapestry that creates Cruzer and the ramifications this has for him."

"Ramifications of taking flyers?" I asked, "Do you think that I'm taking advantage of him here, Malificent?"

"No, your first priority is finding your missing student, of course I don't think that you're taking advantage of him. But who was this man who asked Cruzer to remove the flyers? What were his motives? Was he aware that his actions could have dire consequences for Cruzer?"

"Well, hopefully Chief Morreale will be able to figure that out, but in terms of dire consequences, I think that we understand that Cruzer acted out of innocence."

"I'm not referring to his actions in this case."

"Then to what are you referring?" I blurted, more loudly than I had intended, "Malificent, you're speaking in code. In one breath you're saying call the police and in another you're saying that there are dire consequences."

"I'm sorry to be cryptic, Doug. But much like a personal counselor, as a person of the cloth I have certain confidentiality ethics that I can't breach."

"Malificent, I deal with counseling issues every day and I know that confidentiality can only be breached if the individual has the potential to cause harm to himself or others. Do you think that Cruzer's hiding something relating to this case?" Malificent sat down in her desk chair and looked at me sympathetically. Finally she replied, "Yes, Doug. Unfortunately I know he is."

15

By 9:30am, Chief Morreale had arrived at the church. Malificent whisked him away very shortly after I filled him in on the details of what had happened, and I had since been relegated to the front porch. I sat on the front steps, still in my sweaty running clothes, like a dejected adolescent who had been picked last in gym. I was mad at Malificent, although in actuality, I wasn't sure why. She had helped me speak with Cruzer and also to contact the police. But she was hiding something and I couldn't help but think that she was stopping me from finding Jessica.

It was quickly approaching a week since we discovered that Jessica Philmore was missing, nearly two weeks since her actual disappearance. Seeing the Ladies Auxiliaries flyers in Cruzer's wheelbarrow, and then hearing him talk about a strange man, was the best information we had yet even remotely related to the case. Did this man know something about Jessica's missing mother, too? What sort of additional information did Cruzer have, and why was Malificent hiding it from me? My mind raced as I kept mulling over the possibilities. My thoughts were interrupted when Malificent walked out the front door of the church and onto the porch behind me.

"Chief Morreale's in with Cruzer now," she said toward me. Still sitting on the steps, I craned my neck to glance at her, "Great, thanks," was all I could manage.

"Doug, I'm sorry if you're angry at me." This caused me to turn fully around to look at her before rising to the porch to meet her. "I'm not mad at you, Malificent," I said, "Confused, perhaps. Curious, maybe. But mostly, I'm just anxious. This is the first tangible connection to Jessica that we've had in two weeks." Malificent nodded, holding her fingers at her mouth as if she was holding a cigarette. I was sure that she was dying for a puff, although I knew that she never smoked in full public view. She was silent for a long time and then spoke again, "Doug, I'm confident that Cruzer has no information about Jessica Philmore's disappearance."

I gave her a quizzical look, "But an hour ago you told me that he was hiding something?"

"Yes, that's what I said, and it's true. But it's not what you think. That's all I can say." I looked at Malificent coldly, "That's not really helpful to me, Malificent. In fact, it's really frustrating to have you speak in riddles." I was responding in a biting tone and I could tell by the look on Malificent's face that my words stung. She folded her lanky arms around her self and fought back the tears welling in her eyes. Although this had not been my intention, I wasn't ashamed that I made the Reverend cry. In the same icy tone, I continued to look at her and asked, "Did the Chief say how long he'd be? I need to get to my office." With this, Malificent's lips began to quiver and I could tell that she was angry.

"Doug, this isn't about *you* or what *you* need," she said, continuing to hug herself for support.

"I'm sorry?" I asked.

"This is not about *you*, Doug. You are *not* the victim here."

"I'm not playing the victim, Malificent, I need to find my student!"

"You're not the official investigator, either," she bit back, resolute. Her words struck me like a slap in the face. I wanted to lob back a response, but I had nothing to say, except that I had had enough. I turned to the steps and said, "Tell the Chief that he can reach me on my cell phone or in my office." I stepped quickly down, onto the sidewalk and headed home, not turning back to look at Malificent. On my walk home, her words poked and prodded at me.

Victim? Was I acting like a victim? And what about the

investigator jab? I continued to mull both of these questions over as I entered the gate to my front yard. As I did, I realized that I hadn't called Barbara to tell her where I was for the last three hours. I picked up my key from the usual outside hiding place and went inside. Ethan had long-since been at school and I found Barbara standing in the kitchen.

"Doug," she said, "Where have you been? I was worried."

"I'm sorry, I'm so sorry. I've had one shitty morning already and I haven't even gotten to work." Barbara moved closer to me, if she was angry, she momentarily hid it in order to comfort me. Hmmmmm. Maybe I was playing victim.

"What happened?" she asked, "At first I thought that you went to the office early, but after I got Ethan off to school I noticed your wallet and keys and your briefcase still on your desk. Then, a few minutes ago, Judy called asking for you. You just got back from running?" Crap. Not only had I been MIA and forgot to tell my wife where I was, I was late for work and my office had no idea either. "Among other things," I said, "I need to get going, come talk to me while I get ready and I'll fill you in." I immediately began stripping on my way up the stairs and explaining the course of the morning's events to Barbara. I quickly called from our bedroom phone to tell Judy that I was on my way. While I was in the shower, Barbara sat on the toilet listening intently, asking for clarification whenever I wasn't clear or dropping water drowned-out my voice. By the time I turned the shower off, I had pretty much finished, omitting the part about my concluding spat with Malificent. Although I'm not good at withholding personal information, especially with Barbara, I wanted to finish processing Malificent's accusations myself before sharing with anyone. This resolve lasted at least ten minutes.

As I stood all deodorized and coiffed, but naked, in front of my bedroom closet, I asked Barbara, "Have I been acting like a victim?"

"With your clothes on, or without?" she mused, sitting on the bed.

"At any time." I responded seriously.

"I don't understand?"

"A martyr, a victim. Have I been acting like that?"

"I don't think so, Doug. Why?"

"Well, after Malificent took the Chief to see Cruzer, we had a fight on the front porch of the church. Now if *that* won't make you go to hell." I said, stepping into my briefs.

"Either that or those tighty-whities," Barbara said playfully. Clearly my nakedness was detracting from the seriousness of my point. "I like my tighty-whities, and I'm being serious. Malificent told me to stop acting like a victim and also insinuated that I was over-stepping my role in the investigation. Do you think that's true?" Of course, this was one of those loaded spousal questions that left little response time and even lesser margin of error.

"No, I haven't noticed either of those. I think that you've been a little preoccupied, but that's understandable. I haven't noticed martyr-like qualities and even if I did, you would be somewhat justified. You have a lot of people looking to you to fix a problem that is out of your control. It's got to be overwhelming." This just solidified why I loved this woman.

"Are you sure you're not just saying that?" I asked, buttoning my shirt. She moved off the bed to give me a kiss, "I think you're doing a great job." We hugged, I thanked her, grabbed my tie and sport coat and ran down the stairs headed for the office. Although I certainly appreciated and needed to hear Barbara's comments, Malificent's words still left me unsettled. There's nothing like a little criticism to bring out all your insecurities. With the weight of the world that I was feeling lately, was I behaving like a victim and losing sight of Jessica's pain? Was I overstepping my role in the investigation? Should I stop wearing tighty-whities?

As I walked, I decided to shelve the question of

martyrdom, and considered the investigation issue further. Although to outsiders I understood that it may seem odd, but my role as the Dean of Students required me to be intimately involved with the case. It seemed as though the only major difference between me investigating an incident that occurred on Westmire College campus and the police conducting an investigation in town was the difference in scope. My efforts seemed to be much more focused on Jessica and her welfare. Although I was concerned about her mother's whereabouts, my responsibilities focused on finding Jessica. Or maybe not finding her, but facilitating the investigation. This made me consider Cruzer.

Although when I saw Cruzer with the flyers I wasn't on campus, I still felt it necessary to respond in order to facilitate the investigation. As Dean, this is my role both on and off campus. This line of thought made me remember some of my doctoral coursework and the words of educational philosopher, John Dewey. Dewey contended, paraphrasing as well as my memory serves, that individuals in society are one person. Regardless of a person's role in work or out of work, he or she remains the same individual, unable to separate their conduct between one area and another. Thus, conduct whether in or out of work remained the same. Therefore, I acted on Cruzer off campus just as I would on-campus. My actions didn't changed regardless of my location.

I found some comfort in this lofty recollection pulled from the far reaches of my memory. I was pretty convinced that I wasn't overstepping my role in investigating Jessica's disappearance; I had a responsibility to the Westmire College community to do just that. Malificent simply didn't understand. Perhaps it was because she was hiding something, or better yet, hiding a secret for Cruzer.

Discussion with my wife and the walk to work had certainly helped my mood. I had effectively wiped away any glimmer of truth that Malificent spoke and absolved myself of any wrongdoing. Whether fully accurate or not, I felt better. I walked into my office at 10:45am. Judy greeted me with her hand on her hip, "Well fella, where have you been?"

"I'd like to say recovering from a wild night and a hangover," I said since there weren't any students in the office, "but it wasn't nearly that much fun. I'll fill you in on the details later. What'd I miss?"

"You had a 9 o'clocker with the provost, I rescheduled for later this week. You had a 10 o'clocker with a student upset about the vegetarian selections in the dining hall, I told her to get a cheeseburger and go talk to Jerry." She smiled and looked over her glasses, "Jerry handled her. Go ahead into your office, I'll follow you."

I walked into my office, set my briefcase down and sat behind my desk. Judy came in behind me and laid a stack of papers on my desk, "These are for your signature, I need the top two right now and the rest by the end of the day. And here are your phone messages; one of them is from Chief Braggish asking about last night. What happened last night?"

"There was a vigil for Jessica, it was no big deal, pretty low-key. But Al Towers called me to let me know, so I stopped by. Oh, that reminds me, can you call Chris Fagan into the office, please?"

"I thought you said it was low-key?"

"It was for the most part, but Chris was too busy giving me the double bird salute to go and sing Kumbaya."

"You know, with a shower and a haircut, that boy'd be a looker."

"Well when he comes in, why don't you tell him that?" I responded sarcastically, "In fact, I bet that you could do a makeover right here in the office. In fact, it could be a new series, 'Menopausal Eye for the Dirty Guy'. It'd be fabulous."

"It's a good thing that I like you," Judy smirked, "or I'd file harassment charges." We finished discussing my calendar for the rest of the day and I started looking at the forty-seven new e-mail messages in my inbox. Within twenty minutes, Judy buzzed me, "Mr. Philmore's on the phone." I hadn't heard from him in a few days, maybe he knew something new.

"Mr. Philmore," I said putting the receiver to my ear, "How are you?"

"I just called for an update. Any news?"

"Well, I saw the Westmire Shores police chief this morning and I know that he's actively investigating." I didn't feel that it was appropriate to share any information about Cruzer, the flyers or the tattooed stranger. Overstepping my bounds in the investigation, indeed. I continued, "And there was a vigil for Jessica last night that the students organized. They are all very hopeful, Mr. Philmore, as are we." What else could I say?

"Any word on Susan?" I had to consider this a moment, since Mrs. Philmore had only given me her first name reluctantly.

"Not that I know of," I responded, "But that's a bit out of my jurisdiction." Where was Malificent now?

"I just thought that you'd be kept in the loop."

"Well, mostly about the details relating to your daughter. She's been my focus."

"I just can't believe it." Mr. Philmore spoke as if in shock, "All weekend I racked my brain. Who would do this, I mean, who wants to get me that badly?"

"What do you mean, 'get you'?"

"I mean it can't be a coincidence that my daughter and ex-wife go missing in the same week. Someone's got to be after me, they've got to want something."

"But you haven't received any ransom request, right?" Suddenly this felt surreal.

"No, the police have been checking in with me. Nothing. I just can't believe this is happening." In the background, I could hear some raised voices in Mr. Philmore's office, "Excuse me, please," he said to me, cupping his hand over the receiver. I could still hear loud mumbles, including the raised, muffled voice of Jack Philmore. After a brief albeit heated interlude, he returned, "Sorry, Dean. We're having labor negotiations and everyone's a little jumpy. As if I didn't have enough to worry about." Mr. Philmore had actually told me about his trouble with his workers' union a few days earlier, but obviously had forgotten.

I asked him a few polite questions about the migration habits of carnival workers and their relationships with powerhouse unions, we made small talk for a few minutes more, and then hung-up the phone. It seemed as though Jack Philmore called me in place of a personal counselor. I was the only lifeline to his daughter, and martyr or no martyr, that was a big responsibility. As I hung-up the receiver, Judy approached my office doorway, "Chief Braggish is here to see you, she says it's important."

"Sure." I responded, shuffling some papers on my desk. She was probably here to get a first-hand account of the vigil. Within seconds, Quacky Braggish lumbered her ample frame into my office like an oversized weeble-wobble.

"Hello, Dean Doug," she said out of breath, "I just got this and brought it to you right away." She then flung a manila folder on my desk.

"What's this?" I asked.

"Report on the vending machine. Thought you'd like to have it. Very suspicious."

I opened the report from the Westmire College Security Department, which included a statement from the vending machine company. I skimmed it over quickly and didn't actually find anything any more suspicious than when the incident occurred. As I read, I didn't see anything new at all.

"Well Tina, since you're here and more intimately knowledgeable about the report, why don't you give me the short version."

"Right!" she said, straightening her white polyester security officer's blouse. The blouse's buttons were straining so much to conceal Tina's abundant bosoms that I was afraid that one would pop off and hit me in the eye. Nevertheless, she persevered, "Well, the machine was tampered with." She said as though she was making a speech on the discovery of the eleventh Commandment, "and some of the animals, the fetal pigs, were stolen from our biology lab on campus." This is what we suspected all along. She continued, "and according to the lab report, I called in a favor with the folks in the chemistry lab, the red substance wasn't blood, it was dyed corn-syrup." Again, not a revelation, we already knew this.

"So," I interrupted, "what's in the report that we didn't already know. Do we know who did it?"

"We're still working on that, Dean," Tina said, with the straight face of Sgt. Joe Friday, "But we do know how the perpetrator allegedly gained access to the inside of the machine."

"How?"

"They had a key. You see," I settled in, knowing that this could take some time, "vending machines can only be opened with a special key unique to the machine. Much like a key that you'd use to access your front door, only different." Tina's enthusiasm for gaining access to the contents of a vending machine were clearly effecting her ability to focus, "It's more like a round cylinder..." She continued, as I drifted off to my happy place. Chief Braggish actually had also speculated that the person who did this had a key when she completed the initial investigation. I waited for her to finish her breath, and then interrupted again, "So where would they get a key?"

"Well, I talked to the folks at Oceanside Vending, and they aren't missing any keys. The deliveryman, Thomas Reynolds, has been working this route for over ten years, I spoke to him and all of his keys are accounted for. He's a really nice man, he was nice to talk to." A match made in heaven, Quacky was hot for the vending machine guy. "The interesting part, though..." Finally, the moment I had been waiting for, "is that according to Tom, he asked me to call him Tom, is that he had an emergency appendectomy three weeks ago and someone had to cover his route." Ah, yes. Truly fascinating indeed.

"Why is an appendectomy interesting?" I asked.

"Because if access to the machine wasn't gained through Tom's devices, the guy who replaced him for a week may have something to do with it. Maybe the guy lost one of *his* keys and just didn't tell the company... I'm still working on locating him. Tom's helping me out." There was a twinkle in Quacky's eyes that I could only imagine was conjuring up visions of quiet, cozy nights with equal and full access to both Tom and the contents of his truck. It reminded me of an incident that occurred during my first year in college when one of my housemates hooked up with his ex-girlfriend after a nasty fight of throwing Devil Dogs at each other. In attempts to clean up the mess, they ended up in a passionate heap, still covered head to toe in preserved devil's food cake, locked in the downstairs bathroom. Moans of ecstasy could be heard throughout the house. Perhaps Tina was on to something.

After we finished discussing vending machine love, we moved onto the subject of the vigil. I praised Al Towers' great work and Chief "Quacky" Braggish left my office with the smile of a pleased supervisor. Despite her faults, Chief Braggish is a dedicated worker who takes great pride in keeping Westmire safe. Who can argue with that.

After a quick lunch and a couple of afternoon meetings out of my office, I went back to my desk to do more paperwork. Although it felt good to get out of my office, I was consistently bombarded with questions about the Philmores whenever I left. There were benefits to hiding behind my desk with Judy acting as sentinel. As I walked, I thought about Cruzer and what had happened earlier in the morning. What was going on with him? I decided to give Chief Morreale a call for an update.

Upon returning to my desk, Judy informed me that Chief Morreale had already called and asked me to call him back. Perfect. Malificent couldn't accuse me of overstepping my bounds by fishing for information. The Chief was bringing the pond to me. We played phone tag for nearly an hour and finally connected around 4pm.

"Hi, Chief," I said, "How's your day going."

"Oh, not bad." Chief Morreale replied in his usual chipper way, "I called to give you an update. You know, that Cruzer's not a bad guy. I think that someone just took advantage of him."

"So you don't think that he's involved in Jessica's disappearance?"

"Cruzer?" the Chief responded with surprise, "No, not at all. He took the flyers because he wanted the money. Period." OK, now was the time for some fishing.

"Oh, well Malificent alluded to the fact that Cruzer may have some motive for involvement."

"Well, he has a link, but a motive for murder. There's a lot more than meets the eye with Cruzer, he's had a tough life." It seemed that although Cruzer had some sort of secret past, a lot of people were in on it. I was determined to find out, "Oh?" I said, both casually and sympathetically, "What happened?"

"He was abandoned as a child," the Chief replied without hesitation, "Father died when he was ten or eleven, mother went missing when he was 16 or so. Turned up dead a few months later. From what I know, he wasn't really right after that. Sad." That was it? That was the secret? Although Malificent had a personal code of silence, I was glad to know that Chief Morreale did not.

"Is that the connection?" I asked.

"Well, that's what Malificent thinks. She's been working with him to deal with the disappearance and murder of his mother. You know, through the scriptures. She was worried that if Cruzer was questioned too much about Jessica's disappearance, it might bring a flood of bad memories."

"But Cruzer must have known that Jessica was missing, that *was* what the flyers said. My God, Chief, he had at least fifty of them in his wheelbarrow."

"Yeah well, Doug, like I said, he's not right. You know that. And he doesn't read, so actually, he had no idea what the flyers said." All right, it was time to concede and let Cruzer off the hook. Although I wasn't anxious to persecute him, I was hoping that we were onto something. The chief continued, "But let me tell you, if the Ladies Auxiliary knew who took their flyers, Cruzer'd be in big trouble. I had two little old ladies in my office today ready for a lynching."

"What'd you tell them?"

"I told them it was just a cruel prank and that they should make more. I let them file a police report, at their insistence, and they walked out the door ready to take on the world."

"What about the tattooed man that Cruzer talked about?" I asked.

"Well, he gave us a pretty good description, we're working on it."

"It's a long shot, right?"

"Well Doug, it ain't easy, but it's something. We'll do what we can."

"What do you make of what he said about mittens and camping?"

"Yeah, that's a tough one too. I'm not sure where to begin on that one, but we're trying our best."

"Anything on Jessica's mom?"

"No. Dead end so far. It's like she vanished. What about your anonymous e-mailer? Get any response." It was as if we were sharing dead end ghost stories.

"No, nothing. Seems like a pattern, huh?" I said.

"Doug, something will break... usually when things seem the dimmest, something breaks," the Chief said reassuringly.

"Thanks for the update, Chief. I appreciate your help."

"You got it, Doug. I'll talk to you later." What the chief didn't realize was that actually, he'd be talking to me in about ten minutes, because something *was* about to break.

As I hung up the phone, I saw that my "message waiting" light was flashing red. In our automated phone system, people can leave messages while we're on the phone. I dutifully hit the message button, entered my password and prepared to listen to my messages. However, I wasn't prepared for its contents. It began with some static and then a tense man's voice came on, "Jessica is fine [pause, static]... you just leave her be... she's fine. I'm the professor here. You never mind her spot, she'll be jumpin' soon anyway, so forget it. [click of the phone; line goes dead]."

Chills ran up and down my back as I clutched the receiver with a death grip. As I hit the replay button, I screamed for Judy to come into my office. We had something. Finally, something. And it was big.

16

It really was a scream. Although I only meant to call Judy into my office, my excitement and adrenaline transformed my normal holler into a type of frenetic screech. Within moments, Judy ran like I've never seen before, adjusting her skirt as she moved into my office, "Doug, what's wrong?"

"Did you just transfer a call to my voicemail?" I asked, still in a frenzy.

"No, I was in the ladies room," she replied, adjusting herself again, "I heard you yell and I ran out, I thought you were going to be dead or something." Her voice moved into the lower register of hers, always saved for gossip, "I barely got my bloomers up. What's wrong?"

"We need to find out who transferred that call!"

"What was the call, what's wrong?"

"I'll explain in a minute, you find out who transferred the call, I need to call Chief Morreale."

"But you were just talking to Chief Morreale."

"I know, but this call changed everything. It was about Jessica, Judy. It was a message about Jessica!" With that tidbit, Judy ran out of the office to find the call transferer, while I called the Chief. A few minutes later, Judy came back holding Kristi, one of our student workers by the hand. The Chief said that he'd be right over, and I hung-up the phone.

"Kristi took the call," Judy said excitedly, "Go ahead, sweetheart, tell Dean Doug." Kristi is a pretty sophomore with curly brown hair and lots of teeth that are usually bared in a huge smile. Now, however, Kristi just looked as if she had entered the gas chamber. "I took the call," she said meekly, clearly unsure of the consequences, "Was that wrong?" In our attempts to calm her, Judy and I replied in stereo, "No!" which was much louder than we both expected. Kristi jumped back.

"No, Kristi, you didn't do anything wrong," I said, attempting to compose myself, "What did the man say?"

"Well, didn't he leave a voice message?" Kristi asked, innocently.

"Yes he did, but I need to know what he said to you *before* he left the message," I replied.

"He just said that he needed to speak with you, the Dean. I told him that you were on the phone and asked to take a message. He said 'no' and said that he wanted to speak to you in person. He acted really weird. I told him that you were on an important call, I didn't know whether you were or not, but I just told him that, and said that he could leave a voice message if he wanted to. After a little while, he seemed to get panicky, and then he said, 'ok' so I transferred him right to your voice mail. Was I not supposed to do that?"

"No, honey, that was fine," Judy said giving Kristi a hug.

"No, Kristi, you did fine," I reiterated, "Did he say anything else? Give his name or phone number?"

"I asked him who was calling and he just kept saying, 'the professor', 'the professor', over and over. I figured he was a professor."

"And he didn't leave a number?" I asked.

"No, he wouldn't. He said that he couldn't be reached. Well, actually, I think he said something like he, 'wasn't near no phone.' I thought that was weird coming from a professor, talk like that."

"And that was all?" I asked with a continued sense of urgency.

"I, I think so?" Kristi said hesitantly. Obviously I was making her nervous.

"Judy," I said, "Why don't you take Kristi downstairs

and grab a soda. Then, Kristi, you can relax. Chief Morreale from the Shores Police Department is going to be stopping by soon. I'm sure he's going to want to ask you more questions when he gets here." Judy continued with her arm around Kristi's shoulder and steered her out of my office. I suddenly got panicked that I hadn't saved the message, so I ran back to the phone. I saved the message, checked to make sure that it was saved, and then replayed it over and over. Who was this guy? How did he know Jessica? Did he kidnap her? If he did, why no ransom request? How did this man know me or get my number?

I continued to replay the message repeatedly for about fifteen minutes until Chief Morreale came into my office. I was harried, he was calm, cool, and collected as usual, munching on an apple, "So, let's hear the message!" he said in a peppy tone. I put the phone on speaker and played the message a few times for the Chief.

"And who took the call?" he asked.

"One of my student workers, Kristi. She's with Judy right now, they'll be up shortly so you can talk to her."

"Interesting voice," the Chief said, still crunching away, "a slight southern accent, and a strange dialect. What'd he say? 'leave her be?', 'never mind her spot?'" I replayed the message again while the Chief threw away his red-delicious to take some notes. Moments later, Judy returned with Kristi. I introduced the Chief and he began questioning her in my office with me present. He asked her many of the same questions that I had, and her responses weren't much more enlightening than they were a few minutes earlier. After about fifteen minutes, Kristi insisted that she had shared all she remembered.

"All right, Kristi," the Chief said, "I just have one more question. What did you hear in the background when the man was talking."

"Static." Kristi said, without much reflection.

"Anything else? Beyond the static?" Chief Morreale

continued, "Horns, music, traffic?" Kristi thought for a moment, "No, not really. All I remember was static, or like he was talking low, like he didn't want anyone to hear him."

"OK, well Kristi, if you remember anything else, you let me know. Dean Doug knows how to find me." We sent Kristi on her way, and shut my office door.

"Doug, I'll need a copy of that message,"the Chief said.

"Sure. Our voice mail is digital, so I think our people can make a recording right off the system. I'll ask Judy to check." I offered the Chief the wastebasket for his apple core, and as he put his hat on he said, "This is a good one, Doug. Like I told you earlier, just when you think that the case is dead, something comes up."

"But can we believe it? That she's alive?" I said hopefully.

"Well, what adds to the possibility is that the guy didn't make a ransom request. He just wants us to leave her alone."

"But why?"

"Well that's the next piece that we tackle." It was almost 5:30pm and I was ready to go home. I grabbed my briefcase, and the Chief and I walked out of the Student Center together. On our way out of the building, I noticed that someone had taped bright green flyers in the foyer of the building, not on the designated bulletin boards. I stopped and read one, "SAVE THE TREES! Help us fight deforestation...WHEN? Tomorrow! WHERE? Meet on the front lawn, 9:00AM, sharp. Poster board and markers provided." The Chief stood behind me and chuckled, "How many trees did they kill making these flyers?"

"Maybe it's recycled paper?" I responded jokingly.

"Haven't you had a lot of student protests this year?"

"Yeah we have, more than usual... and the semester's young." As we continued our way outside, Chief Morreale asked me if I wanted a ride home, but even though a light rain had begun to fall, I declined. I enjoy my walk and owed it to Barbara and Ethan to decompress before I walked into our house. I pulled out my trusty umbrella and headed home.

Although the rain ordinarily might have dampened my spirits, I was feeling pretty good. There was a possibility that Jessica Philmore was alive. It was the best news I could have received. But where was she? Had someone abducted her or had she just run away? Who was this man, or men, who were talking to Cruzer and calling me? Although I was more confused than ever, I felt like we were finally getting somewhere. I continued on my walk to the cadence of raindrops on my umbrella.

As I crossed Main Avenue, I glanced down at the ocean. It was steel grey to match the sky and churning softly. Although I wanted to get home, I stopped and marveled at the Atlantic's quiet strength. When I first moved to the shore, I promised myself that I would never take the sight of the ocean for granted, and I never have. It was the perfect setting for my current mood: unsettled, but content. I continued home and found Barbara and Ethan sitting on the front porch enjoying the rain.

"Daddy!" Ethan called, and ran down the front walk to greet me. He reminded me of Christopher Robin in his shorts and red rubber boots nearly to his knee. I picked him up and carried him back to the porch where Barbara was waiting with a kiss. Yup, it's cliché and a little cheesy, but that's my life and I love it. That night we ate dinner on the front porch and watched the rain get heavier as if it were a television program. By eight o'clock, Ethan was in bed and Barbara and I went back to the porch and had another glass of wine. What's a bottle or two of pinot grigio between partners?

I had already filled Barbara in on the latest news, but hadn't gotten into the specifics. "So," Barbara began, "Did you actually *talk* to this man on the phone?"

"No, he left a message on my voicemail," I said.

"How'd he get your private line?" I have a private line directly in my office that very few people know the number to, such as Jerry, the President of the College, and Barbara. I usually refer to it as the "Bat-phone".

"He didn't call the private, he called the main number and asked for me. Judy was away from her desk, so one of our students took the call and transferred him to voicemail." I told her what Chief Morreale had to say and went on to tell her about the latest, impending protest.

"They're coming at you like nor'easters," Barbara joked, referring to the strong coastal storms that often hit the East coast from fall to spring, damaging the beaches, bringing heavy rain, or dumping a foot or more of snow.

"Well, we'll see what this one brings. It should be relatively quiet, tree-huggers are pacifists aren't they?"

"I think so, but aren't they also the people who go up in a tree, chain themselves and live in order to save it?"

"None of the trees on our campus are in danger and don't need saving."

"You tell that to your 18 year old protestors who need a cause," Barbara smiled and winked at me. I shuddered to think of the possibilities and changed the subject.

"So, how was your day?" I asked.

"It was fine. I actually started my research on the carnivals."

"Madame Dread not freaking you out anymore?"

"No, she freaked me out, but I'm not going to let that stop me from doing this story. I've changed the slant a little bit. At first I was going to talk about the fun, kitschy psychics that you find on the boardwalk. Now, I'm ready to blow them out of the water as phonies."

"Piss-off Barbara Carter-Connors and she'll stab you with her pen," I quipped, "Metaphorically, of course."

"This revenge is sweet, as well as a little bit of therapy. She *traumatized* me, Doug!" Barbara replied, laughing, but with a note of seriousness.

"So what've you found out so far in your research?" I asked.

"I really just started."

"I should have you talk with Jack Philmore," I said, "He owns and manages a string of boardwalk amusements up and down the East coast."

"Jessica Philmore's father?"

"Yes, he was just telling me the other day some of the problems he was having with the labor union."

"Carnival workers have a labor union?"

"Doesn't everybody have a union of some sort?"

"Except for stay at home moms."

"Are you being overworked?" I asked, kidding.

"I'm not complaining, just commenting on society." Barbara replied, seriously, "And I think I'll pass on Mr. Philmore, he's got much more to worry about than my hometown story for the *Shores' Sentinel*."

The rain had passed, leaving behind a humid stew of warm air conducive to outside lounging and warm conversation. We chatted until nearly midnight, losing track of time finishing the pinot, refueling with some decaf coffee, and simply enjoying each other. Finally, we gave in to the impending pressures of the next day and went up to bed.

Although not typically a cuddler, I cuddled-up to Barbara in one last-ditch effort to make our perfect evening last a little bit longer. However as I drifted off to sleep holding my soul mate, Jessica Philmore once again infiltrated my thoughts. For once, she wasn't lying dead somewhere along the beach, but sleeping. She was alive, and although we had no idea where she was at the moment, this was all that mattered. I fell into a peaceful sleep that night, still thinking about Jessica. I was hoping that somewhere, wherever she was, she was sleeping peacefully, too.

17

I turned my alarm off at the usual 5:45am and immediately decided to forego my run. Instead, I lounged in bed until 6:30am. Actually, I wasn't lounging; I was sound asleep and probably would have slept longer if Barbara hadn't woken me up. The previous night had left me tired due to lack of sleep and overindulgence of Pinot Grigio, but surprisingly rested and feeling well. While Barbara and Ethan ate their breakfast, I hopped in the shower. I was feeling so peppy that I even used my "Mountain Mist" shower gel that I save for special occasions and times when I want to get lucky-- which I suppose is a special occasion.

I dressed in my favorite navy blue suit, added a light blue dress shirt and a bold blue and pink striped tie to reflect my mood. I was feeling sassy. I bounded into the kitchen, kissed my family, ate a bowl of honey-nut Cheerios and practically skipped out the door. I felt renewed. We were finally getting closer to Jessica Philmore; not merely her ghost, but her. Although I wasn't naïve enough not to consider that she may be in trouble, my euphoria at the possibility of her being alive shadowed all else.

As I arrived on campus, I was quickly reminded of the tree-hugging rally. I was also reminded of the level of human development for eighteen through twenty-one year olds. Protesting on a college campus is a slippery slope greased with olive oil. It seems that at this point in college students' lives, once they've decided that they've been wronged, indeed society's been wronged, there's no stopping them. They'll protest anything. Given the spike in protests, obviously the students on my campus felt wronged quite a bit lately.

Unlike the previous protest, however, this one wasn't nearly as well attended, although it was still barely 9am. There were as few as seven students on the front lawn, sitting in a circle, holding various signs that said, "Killing trees = murder!" and, "green = clean, not mean". Funny, I had never realized that there was so much math involved in being an environmentalist.

I could see that one young woman had loosely chained herself to a Japanese maple. Propped-up against her was a sign that read, "Save the Trees." As I had said to Barbara, I thought that this type of demonstration was usually saved for the giant redwoods or other rare variety of sapling. I didn't have the heart to tell her that her Japanese maple was in no danger of deforestation whatsoever. It had been deforested from a nursery out on route 35 several years ago. One young man must have thought that it would be mean to use a piece of poster board for his sign, so he simply painted his message on his torso. On his chest was a rough outline of a green tree, on his back was a smiley face. If his back was smiling, I didn't want to see what was painted below his belt.

As I walked past, I called, "It's a lot of dedication to be protesting a cause at 9am." One of the young women happily responded, "We've been here all night!" I simply waved and decided to call Quacky just to make sure that she realized that our front lawn had turned into a campground.

The remainder of my morning was relatively uneventful. I didn't have any appointments or interruptions, which allowed me to catch-up on all of my e-mail and paperwork. Judy let me know that my buddy, Dirt, was coming to see me at 1:30pm as I requested. After lunch, Jerry, Keesha and I made our way back out to the front lawn to check the progress of the tree-huggers. Their mass had only doubled in size to about fourteen, and most of them were just napping with signs lying next to them on the ground. Silent protesting must be exhausting.

When we returned to the office, Dirt was sitting in the waiting area looking, in ill-humor as usual. His hair was greasy and matted and he appeared to be wearing the exact same denim ensemble of two weeks ago. It's true, denim gets better with age. Since I was still in my good mood, I greeted him chipperly, "Hey Chris, thanks for coming in. C'mon back to my office." I stood in front of him gesturing with my arm toward my office. He rose from the cushioned chair in the reception area slowly and proceeded down the hall. As I followed behind him, the smell of patchouli that he left in his wake was almost overpowering. And I could swear that he also left a cloud of dirt lagging behind him like Pigpen in the Peanuts comics. As I passed her desk, Judy looked at me holding her nose and shook her head, already holding a can of Lysol in her hand.

Dirt and I entered my office and both took our usual seats, me behind the desk, him in front of it. He draped his arm over the back of the chair and cocked his head to one side, "You called?" he said flatly.

"Yes, do you know why, Chris?" I responded.

"Because of the other night?"

"Yeah, and what happened the other night?"

"You were harassing me and I got frustrated." His comment made me reflect on that night of the vigil, when I found him sitting in a booth in the cafeteria reading a comic book. Although I found it odd, and did approach him, I hadn't intended to harass him.

"You felt harassed?" I asked, "I remember very simply asking you about the vigil, that's all."

"Yeah, and I was minding my own business."

"Yes, you were, but you were also sitting in a public place out in the open for everyone to see. It just struck me as odd that you weren't out on the lawn."

"Why?" Dirt responded a little more defensively than I had expected, "I wasn't there, ok? Maybe I forgot about it, ok? It's none of your business."

"Forgot about a ceremony in honor of your girlfriend?" I asked. It was a harsh question and I knew it.

"I didn't plan it, so why would I know about it or go to it?" He spoke so matter-of-factly that I couldn't tell if he just didn't attend, or wasn't informed about the vigil at all.

"You didn't know about the vigil?" I asked, softening my tone, which didn't help. Chris jumped to his feet, "Whatever! Look, I didn't mean to flip you off. I'm sorry. Can I go now?" He was agitated, but so hard to read that I couldn't tell why. Either no one told him about the vigil, which would certainly hurt even a dirty boy's feelings, or he forgot about it. Which was worse?

"Chris, have a seat." I said.

"No. I'm done. I want to leave." He stood resolutely behind the chair, clutching the back cushion with talon-like fingers. Although these impasses were rare in student conduct cases, they happened. The way to maneuver around situations like these is to take ego out of it. If I made him sit back down as a show of my power over him, I would never get anywhere in the future. I had to simply ask myself if I had made my point. I decided that I hadn't, so I simply said, "Chris, I'm sure that you're going through a hard time right now, but flipping me off, flipping anyone off, isn't acceptable."

"I said I was sorry, all right?" Dirt said looking away, under his breath he muttered, "just mind your own business."

"Excuse me?" I responded, a bit surprised by Dirt's tenacity.

"Just leave it alone!" Dirt implored.

"*It*?" I asked. I could understand, 'leave me alone', but "it"? It didn't make sense. With this question, Dirt lost his confidence for a moment. I could see his stare turn fearful for a brief second before he iced it over again and responded coolly, "Just leave me alone and let me mind my own business." Although I was convinced that Dirt Fagan had a great deal more to tell me, I let him go. Full-fledged interrogation had to be left to the police, and I would simply tell Chief Morreale.

There was something wrong with Dirt's behavior, his responses, even though I couldn't quite put my finger on it. Why didn't he ask about the status of the case? As Jessica Philmore's boyfriend, wouldn't he want to know what was going on? But he didn't ask one question, his only concern seemed to be leaving him alone and staying out of his business. It was guilt by omission. The fact that he *didn't* ask about Jessica didn't sit well with me, Dirt knew something more.

I followed Dirt's filthy cloud out of my office and collected my messages from Judy. She dutifully followed me back to my desk armed with her trusty can of Lysol, "I'm telling you," she said spraying with all her might, "That'd be a good lookin' fella if he'd clean up his act. Why would any girl even want to get near him? Especially that cute Philmore girl?"

"Adolescent rebellion," I stated casually.

"Well, as a mother of five, the adolescents that I know like to shower," Judy responded through the mist. Between the aerosol spray and Dirt's stench, quite a haze had developed in my office, "I just don't understand some kids," Judy lamented, leaving my office.

The next couple of hours were uneventful, filled with e-mail, phone calls and a meeting with Jerry. The events that followed at the end of the day, however, were not. I was sitting at my desk, sifting over the afternoon mail when suddenly I heard yelling coming from the outer office. "I need to see the Dean!" I heard a young woman shriek, "I need to see him, now!" By her tone, I could tell that she was on the verge of hysterics. I immediately got up from my desk and went to see what was happening. I saw Judy standing in front of Sarah Borden, Jessica Philmore's blue-haired Wiccan roommate, trying to calm her down. A few students outside of the office were staring, Keesha stood in her office doorway assessing the situation.

"Honey," Judy was saying, trying to calm Sarah, "Honey, calm down. What's the matter?" Sarah began to sob and continued to insist that she see me.

"I'm right here," I said, entering the reception area, "Sarah? Let's go into my office and you can tell me what's going on." Since she seemed more fragile than normal, I didn't want to meet with her without someone else present. In today's litigious society, false accusations of harassment and inappropriate behavior come easily, especially to Deans by students who aren't wound too tight. This was the reason why I rarely closed my door when I met with students. I looked to Keesha and asked her to join me.

We ushered Sarah into my office and offered her a seat while Keesha and I sat on the couch. Sarah looked sullen, confused and mildly paranoid. I immediately wondered whether or not she was on a bad drug trip, "Sarah," I began, "This is Keesha Cribbs. She's on my staff and I've asked her to join us. Now, what's wrong?"

"Someone was in my room, they broke into my room!" she blurted, leaning toward me for emphasis. Her blue hair was melting into her normal mousy brown and hung in front of her face in greasy strands. Her eyeliner and lipstick were still dark, nearly black, but smudged. In a word, Sarah was a mess.

"What do you mean someone broke into your room, when?" I asked.

"Today, a little while ago, they were in my room!"

"You found someone in your room?"

"No, but the door was open when I came back from class. I know I shut it, I know I did!" She was becoming increasingly anxious.

"OK, OK," I said in my calming tone, "Just try to tell me what happened, take a breath." Sarah complied, and immediately began again, this time a bit slower, "When I got back from class, my door was open, not much, just a crack. When I went in, some of my stuff had been moved... I think some things are missing. Some of Jessica's stuff had been moved, too!" I glanced at Keesha who gave me the, 'is this girl crazy?' look. Sarah started in again, "They're trying to get me! I know it, they're trying to get me!" Now I returned the look to Keesha.

"Who's trying to get you, Sarah?" I asked.

"Those girls on my floor! They said that I should watch my back or something would happen... they hate me because they think I did something to Jessica, which I didn't. I didn't do anything to her, it just wasn't working out, you know that, right?"

"Right, we've talked about that," I responded, "What did your room look like when you went in, was it torn up?"

"No, not really," Sarah said beginning to calm a bit, "Some things were just moved around a little. But I could tell, and they took some of my things!"

"What do you think was missing?"

"My crystal ball and my Tarot cards, they're gone. I'm not sure what else, but there's probably more."

"You're sure they're gone, you didn't just misplace them?"

"No, I got my crystal ball last summer in England, it's very special. I got it in a little shop near Stonehenge. I keep it right by my bed on my dresser, and my Tarot cards were on my desk and now they're gone!"

"And what about Jessica's stuff, you said that it had been moved, too?"

"I didn't look really closely, but it looked like some of her clothes were gone, and maybe some stuff from on top of her dresser, I'm not sure." Sarah was almost speaking in a normal voice now allowing her story to become more believable.

"Did you see anyone in the hallway before you went in

to your room?" I asked.

"Not really, not right by my door."

"OK, let's do this. I'm going to call Mr. Ricardo from Residence Life and Chief Braggish from Campus Security and we'll all go to your room to see what's happened. Is that OK with you?" Sarah simply nodded. I picked up the phone and dialed Jerry, who met us in my office right away, and Quacky who promised to meet us at Sarah's room. I thanked Keesha for her help, and led Sarah and Jerry to the scene of the crime.

We arrived at Cambridge Hall and saw Quacky's security mobile parked next to the sidewalk outside. The vehicle is an intimidating, souped-up golf cart painted bright yellow complete with a revolving red siren light on the top. If it didn't have, "WC Security" written on the side, it would look like something better suited to be the clown car at the circus. Although walking was faster, Quacky drove the security mobile around our tiny campus whenever possible.

"Well, looks like Chief Braggish beat us," I said, making conversation while Sarah let us into the residence hall. We made our way to her room and saw Quacky waiting outside, inspecting Sarah's door, "Hi, folks," she said, waving something in her hand.

"Hi, Chief," I said pointing to her hand, "What've you got there?"

"Latex gloves. Before we enter the area, we all need to put these gloves on to protect any evidence inside. And until we get a better look, don't touch *anything*." It seemed a bit extreme to me, but I didn't say anything. Sarah immediately got her look of panic back, "Am I not going to be able to stay in my room?" she asked. Quacky began to answer but I cut her off, "We'll know more after we go in, right Chief?" I shot Quacky a look that said, 'don't upset her' to which she responded, "We'll have to see what we find." With that, we all donned our gloves and Quacky opened the door with her master key.

The room was just as I remembered it: Dark. I hadn't been in the room since we discovered Sarah Borden's Wiccan Ways over a week ago and she hadn't redecorated much, save the fact that the pentagram had been removed from the middle of the floor. Even though it was the middle of the day, the interior had a darkroom like quality. The blinds were all closed and heavy black curtains shrouded any light. Quacky flipped on the overhead light with a latexed finger which, unlike the last time, illuminated the room. "Ms. Borden," Quacky said, "without touching anything, show us where the locations of the removed property."

As Quacky pulled out a note pad, Sarah walked over to her dresser, "My crystal ball was right here," she said, pointing to a dust-free imprint, then walking a few steps to her desk, "...and my Tarot cards were here on top of my desk."

"Can you describe the items?" asked Quacky.

"I got the crystal ball in England last summer, it's very special. I got it in a little shop near Stonehenge." It must have been very special because I've been to Stonehenge and didn't remember any cute shops other than the touristy on-site gift shop near the premises. Indeed, it's an awe-inspiring collection of rocks, but it's in the middle of a very large field. Clearly, Sarah had sought out some specialty shop nearby that sold mystic items.

"Can you describe the crystal ball?" Quacky asked.

"Well, it's about this size," Sarah said holding out her cupped hand, and Quacky interrupted, "So about five inches in diameter?" Sarah continued, "Probably, and it sits on a black base with ancient carvings etched into it, they're painted with gold."

"You said, 'etched'," Quacky responded, referring to her copious notes, "so is it made of wood?"

"Teak," Sarah responded proudly. Good thing the tree-huggers weren't nearby or she'd have been in double-trouble. Quacky wrote feverishly, what I'm not sure since Sarah only uttered a one-syllable word. "Do you know the value?" Quacky asked.

"It's very powerful," Sarah said rolling her eyes in the back of her head for effect, "It's priceless."

"But how much did you pay for it?" pursued Quacky.

"Fifteen pounds." Sarah responded sheepishly.

"So that's what, twenty dollars, American?" Quacky asked all impressed with herself. I must admit, I was impressed too.

"Yes."

"OK, what about the Tarot cards?"

"Well, I was using them last night, and they were here on my desk. I normally keep them in my desk drawer."

"Were they in a box?"

"They are old, I got them at the flea market in Collingswood, so they didn't have a box." Collingswood is the site of a very big weekend flea market about twenty minutes west of campus.

"And what do they look like?" asked Quacky.

"Tarot cards." Sarah answered, seeming annoyed.

"Miss, I'm not familiar with Tarot cards, can you describe them please? Are they like regular playing cards?" I shot Jerry a wink, obviously Quacky never watched Miss Cleo.

"No, they're bigger, probably three times the size of a playing card. The backs are plain black." Boring, I thought.

"And their value?" Quacky asked.

"They are fifty dollar Tarot cards..." Sarah began, but then anticipated Quacky's follow-up question, "but I paid five." Quacky smiled and documented the amount on her pad.

"Anything else of yours missing?"

"I didn't really look. Maybe. I noticed those right away and freaked out." Sarah said, turning to my direction, "I ran right to DOSO." I stood with my gloved hands inside my pants pockets (an odd feeling) and decided to jump into the discussion, "Sarah, you mentioned that some of Jessica's items were missing too?"

"Yeah, well, I think so... she had a laundry basket filled with clean laundry over there. It was piled way over the top and now it's not." We all turned to look at a half-full blue laundry basket, Sarah continued, "and then maybe some things from her dresser? I'm not sure, I looked quick and I don't really know much about Jessica's stuff." Quacky went over to the dresser to look and put her nose about three inches from the top, "Yup, something's been removed alright, a couple of things..."

I went over and saw the same conspicuous dust-free spots on the dresser, like undusty crop circles. Like most college students, it was clear that dusting wasn't top on the list of Sarah or Jessica's chores. Quacky was once again writing feverishly and then suddenly moved toward the door, "Dean Doug, can I speak to you in the hall?"

"Sure." I said.

"Mr. Ricardo and Ms. Borden, you can stay in the room but DO NOT touch anything." This seemed to make both of them uncomfortable, causing Jerry to stuff his lanky arms into his pockets. I walked into the hallway and Quacky shut the door. Quacky began speaking in a hushed voice, "I think we better call the Shores PD."

"You do?" I asked.

"This is a crime scene, Dean." Quacky snapped, obviously offended by my question, "This is the former room of a missing female, which has been unlawfully entered and personal property stolen. I'm not comfortable leaving possible precious evidence in there that could be destroyed." Quacky finished, sniffed, and raised her head back to look at me. She had rested her case.

"Tina," I said, forcing myself to remember her real name, "I wasn't questioning your judgment, I was just asking. Do you want to call them?" Tina looked down at her pad, looking a little embarrassed by her defensiveness, "Yes, I'll call them. Sorry."

"It's OK," I said, "We're all a little on edge these days. So I should move Sarah out of this room?"

"Yes, indefinitely I would assume, until a team can come in and collect evidence."

"But the police have already searched the room for evidence."

"Yes, but I bet this time, they're going to want to dust for fingerprints, look for hair samples, etc. in order to determine who's been in this room. Most likely, the FBI will be here."

"OK," I said with a sigh, somewhat daunted, "Let's tell Sarah."

We called Sarah and Jerry out into the hallway to limit the potential of someone accidentally sneezing, thus, damaging evidence. I explained the situation and broke the news that Sarah would have to move out of her room. Sarah was obviously upset and I could tell that Jerry was worried about finding her another bed on campus. Sarah protested that she needed her room and needed her things, but Quacky remained firm and explained that this was not possible at this point. We all headed back to my office, including Sarah, under duress.

When we got outside, Quacky hopped into the Security Mobile, "All aboard!" she called. I wanted a few minutes to speak with Jerry so I answered, "Chief Braggish, why don't you take Sarah with you and Jerry and I will meet you at my office."

"Are you sure?" Quacky responded like a dejected cab driver, "There's plenty of room."

"No, it's fine. We'll see you in five minutes." Tina waved and with the push of a few pedals and the turn of the key, the Security Mobile ignited and spun out a bit on the lawn in front of Cambridge Hall. Sarah Borden sat alongside

Quacky, hugging herself and looking completely mortified.

"Doug," Jerry began immediately, "I don't know where I'm going to put her." We began walking slowly back to the Student Center. "But we have a few empty beds, right?" I asked.

"Yes, but who wants to live with her? Her RA, Jenny, says that no one will talk to her... I wouldn't be surprised if someone got into her room just to freak her out enough to leave." I thought about this for a moment and it made sense. After some intelligent reflection, I finally came up with this gem of a response, "Well we've got to put her somewhere." That's why they pay me the big bucks.

"I'll look... but this won't be easy. When the new roommate's parents call, *you* tell them that we bunked their daughter with a witch." I agreed because, well, that *is* why they pay me the big bucks. Well, mediocre bucks anyway.

We got back to the office and found Quacky and Sarah sitting in the waiting area. Tina indicated that she had already called the Shores PD and that she was going to head back over to Sarah's room to meet them. Jerry ushered poor homeless Sarah over to his office to find her a new place to live. I filled Judy in on the latest as she packed-up her things to go home.

"Any news on the tree huggers?" I asked as she traded her heels for sneakers.

"There's not a soul out there. By three o'clock there we only three kids taking a nap using their signs as blankets. Keesha went out at four and there wasn't a soul to be found. Either they decided that the trees were safe, or decided to screw the trees and go get dinner." Judy briefed me on a few other calls as I walked to my desk. As I sat down, my private line rang, "Hello?" I answered.

"Are you up for an outing this evening?" It was Barbara.

"Sure, what'd you have in mind?"

"Something greasy and beachy, like the Windmill." The

Windmill is a small chain of restaurants that specializes in, "gourmet fast food". Their hotdogs are huge, their burgers are immense and everything is delicious. There were a couple of them near Westmire Shores, the most notable a couple towns north in Long Branch that was built to look like a real windmill. It had a top deck where you could bring your food on a plastic tray, sit on a picnic table and enjoy a view of the ocean. You typically also had to fight the seagulls that apparently liked Windmill gourmet too, since they would often swoop down and grab whatever was in your hand. It was all part of the ambiance.

"Greasy and beachy are my favorite combination," I mused, "I'm finishing up here and I'll be on my way."

"How was your day?"

"Yet another day at the funhouse, here. I'll tell you all about it. What about you?"

"Well, while you were in a funhouse, I was researching them."

"So more research on life as a carnie?"

"Yes and Doug, it's fascinating!" Barbara said, clearly energized.

"Really." I responded in more of a statement than a question.

"Did you know that they have their own language? I mean it's English, but they have their own dialect. One of the things I found out was that a psychic booth is referred to as a 'mitt camp'."

"Still after that psychic, huh?"

"Well, all in the name of research. Come home soon?"

"I'm cleaning-up my desk and walking out the door."

"Good, I love you."

"I love you too."

I loved to see Barbara when she got excited about a story. A great quality of living with a writer, she would pick a topic that I never even considered and find out unique gems of knowledge. I always think that if I was ever on the game show, "Who Wants to be a Millionaire", she'd be my lifeline.

I organized my desk a bit and walked straight out of the office, as promised. As I made my short walk home I relived my day in fast forward. This place was crazy. I then began to think about Barbara's research. Maybe I should become a writer. Then at least I could document the craziness and make a little extra money. So carnies had their own language, huh? Who knew. What'd they call they psychic booth, mitten camp? I came to a dead stop on the sidewalk. Mitten camp. Mittens and camping. That's what Cruzer said that the man who approached him was talking about, "mittens and camping". 'Mitt Camp' could very easily morph into 'mittens and camping' to the uneducated ear. This was too close to be a coincidence. I got excited. I hugged my briefcase close to me and jogged the rest of the way home to talk to Barbara.

18

I ran in the front door still hugging my briefcase under my left arm, my shirt collar unbuttoned and my tie thrown over my shoulder. I ran through each room looking for Barbara and Ethan, who I ultimately found in the backyard. They both got up to hug me and Barbara looked at me curiously, "Did you run home?" I looked down at my clothes and saw my disheveled self, "Actually, I did."

"When I said hurry home, I didn't mean you had to run," Barbara laughed.

"Tell me more about the carnies," I said quickly.

"Are you going to put that down?" Barbara said, pointing to my abused briefcase that I was still clutching. I shook my head urgently, "Tell me more about the carnies," I repeated, "What did they call the psychic booth?"

"Well my notes are in my study, honey. Are you OK?"

"Yes, I'm fine, get your notes."

"OK," Barbara said looking at me as if I had lost my mind, "What's wrong?"

"Nothing is wrong, in fact, I think something is *right*, really right! Get your notes!"

"OK, OK, I'm getting them."

I put my briefcase down, took my blazer off and spent more time hugging Ethan as Barbara got her notes. She came through the screen door to the backyard with a pad, "Mitt camp," she said, "Doug, why do you want to know that?"

"Tell me about the psychic you saw."

"What? Doug, you're acting very strangely."

"I know, just tell me about the psychic you saw last Saturday."

"We've already talked about her." Barbara said, but I

didn't respond. I stood-up and stared at her.

"OK," she said, giving in, "She looked like a psychic, lots of scarves and a turban."

"Young or old?"

"What?"

"Young or old!" I said insistently.

"She was young," responded Barbara, "Doug, what's wrong?" I was reeling with excitement. My newly conceived hypothesis was right.

"Mine was *old*!" I blurted out excitedly.

"What? *Yours?* Doug, what are you talking about?"

"Remember when I went into the psychic booth after you, to give her a piece of my mind?"

"You're saying that they psychic that you saw a couple of minutes after the one that I saw was a different psychic?"

"Exactly!" I shouted excitedly, "That's exactly what I'm saying!"

"So the woman that you saw was old?"

"Yeah, older anyway, she looked like Miss Piggy in a turban... dark hair, pushed-in nose. Now describe yours..."

"Well it's hard to say... but she definitely wasn't Miss Piggy. She was thin, younger. Again, it's hard to say because she had a bright orange turban on her head and a veil covering most of her face. But she was definitely young, twenty tops."

"Did you see the color of her hair?" I asked. Barbara thought for a moment, "No, it was hidden under the turban."

"You didn't happen to notice her ankles, did you?"

"Her ankles? No, I think they were covered by an orange robe that matched her turban, it really was quite the outfit. But, Doug, I'm really losing you. What are you thinking?" I almost couldn't contain myself, "I think that your psychic was Jessica Philmore!"

Although I hadn't figured it all out yet, I was beginning to fit the pieces of Jessica Philmore's disappearance together. Barbara looked at me with a quizzical stare, "You think that my cruel psychic was your missing student?" she said, not yet believing me.

"Yes," I said, "that's why she was mean to you. She wanted me, us, to leave the boardwalk."

"Why would she leave school to be a carnie?"

"I haven't figured that out yet, but I'm sure it's no coincidence that her father owns all of the amusements."

"So what made you connect her to the psychic booth?"

"When I saw Cruzer the other day with the flyers, he talked about this man with lots of tattoos who told him to take them down. Cruzer said that the man said something about 'mittens and camping'. Sounds an awful lot like 'mitt camp' doesn't it?"

"Maybe he was just cold," Barbara joked. I gave her the icy stare.

"I'm serious," I said, "there's a connection. The man who tells Cruzer to remove flyers announcing Jessica Philmore's disappearance talks about a mitt camp, where coincidentally, you had the scare of your life just a week ago. This is it, I'm telling you."

"Doug, are you sure it's her? What are you going to do?"

"I don't know… no, I'm not sure, but I think I'm right. Maybe I should go pay her another visit?"

"Are you going to tell the police?" Barbara asked. It was a good question and I hadn't considered it yet. My theory was so new, twenty minutes new, that I hadn't really thought about a course of action.

"I don't know," I said, beginning to second-guess my sleuthing abilities, "It's only a hunch, I feel like maybe I should check it out first before I raise hopes and include the police."

"But what if it *is* her and she runs farther away when she sees you?" asked Barbara, "If your hunch is right, it's clear that she doesn't want you around." It was a good point. Perhaps me going to investigate wasn't such a good idea.

"You're right. I'll call the police," I said, a little disappointed.

"There is another option."

"What's that?"

"I could go," Barbara said with a coy smile.

"You could!" I said excitedly. I wished that I had thought of it, it was brilliant, "But won't she recognize you, too? After all, if I'm right, she intentionally terrified you."

"If you are right, I'm sure that the only reason why she recognized me is because of you. She must have seen you first." I nodded in agreement and she continued, "Besides, I can wear a hat and some glasses, she'll never know."

"So you're going to wear a disguise? Who are you a Charlie's Angel?" I joked.

"Anything to get the job done. When should I go?"

"As soon as possible, but the amusements on the boardwalk are only open on the weekends now, is the Psychic booth even open during the week?"

"I don't know, but I'll check it out tomorrow... the aquarium, the shops and the restaurants are still open. It's still September, it won't turn into a ghost town for another few weeks." I hugged Barbara and thanked her for being such a supportive partner. Then, I went upstairs, changed into shorts, tee shirt and Teva sandals and the three of us headed to the Windmill.

If our child grows up to have high blood pressure and high cholesterol like his father, Barbara will have to take equal blame. After selecting a primo picnic table on the top deck of the Windmill "gourmet" fast food restaurant in Long Branch, we all dined on fries and hot dogs. In fact, I had two hot dogs. The excitement of thinking that I knew where Jessica was made my adrenaline pump and clearly affected my appetite. As we ate, guarding our "gourmet" hot dogs from the hovering seagulls, Barbara and I continued to pursue my theory. Ethan tried to feed his french fries to the gulls, which was one of the reasons that they were hovering.

"So," Barbara said, "If I do see the same psychic again, how will I know that it's Jessica?"

"Well, as I said, she's blonde, twenty, pretty..."

"But before she had a veil, how else will I know?" This one stumped me and I had to think a moment. I thought about any distinguishing marks. Birthmarks? Twitches? Tattoos! Again, I couldn't contain myself, "She has a tattoo!" I shouted, scaring all of Ethan's sea gulls and the other patrons around me, "She has a tattoo of a leaf on her right ankle!"

"How do you know that?" Barbara asked, surprised.

"Because Keesha told me! When we were at the funeral home!" I was still shouting, and given the stares it was obvious that I was making the people around me nervous. I lowered my voice; "When Keesha and I went to the funeral home to identify the body of that young woman, Keesha made a point of asking to see the victim's feet... because she knew that Jessica had a tattoo of a leaf on her right ankle!"

"OK, that may be an option, but if I remember correctly, she wore a long flowing gown. What if her ankles are covered?"

"I don't know, pretend to drop a nickel, crawl under the table and hike-up her skirt?" I teased.

"Anything else?" Barbara asked. I thought again, and another bolt of lightning hit me, Sarah Borden's crystal ball. It was just another piece of this puzzle that was too coincidental not to be connected to "mittens and camping." "Look at the crystal ball that she uses," I said.

"Don't they all look alike?"

"Apparently not. I'll bet you that the one in the psychic

booth has a black base with gold markings on it."

"And how do you know this, Jessica had one?"

"No, but her roommate did, and she was just in my office today horrified that someone got into her room and took her crystal ball and Tarot cards."

"*Another* coincidence, huh?" Barbara smiled.

"It can't be." I could feel the excitement building in my stomach, "This has to be it, Barbara. It *has* to be her!"

We left the Windmill stuffed to the gills and satisfied. We took a quick walk across the street to the Long Branch boardwalk and stared at the ocean in the warm evening air. I breathed deeply. More deeply, it seemed, than anytime in the last two weeks. Was I right? Had Jessica Philmore been only twenty miles away all the time? As I watched the waves lap over the sand and held Ethan tight, I couldn't help but think about the same ocean waves hitting Prospect Point Beach. What if Jessica was dipping her feet right now? She felt closer than ever to me, but I had to be sure. I didn't want to call a false alarm and raise anyone's hopes unnecessarily. If my hypothesis was right, Barbara would confirm it with a quick trip tomorrow and then I would call Chief Morreale immediately. It would be easy, quick and painless. Or so I thought.

19

I woke up at 5:30 the next morning like a kid on Christmas morning. I turned off my alarm before it's usual 5:45 calling time, went downstairs (naked, of course), threw on my running clothes and bounded out the door. Even though I had tossed and turned all night, the adrenaline rushing through my body was like a drug. Today was the day we were going to find her. Regardless of the reason for her disappearance, we would find her today and all questions would be answered.

As I walked and stretched my way to the boardwalk, I passed Cruzer pushing his wheelbarrow on the opposite side of Main Avenue. He deliberately avoided my gaze, so I called out to him, "Good morning Cruzer!"

"Morning, Dean," he responded quietly, still looking at the contents of his wheelbarrow. It was obvious that he was still embarrassed by taking the flyers, which made me feel bad. It wasn't his fault and it didn't matter. Everything would be back to right after today. As long as the psychic booth was open and Barbara could get in, everything would be back to normal.

I did my run, savoring the cool mist that collected on my face. The sea was calm and the air was still. Everything, it seemed, was at peace which matched my mood perfectly. I was ready for the turmoil of the past few weeks to be over. I was ready to have my only preoccupations be R.I.P.'s latest tirade and Ethan's latest toy-obsession. Would it be dinosaurs next week and then monster trucks the week after? I couldn't wait to have the time and attention to find out.

I stretched on the boardwalk, enjoying the last few glimpses of the scenery before I headed off to work. There were a couple of men fishing on the beach, enjoying a cup of coffee as they lounged in their beach chairs and waited for a bite. A few other runners were dodging the tide near the water's edge. We were all being serenaded by the gulls and the sound of a distant garbage truck, slamming and beeping in the distance. Another beautiful day at the Jersey shore.

I walked back home, taking the time to stretch my arms out in front of me as I went. As I walked, I began to think about my day in the office. What was on my calendar for the day? Nothing much was coming to mind, which either meant it was going to be a light meeting day or I was blocking it out. Hopefully, Barbara would be able to see the "psychic" by early afternoon, which left plenty of time for me to call Chief Morreale. Was it possible that the police could go to Prospect Point Beach, pick-up Jessica and bring her back to campus by the end of the business day? It seemed likely. Although it seemed too good to be true, it seemed likely.

I reached the gate to the front walkway of my house with a smile on my face. This day was going to put an end to a two-week nightmare. I took a moment to revel in that comforting thought and to survey my home. My garden still looked great, still a treasure in early September, and all of the shutters that we had to nail back in place after a mid-summer windstorm were still holding. The wind had been so strong that it literally ripped four of my shutters off the house. Luckily, three out of the four were on the first floor, which meant that Barbara only had to go up on the ladder once and do the high job for me. Hey, I do garden and garbage, she does cooking and high stuff; that's the deal.

I walked around back to find Barbara and Ethan eating breakfast on the patio. "Good morning," I said, giving both of them a kiss. Ethan offered me a bite of his half-chewed toast, which I graciously declined. Not offended, he continued to busily munch away while playing with a red plastic fire truck. "So," I said to Barbara, "When do you think you're going to the boardwalk?"

"I was thinking that the best chance of it being open is lunchtime and after... so I'm planning to get there around noonish," she said, "That way I can be home by the time Ethan gets home from school." Luckily for us, Ethan has full-day kindergarten and his bus doesn't arrive home until 2:30 in the afternoon. "If for some reason I'm running late," Barbara continued, "I can have Polly pick-up Ethan at the bus stop." Polly is our next-door neighbor.

"Are you sure you want to do this?" I asked.

"Yes, I'm excited. It reminds me of my old college days as an investigative reporter."

"Well I don't want you to do any investigating beyond seeing Jessica and coming home. *Right*?" I asked with emphasis. Although I had no real reason to believe that there was any danger, I didn't want Barbara getting into anything alone.

"Right," she said, standing up to give me a kiss, "I'm going to see your psychic student, or identify your witch's crystal ball and come straight home. I promise."

"And if the booth is closed, we'll go on Saturday."

"Right," Barbara said smiling and clearing her breakfast dishes, "Don't worry, it's an easy job." I gave her another kiss and avoided a hug given my sweaty state, "Thank you," I said.

"You're welcome. Hopefully I can help."

"You're great," I said admiringly, "Maybe tonight we can go out to dinner to celebrate." Barbara looked at me surprised, "Douglas Carter-Connors is being an optimist? That *is* reason to celebrate." She was right. My normal philosophy of life is, 'don't count your chickens before they hatch', but I was being hopeful.

"Maybe I'm turning over a new leaf," I joked.

"Where do you want to celebrate?"

"How about Moonstruck?" I said, referring to our

favorite restaurant just north in Asbury Park. Although not new, Moonstruck had moved to a freshly renovated three-story building in Asbury a few years earlier. It is classy but casual and the food is excellent. Walking into the first-floor bar area always reminds me of something out of *Casablanca*.

"Mmmmmm, sounds good, maybe I'll see if Polly will watch Ethan."

"Maybe she can watch him a little longer and we can have an after-dinner quickie," I said, smiling. Barbara laughed and we lingered for a moment until Ethan began making funny kissing noises on his arm. I took that as a cue to get ready for work.

I ran upstairs, got undressed, and jumped in the shower. I clicked-on my shower radio while I shaved-- in the shower. If I could eat my breakfast in the shower, I would. I bopped to the music, hummed along only to be interrupted by the weather forecast, "Mostly sunny today, highs in the low 80s... Chance of a late afternoon thunderstorm." It was another typical forecast. I wondered for a brief moment when our summer weather would end, but I wasn't complaining.

I finished in the bathroom and lingered at my underwear drawer. If I was getting lucky later in the evening, I wanted to look good. I rummaged past my tighty-whities and uncovered what was at the bottom of the drawer, you know, where the Christmas gift and old bachelor party underwear hide. I must admit, I didn't have much in the "sexy" department. All I could find was a pair of bikini briefs that came equipped with an elephant trunk, fun maybe, but not sexy; a pair of red boxers with Santa's face smack dab on the front, and a black thong that Barbara got me one year for fun. I had never worn any of them for more than five minutes. My only choice seemed to be the thong, but could I actually wear a string up my butt all day long? What the hell, I was feeling frisky. I grabbed the thong with my thumb and forefinger and wondered for a moment if all of me would actually fit inside such a small piece of material. Since I don't usually have to worry about such things, it was all the more incentive to wear it.

I maneuvered the thing around my legs and stuffed myself into the front. I did a quick shimmy to even everything out, and I was ready to go. Maybe I would forget about the string up my crack once I got to work. I finished my underwear selections with a white V-neck tee shirt that I tucked through the side strings of the thong and donned some black socks. I had succeeded. Damn, I looked sexy. I spritzed myself with cologne, threw on a white shirt and my favorite khaki suit, even though I was never sure if khaki was appropriate after Labor Day. What the hell, it was my favorite and I was feeling good. I chose a yellow, print tie, my brown loafers, and I was finally ready for the day.

I ran down the stairs and ate a quick bowl of cereal while Barbara finished getting Ethan ready for school. A few minutes later, the three of us walked out the door together, them on the way to the bus stop and me off to WC. "So," Barbara said as we walked, "Any last minute details that I should know about?"

"No, I don't think so," I said, "Just be careful, OK?"

"I'll be fine," she said, giving me a peck on the cheek and then moved to my ear and whispered, "I'll see *you* later." If she only knew. I gave Ethan a kiss and we walked down the front walk and parted in opposite directions at our front gate. Barbara quickly looked back and said, "Doug? You're walking kind of funny, did you hurt yourself running this morning?" Just wait until she saw... later.

As I walked onto Main Avenue, someone yelled to me, "Doug? *Doug*?" I turned to look and saw Malificent calling from the front porch of her church. I stopped and waved. "Do you have a minute?" she yelled, already moving down from the porch and toward me. We hadn't spoken since the other day when she called me a martyr, not that I was holding a grudge or anything. She moved her praying mantis-like body and stood next to me in what seemed to be three giant steps. I guess that's what size ten feet will do for ya.

"Doug," she began in a soft, church voice, "I want to apologize for what I said the other day."

"No need to apologize, Malificent, you were just voicing your opinion."

"No, I think I was being hard on you and I'm sorry. I know that you've had a trying couple of weeks and you're in the middle of a crisis. I shouldn't have called you a martyr; I don't really think that's so. Please forgive me." I paused for a minute, but only because I found it hilarious to be standing on our town's main avenue, in front of an apologetic member of the clergy, in a thong. Now *that* doesn't happen everyday. Unfortunately, Malificent mistook my silence as non-accepting, "I know you're mad at me, Doug, but I was only trying to protect Cruzer, which is part of the reason for me being in this community, to protect the innocent. I really..."

"Malificent," I said, cutting her off, "I accept your apology. Thank you."

"Oh!" she said, surprised by my interruption, "Well then, thank *you*." We stood in an uncomfortable silence for a split-second before I said, "Well, I've got to get to the office, but I'll see you later, Malificent. Thank you again for talking to me, I really appreciate it." As I turned to move away, Malificent asked, "Any word on Jessica Philmore?"

"Not yet, but we're hoping for a lead soon," I said, actually hoping that "soon" would mean a matter of hours.

"Well, please keep me posted and if there's anything that I can do..."

"I'll let you know, Malificent, thank you," I responded, walking in the opposite direction toward campus.

I made it to the office early, by 8:35am or so, before the campus was fully awake. As I walked into the Student Center and up the stairs, I was met by Miss Bettie, our building's resident custodian. Miss Bettie possesses the wit of a philosopher and the tongue of craps-shooter. Although she works for Facilities Management, she calls me her boss and uses our office as her home base in the building. She keeps her coat and her lunch in our copy room and parks herself in one of the reception area's chairs during her breaks. This is where I usually find her, presiding like a queen, eating her bologna sandwich, spouting rhetoric like an irreverent preacher. I am honored that she graces us with her presence and wisdom.

"Good morning, Miss Bettie," I said.

"Morning, Doug." She said. Miss Bettie was practically the only person on campus who didn't refer to me as "Dean Doug." She was busily washing the windows in the entryway of the building, "How are you this morning," she asked, showing me her southern hospitality.

"I'm doing well," I replied, "how are you?"

"Pretty good," she said, "Except for all these flyers that I've been finding all over the building." She pulled out a blue sheet of paper from the front pocket of her uniform, "I saved one here to show you." My heart sank for a moment, but then saw that it was an old flyer about the tree-hugging protest. "For the past week, stuff like this has been littering-up my building," Miss Bettie continued, "There sure have been a lot of protests, lately, huh?" she asked.

"Yeah, there have been."

"These kids have got to realize that they're here for school. The sixties are over. Move on. They don't have time for protesting, they should be doing their schoolwork." "These kids," she continued, rolling her eyes and getting back to her window washing, "They're crazy."

"I'll see you later." I said, smiling and walking up the stairs.

"How's the baby?" she called up to me, the "baby" referring to five-year old Ethan, whom she adored.

"He's great," I called back, "Barbara will bring him in some day soon."

"Good," she called back, "I got him a gift."

"For what?" I asked, stopping on the stairs. She put her hand on her hip, and waved her cleaning rag at me, "I don't need a reason," she said, "For the fact that he's a child. Children aren't children very long." I thanked her, and headed to my office. Before I even stepped foot into the office, Judy greeted me, "You're early today, what's the occasion?

"No occasion, I just got out of the house early today." I wanted to tell Judy the truth, that I was so excited for the outcome of the day that I couldn't contain myself, but I didn't. Although I knew that Judy didn't totally buy it, she moved on, "Your morning is pretty packed, but your afternoon is clear." *Perfect*, I thought.

"Did you do anything fun last night?" she asked.

"Went to the Windmill."

"Oh, my favorite. Did you get a burger?"

"No, hot dog." I replied. This made Judy wince, "Oh, no. You get hotdogs at Max's and burgers at the Windmill. That's the rule of the shore, I thought I taught you better?" Max's hotdogs was a famous joint just down Ocean Avenue from the Windmill in Long Branch. The food is legendary, so much so that many legendary people visit the place. The walls are lined with signed photos of famous people from Frank Sinatra to Bruce Springsteen. The place is led by Max, the name of the woman who owns it.

"Sorry, I let you down," I answered, "How about I make it up to you by taking you to Max's next week for lunch."

"A date with my boss? I'm yours. You name the day."

"How about you name the day, and put it in my book."

"I don't know about etiquette, having a lady schedule her own lunch date, but OK," Judy winked and I went to my desk. I sat down, turned my computer on and began to get organized for my 10am meeting with Jerry, followed by an 11am with Keesha and some students who wanted to discuss ideas for a dance marathon. Then lunch, and by early afternoon, hopefully I would have some good news from Barbara.

Although I was busy, the morning seemed to drag. I felt as though I was looking at my watch every few minutes, which I fought to avoid doing. I got through my meeting with Jerry, but found myself really antsy by the time the dance marathon meeting came around. While two peppy students were enthusiastically raving about the prospects of dancing for twenty-four hours straight, I was thinking, 'OK, Barbara's on her way now.' Then a few minutes later, 'Barbara should be in Prospect Point Beach right now.'

The meeting ended at 12:10pm and Keesha asked me to go to lunch, which I declined.

"You? Missing lunch? Is something wrong?" Keesha asked.

"No, I'm just going to catch-up on some things, I'll grab something later," I replied, lying about the fact that I was too anxious to eat.

"OK, we'll be downstairs if you change your mind."

I sat at my desk and pretended to work. It was now 12:20pm and I was having trouble concentrating on anything. I knew that by this time, Barbara was probably at the psychic booth. At that moment, Judy appeared in my doorway, "What, no lunch for you? You have a totally free afternoon, what's wrong?"

"Nothing's wrong," I lied, "I'm just working on some things and I'll take lunch later." Judy looked at me over her half-glasses, "Are you sure you're alright?" she asked.

"I'm fine," I said, looking down and pretending to work.

By 12:35pm, I stopped pretending to do paperwork, and jumped on the internet to occupy myself. I looked at a few TV websites, I hopped over the Walt Disney World site to see what was new since our last vacation, and ended up at my favorite garden site to look for bulbs. 12:45pm. I was beginning to get worried. Why hadn't Barbara called? She must have arrived. Either the place was closed or it wasn't.

As my thoughts wandered again, Judy suddenly ran into my doorway, "Doug, you need to pick up line 1... it's important." It couldn't be Barbara, I thought, she'd either call me on the Bat-phone or my cell.

"What's wrong?" I asked, "Who is it?"

Judy paused, "She says she's Jessica Philmore's mother."

20

I was stunned, and looked at Judy as if she were speaking another language, "What?" I said emphatically. Judy looked dazed, eyes wide, "That's what she said, 'Jessica Philmore's mother'. The line's not too good, she must be on a cell phone, but that's what she said. Let me put her through, I don't want to lose her!" Judy said urgently as she ran back to her desk. Could it really be Mrs. Philmore? Or was it a hoax? If it was her, why had she disappeared? Judy buzzed me and I picked up the phone hoping to find out.

"Hello, this is Douglas Carter-Connors."

"Dean Carter-Connors?" came the voice on the other end. Judy was right; the woman was on a cell phone that was cutting-out consistently.

"Yes," I answered loudly, "Who is this?"

"It's Susan Philmore," the woman said, straining to be heard, "Jessica's mother."

"Mrs. Philmore, where are you?" I asked right away, hoping to get an answer before we lost the connection.

"I'm fine," she responded, and then the line became lively with static, "I...(static, line break-up)... things... (line break-up)... horribly wrong... (line break-up)... not what I intended... (line break-up)... the point... (static, connection lost)."

"Mrs. Philmore?" I called into the phone, "Mrs. Philmore?" But it was of no use, she was gone.

In the next few minutes, then hours, things were going to happen at lightning speed. I hung-up the phone and froze. First Mrs. Philmore disappeared like her daughter and now she called me out of the blue? Something had happened. Something caused her to come out of hiding to speak with me. From the garbled sounds, something was going terribly wrong and it involved Jessica. And if my hypothesis was right, I had sent Barbara right in the middle of it.

I picked-up the receiver to call Barbara's cell phone. As I dialed, Judy reappeared in my doorway, "Judy, something's wrong... can you call Chief Morreale right now?"

"I don't have to, he's on the other line for you." As she spoke, Barbara's voicemail picked-up, "Hi, This is Barbara Carter-Connors. I'm not available right now, but..." I clicked the line off and picked up the Chief on the other blinking line, "Chief, what's up?" I asked urgently.

"I just got off the phone with Mr. Philmore. He's received a ransom request for fifty million dollars."

"When?"

"About a half hour ago. This *could* be another indication that Jessica is alive." 'Good news,' I thought, 'this is probably what prompted Mrs. Philmore to call me, and if it is, it *isn't* good news.'

"I'm not so sure about that, Chief," I replied on the brink of panic, "I think something's happened."

"What's that?"

"Apparently while you were speaking to Mr. Philmore, I was speaking with *Mrs.* Philmore."

"Mrs. Philmore? Where's she been all this time; did she say?"

"No, she didn't get to that, she was on her cell phone and it kept cutting out... but she said that something has happened, I think it's about Jessica."

"Did she say where Jessica is?"

"No, but..." I paused, it was time to spill my guts, especially since I now had no idea where Barbara was, "...I think I know."

"What? How do you know?" The Chief sounded a little taken aback.

"Well it's just a hunch, but I think she's working at Jensen's Boardwalk."

"The boardwalk that her father owns? Doug, how'd you come up with that?"

"It's a long story... I think we should head down there right now... there's something else..."

"Doug, it sounds like you've been keeping a lot from me," The Chief stated matter-of-factly, but I didn't have time to worry about that, "Chief, I need to get down there now, I think Barbara might be in trouble as well."

"What? OK, Doug, I'm on my way to pick you up... meet me outside your building."

"OK," I said as I hung-up the phone. I got up, grabbed my jacket and ran out the door. On my way rushing past Judy I said, "I've got to leave..."

"Doug, what's happening? What's wrong?"

"I don't have time to get into it... I'll talk to you later." And I ran out the door. All I could think was, 'What have I done?'

Chief Morreale picked me up in his police cruiser at 1:10pm. He came to a rolling stop and I hopped in. I still hadn't heard from Barbara, even though I kept redialing her on my cell phone.

"Hey," I said, buckling my seat belt, "Thanks for coming to get me."

"What's going on, Doug?" The Chief responded, still in a grandfatherly way, but a little less congenial than usual. I spilled my guts about my hypothesis that Jessica Philmore was the psychic at the boardwalk, and that she attempted to scare me away through Barbara. I talked about my idea that "mittens and camping" was actually mitt camp or psychic booth, and that Barbara went to see if she could see Jessica again to confirm everything.

"Why didn't you just tell me and *we* would have checked it out?"

"I don't know, Chief, I didn't want to waste your time,

after all, I'm a dean not a detective. I wanted to be sure."

"And what made it seem like a good idea to send your wife?"

"There was no danger... she was just going to visit the psychic... if I thought there'd be trouble I would have called you immediately." I turned my head to look out my side window to avoid the Chief's gaze, "That was a stupid move. I'm so sorry that I didn't call you. I just wanted to be sure before I called the police." Thankfully, the Chief both stepped on the gas and moved on from Barbara, "and Mrs. Philmore sounded like she was in trouble?" he asked.

"She was definitely in distress, but the connection was so bad I literally caught only every other word. She said something about a plan going wrong... and she talked about the 'point' which could mean Prospect Point. I think something must have happened at the boardwalk today... something that made Mrs. Philmore come out of hiding."

"You're definitely sounding more like a detective and less like a dean," the Chief quipped. As I began to chuckle out of sheer nervousness, I felt my cell phone vibrate on my belt. My hands moved to it like my pants were on fire, "Hello?" I said anxiously.

"Hi, honey it's me!" It was Barbara and she sounded excited, "It's her! I think it's her!"

"Barbara are you alright? Where are you?"

"I'm fine, I just left the psychic booth and am in my car. I'm sorry it took so long, but I only caught the booth open by chance... I actually didn't see Jessica, but the crystal ball is the one that you described."

"So you saw a different psychic?"

"Yes, I assume it's the one that you saw, heavier set, dark hair... I asked for the other one, but the woman acted strangely and said that she was the only psychic there now. We were right, they really aren't open during the week now, in fact, this weekend is their last weekend there, but I found the woman in the place cleaning it up and I asked for a reading."

"And you're OK, you're on your way home?" I insisted.

"Yes, I'm fine. Doug, are you alright?"

"Yeah, I'm fine, it's just been a crazy hour or so... so you think you saw Sarah Borden's crystal ball?"

"Yes, it was exactly as you described, black with gold markings. And I don't remember it from the last time I saw the psychic, so I think it was definitely new. So, are you going to call the police?"

"I don't have to, I'm with Chief Morreale right now and we're on our way to Jensen's."

"Why? Did something happen?"

"Yes, but I don't want to get into it now..." I didn't want the Chief to know that I share everything with Barbara, so I played it cagey, "I'll fill you in as much as I can later. But I'm not sure when I'll be home... I'll call you."

"OK, then. Are you OK? Is something wrong?"

"I'm not sure, but I'm glad that you're OK... thank you so much, honey..." I said, "I'll talk to you later. I love you."

"I love you too," Barbara answered, and we hung-up.

"Barbara thinks it's Jessica... she didn't see her, but I was right, the crystal ball looks like the one stolen from Sarah Borden."

"Alright," said the Chief, "Good work."

"Yeah, she said that the psychic booth is getting ready to close, but she saw someone in the booth and asked for a reading anyway. Barbara thinks it's the psychic that I saw that Saturday. I wonder where Jessica is?"

"Maybe that's the problem. Maybe someone's got her and holding her for ransom," the Chief speculated, "And if you're right about the 'mitt camp', I'm sure that the guy that approached Cruzer has something to do with this too. You've done a good job, Doug. I think you're on to something, I just wish that you'd told me last night." I agreed with him as we speeded down the Parkway. The bright sunny day had faded and the sky was becoming a foreboding dark grey. It was a perfect complement for my mood.

The Chief parked the Cruiser in a no parking zone right next to the boardwalk. The dense clouds had started to spit rain, making the few visitors that were present run for cover. As I looked down the boardwalk, it was in stark comparison to just a few weeks earlier. There was barely a soul in sight.

Chief Morreale and I got out of the car and he went to the trunk, pulling out a long navy blue raincoat with "POLICE" written on the back. "Sorry, Doug," he said, "I only have one of these."

"Don't worry about it," I said, wiping some raindrops from my face, "I'll be fine. Where do we start?"

"Well, I'm going to start in the psychic booth. You should wait in the car."

"Shouldn't I go with you?"

"No, not right now. If you hadn't sent Barbara here, you wouldn't be here in the first place. Just wait in the car and stay dry."

"OK," I said, not wanting to press my luck. At that moment, the sky opened up and it began to pour. In the distance, I heard thunder, "I'll be in the car." I said, opening the passenger side door and sliding in. I watched as Chief Morreale ran down the boardwalk toward the psychic booth. It occurred to me that you never see a police officer carrying an umbrella, even in a torrential downpour. Apparently, it just isn't part of the uniform.

I sat in the car and watched the rain cascade down the windshield. At this point in the afternoon, I was so emotionally spent, I was mesmerized by the water. The Chief had disappeared inside the psychic shack and I noticed that I was all alone. There was no one on the boardwalk anymore. I slumped down in my seat and listened to the rain, too tired to think. My mind began to wander. I'm not sure that I didn't fall asleep for a brief second. I remembered the first day that Mrs. Philmore came to my office. Where was she now? I remembered going to the funeral home to identify Jessica's body, and how happy I was that it wasn't her.

I replayed the events of the past couple of weeks, which felt like years. I drifted along in thought when suddenly, CRACK! I sat straight up. Lightning had hit very close-by and the sound of angry thunder made my ears ring. The storm was just about on us now, and it was gearing-up to be a bad one. With my eyes widened from the adrenaline rush of being scared awake, something caught my attention through the rain-spattered windshield.

I squinted as if it would help me see through the curtain of rainwater better. Yes, directly in front of me, near the carnival rides, on the other side of the boardwalk, I could see someone moving. Someone dressed in bright orange. Who was out in this weather on the deserted boardwalk? I opened the door and stuck my head outside to get a better view. I saw more movement, now it looked like two people, one holding the other. In fact, it looked as though the one dressed in orange was being dragged. Didn't Barbara say that Jessica the psychic was dressed in bright orange? Was I *looking* at Jessica Philmore? My heart raced, the thunder rumbled again, and I saw her being pulled behind the tilt-a-whirl. I couldn't let her get away from me. I had to go get her.

21

I got out of the car and shut the door behind me; the rain was steady now, but not as strong of a downpour as before. Good thing, since I didn't have an umbrella or an overcoat. I stepped onto the boardwalk, and walked across it toward the amusements on the beach. I shot a glance down the boards toward the psychic booth, but didn't see any movement. The Chief was still inside, but I couldn't wait. I didn't even hesitate to move ahead by myself into the ride area.

Since it was a weekday, the rides weren't running, but the gate that housed them all had been left open. *Probably in haste by the person dragging Jessica Philmore*, I thought. The rain had made all of the rides look shiny and new, bolted conglomerations of slick metal trying to look whimsical. In my opinion, they were still dangerous.

As I shielded the rain from my eyes with my hand, I heard a yell off to the side of me, it was muffled, but it was definitely some sort of cry. It had to be Jessica; she was in trouble. I turned to look and saw that it was in the direction of the Ferris wheel that I had successfully avoided a couple of weekends ago. As I walked in the direction of the Ferris wheel, lightning cracked again nearby making me jump. This wasn't turning out to be any day at the beach, let me tell ya.

I meandered my way through the maze of idle rides and got a creepy feeling. In the summer, all the rides run in endless motion, but today they were like dormant enemies waiting to strike. I passed the Tilt-a-whirl and the bumper cars, and moved toward the sliding-bobs. I never realized how many rides there were at this place; it felt huge. As I continued to head toward the Ferris wheel looming in the distance, I thought I heard another faint cry. Although the sound of the rain clicking against all the metal and plastic upholstery was steady, like peas dropping into an aluminum pan, I was pretty sure that I heard the cry again. This time, it sounded a little more pathetic, like a whine.

I shook-off my hesitation and I began moving swiftly now. Still, the sound came from the direction of the Ferris wheel. I ran passed the Merry-go-round, the sea-dragon and the Cobra and finally, I was standing in front of the dreaded Ferris Wheel that I hated so much. I actually felt my stomach twist, as though someone was wringing it out. I was drenched, with my suit clinging to me like wet paper towels, which added to my discomfort.

This was not your average State Fair Ferris Wheel. This sucker was enormous, with the kind of cars that fully enclosed you in, not the kind like park benches. This terrified me even more… a machine that not only brought you up to unnatural heights, but also locked you in a cage. Although I was already acrophobic, I was pretty sure that a spin on this thing would make me claustrophobic as well. I stopped, like staring at a fierce dragon, in awe of its presence.

As I gaped at the steel beast ahead of me, I saw something move on the ride's metal loading platform. Something orange. I took a breath and walked to the metal stairs that led to the platform where eager riders got their seats for a ride straight to hell. CRACK! Lightning struck again, causing me to crouch on the stairs. Crouching Dean, metal dragon. I looked-up to the sky and saw the black, puffy clouds agitate like dough in a mixer.

I composed myself and made it onto the platform, still hunched over. I think that my rationale was that lightning couldn't strike me if I stayed low. Even though I was standing on a soaking wet, metal platform attached to a 100-foot tall lightning rod masquerading as an amusement, I knew that I should stay low.

A few feet in front of me, I saw that one of the ride's cars, the one sitting on the platform, had its door slightly ajar. Inside, I thought I also saw something orange. Was

Jessica in the car? I ran up to peer inside, and wasn't prepared for what I saw. Not only did I see an orange scarf hanging on the inside door handle, but something else. There was a rain-soaked hand hanging out of the door onto the platform.

I wiped the rain from my eyes and again bent down and opened the car door, being careful not to step on the hand. At that close proximity I could tell clearly that the body was not Jessica. It was a man, slumped down on the floor of the car. He was shaggy looking, fortyish, with graying whiskers and his arms covered with tattoos. His worn, denim shirt was open and I could see tattoos on his neck and chest as well. He was either unconscious or dead, and I was praying for the former. I stepped into the car and straddled his body so that I could bend down and feel his neck for a pulse. However, as I touched his neck, his head tilted to the right side exposing a bloody gash on his forehead. He was dead. I was in a Ferris wheel car with a dead man.

Just as I stood-up in the car to step out of the door, however, I was suddenly propelled back down on the floor with a loud *whirring* sound. My forehead hit the back of the car, opposite the dead man as I fell on top of him. But the part that terrified me wasn't that I was lying on top of a dead man, it was the fact that the car was moving. The car was moving upward, toward the angry sky.

My heart began to beat rapidly and I became nauseous as I felt the car rock in the gusty winds. I was so scared that I actually laid on the cold wet floor, head between a dead man's work boots, for a few seconds before I could even compose a thought. When I did, panic struck again when I realized that the door of the moving car was still open, the dead man's arm now hanging out. Too stunned to move, I forced myself not to panic.

Holding onto the wire cage opposite the door with one

hand, I reached over to the dead man's left shoulder to try to pull him back inside. I'm embarrassed to say that I wasn't worried about him falling out; I was worried about me falling out. Self-preservation caused me to realize that his body was sitting in the way of me closing the door. Although the prospect of being caged didn't wow me, the prospect of me falling out of a moving car at 100 feet wowed me even less.

CRACK! Another lightning bolt flashed as the car continued to rise. I pulled on the dead man's shirt, trying to pull him back inside the car, but couldn't find enough leverage to move him. I was going to have to move closer to the swinging open door in order to move him. Still straddling him, I turned around to face the door while moving my hands on the cage that surrounded the car. When I reached the section right next to the door that was swinging about forty feet above the landing platform, my stomach lurched again. I was facing the open door with a direct view of the platform, now fifty feet below. I had to do it; I had to shut the door.

I moved my left arm to one side of the door, grabbing hold of the cage with my wet hand. I now had a hand on each side of the door, but still couldn't get close enough to move the dead man who was inching closer and closer to the opening. Not only was I going to have to step closer to the door, but I was going to have to let go with one hand in order to pull the dead man out of the doorway.

I inched a step closer, and gingerly removed my right hand from the cage as the car began to sway to the left. As quickly as I could, I pulled the dead man's left shoulder toward me so that he was fully inside of the car. Moving my left leg behind his shoulder, I hunched down and sat on his back, bracing myself inside the car with my right foot against the doorway. As the car continued to lean to the left, the door began to swing inward. As quickly as I could, before I lost my nerve, I reached my right arm out of the car, grabbed the door handle and pulled it toward me.

I latched the door, and sat down with my full weight on

the dead man's back (further pushing his head into his lap) to catch my breath. Now that must have been a sight. As the car continued its ascent, I heard a scream. Not a muffled cry, but a full-fledged scream this time. I raised my body just enough to peer through the cage over the car's seats and was shocked at what I saw. Standing next to the platform on the ground about eighty feet below was Jessica Philmore.

She was soaking wet, her blonde a hair matted a mousy brown and her orange robe clinging to her like plastic wrap, but she was a sight to behold. Although I still hadn't remembered seeing her on-campus, she strongly resembled the picture on the flyer created by the Ladies' Auxiliary. I was looking at Jessica Philmore, and she was alive.

I stood-up in the car and leaned my face into the cage, "Jessica!" I yelled over the sound of moving machinery and rain. She was looking right at me, as far as I could tell given the distance, and gave me a hearty wave as though she was flagging down a ship. We looked at each other like two reunited lovers in a sappy movie. But the moment didn't last long.

Suddenly, a man jumped from behind the platform and put Jessica in a strong hold. With his arm around her neck and her chin in the crook of his elbow, I could see her terrified eyes. "Hey!" I yelled without realizing it, "Leave her alone!" The man just looked-up at me and laughed. CRACK! Another flash of lightning touched down, this time so close that it sounded as if it hit on the boardwalk, and Jessica screamed.

The man reacted with laughter. He was tall, with a baldhead and was wearing a light blue jumpsuit. He looked like a carnival worker. He forced Jessica over to the base of the platform and began doing something underneath. Within seconds, I knew what he was doing as the car that I was sitting in slowly grinded to a halt; stopped dead nearly at the peak of the ride. I looked around the car nervously in an effort to confirm what was happening, and then quickly looked back at Jessica. Both she and the man were gone. What had Jessica gotten herself involved in? Who was this man who was holding her under duress? CRACK! And who was the dead man in the car with me? CRACK!

The lightning was moving from flashes of light, to jagged lines of electricity shooting from the sky. The latest bolt looked as if it touched down 200 yards away. CRACK! This was the first time that I realized that I was in trouble. There I was. CRACK! Sitting inside the biggest lightning rod I had ever seen with bolts of angry lightning touching down every minute or so. CRACK! Not to mention the fact that I was sharing the ride with a corpse. CRACK! Perhaps Malificent was right; maybe I *had* overstepped my place in the investigation... just a little.

22

The lightning was unlike anything I had ever seen. Crooked lines of pink and blue light reached from the churning clouds and touched objects all around me. Sometimes, a pink line and a blue line would join together in a magnificent marriage resulting in a blinding flash. The thunder was now a consistent grumble that I didn't even notice anymore. CRACK! A blue streak hit the idle sea-dragon ride causing spark-like flashes on impact. CRACK! Another streak hit a piece of wooden fencing next to the tilt-o-whirl causing it to smolder. Then came the big one.

CRACK! A brilliant bolt of hot pink light grabbed the Ferris wheel car above me, causing the entire ride to vibrate. My feet tingled with the shock of electricity. This was when I knew that I had to do something. I was a sitting duck. If I stayed in this car, one of the highest on the highest ride in the amusement area, I was going to be hit. Probably killed. I needed to get down... immediately.

But what was I going to do? I was at least a hundred feet in the air? My cell phone! I could call the Chief for help. I grabbed the phone from my belt-clip and pulled-out the antenna. This is where my heart dropped for the fiftieth time that day. "No Service", read the display screen. The storm must have been interfering with the cells in the area. What else could I do? I'd have to reach out and touch someone the old fashioned way, "Help!", I yelled over the din of thunder. "Help!" But I was confident that my voice was barely audible. I was alone. Aside from the dead body under my feet, I was alone and needed to come-up with a new plan.

I shuddered to think of my options. I could either, A) stay in the car and get fried, B) stay in the car and take my chances that I wouldn't get fried, C) try to get someone's attention somehow, or D) try to get down. None of my choices seemed very good. CRACK! Lightning hit the car above me again, causing flashes of hot light. So much for the adage that lightning never strikes the same place twice. My feet tingled again and I knew what I had to do. I had to try and make my way down, at the very least to a car that was closer to the ground.

As I looked out of the door, my stomach churned violently. I knew that I was going to get sick. Dizzy, I turned as fast as I could toward the inside of the car and knelt down. Hunched over the dead man's back, I threw-up all over him. *Sorry, buddy*, I thought, wiping my mouth. CRACK! CRACK! Two flashes in a row. I wiped my mouth with my hand, and then wiped my hand on my favorite khaki suit pants as I pulled myself up. I was shivering with fear and excitement. Maybe I should just stay in the car. CR-R-R-R-A-A-A-CK! The loudest and brightest display yet, this time on the sea-dragon's head. I couldn't stay; I needed to get out quickly.

I braced myself with arms stretched on either side of the door and waited a second to find my balance. The car was still swaying slightly in the wind and it felt like I was in a rowboat trying to find my sea legs. As I gained my composure, I peered through the cage. Could I get down? How would I do it? I examined the Ferris wheel structure closely for the first time, looking both down at the cars below and above at the one car hovering over me.

I could see that each car was connected to the Ferris "wheel" by a series of spokes consisting of heavy metal girders. In fact, as I looked, the girders almost looked like the rungs of a ladder, except that they were farther apart from each other and curved into a circle. From my vantage point, it actually looked, CRACK! as though I could step out of the car's door, grab onto the closest girder and shimmy my way down. One hundred feet down, but down, nonetheless. But first, I had to open the door.

I forced my shaking hand to the door handle and

opened it. The wind immediately grabbed the door and forced it wide-open. This was either a sign from God that I was free to go, or a forceful reminder of the danger involved with attempting to climb down a Ferris wheel. I chose to believe the former.

Still holding onto the inside of the cage, I popped my head out and looked down. I immediately felt a woozy feeling forcing me to sit on the dead man's back again, and in my barf. What a mess. CRACK! I poked my head out of the car again and tried not to look down to the ground, but focus on the Ferris wheel's structure close to me. The way the wheel was positioned, there was a steel girder only a foot below the car. It looked as if I could lower my legs onto the girder, while still holding onto the inside of the car. Once I got my footing, I could lower myself further until I could hug the steel. CRACK! It was now or never as the lightning continued to dance. It was relentless.

I turned my body to face the barf-soaked back of the dead man, and slowly moved my feet outside of the car. I could feel the wind whipping my pant legs and the rain pelting against my calves. I slowly inched my way out, reaching with my feet for the girder below. Since my head and my entire torso were still inside the car, I couldn't see my footing, so I continued to reach with my feet...slowly... slowly stretching until... There! My right foot touched something, then my left foot. I was now standing on the girder.

My heart was racing as I put all of my weight on the steel below me and slowly moved my body downward. When I got to the point of crouching on the beam while steadying myself by holding onto the doorway, I moved my legs and sat down on the steel, straddling it like a tree limb. It was now or never, either I continued to move downward, or pull myself back into the safety of the car. CRACK! I was quickly reminded that I wasn't safe, which was exactly why I was attempting this crazy plan.

I lowered my body down, slowly moving one hand off the cage and onto the girder, and then the next. I had done it; I was now sitting on the skeleton of the Ferris wheel, hugging the steel as if it were a teddy bear. The metal was cold and wet against my face as I rested like a sloth hanging from a tree. CRACK! I had to continue my descent.

Once I got the hang of it, it wasn't as bad as I expected. With each step, I gradually moved my feet to the girder below me while never losing my grip on the preceding beam. CRACK! As the storm continued to rage around me, I remained cautious and deliberate in my every movement. After what seemed to be an eternity, I looked up and was shocked to see that I had only moved a few feet. But I was making progress; with every movement I was getting closer to the luscious ground below.

CR-R-R-A-A-A-C-K! It was this stroke of lightning that changed everything. It had hit directly above me, in the car that I had just been sitting in. As I precariously straddled a girder below, I could see the car rocking wildly and could smell something sickly sweet. Unfortunately for him, not only was he dead, but he had apparently absorbed most of the electricity. I assumed that I was smelling his singed skin and hair. Distracted by the prospect of what could have been, I guess I became careless with my footing.

Still looking at the car above, instead of the beam below, I misstepped on the slick steel. My foot slid off the girder, pulling my entire body down with it. Before I knew it, I was barely hanging onto the slippery beam above me, while my butt swung in the air with only one leg clutching the beam below. As I felt the strength of gravity peeling my fingers loose from the girder above, I could only think of one thing. It wasn't so much about Ethan and Barbara, but something more. *If I fell and died right now, they would find me wearing a black thong.*

I couldn't let Barbara deal with the embarrassment. When Mayor Carcass gave her the clothes off of my dead body, she would probably wonder why he was concealing a smile until she inspected them. At my funeral, townspeople would whisper, *"We never would have suspected that he was kinky."* Or, *"Such a nice man, who knew that he was a pervert?"* I couldn't let Ethan grow up with whispers about his father's tawdry undergarments on the day he died. I had to get better footing and save myself.

As I literally hung-on for dear life, wishing that I had selected my usual tighty-whities, my right hand slipped off of the beam above, forcing my left hand to follow. They slammed onto the girder that I was half-resting on and I quickly gave the beam a bear hug. Hugging it as tightly as I could, I used the beam for leverage as I pulled my butt up. After a brief moment of panic, I managed to rest solidly on the girder as if I was humping the metal. CRACK! Lightning cracked again ruthlessly, not allowing me to relish in my eighty-foot high safety.

I began my descent once again, this time paying strict attention to every movement. Slowly but consistently, I was making headway. After what must have been twenty minutes, I was halfway down. As I got the hang of my movements, I began to move more swiftly, but still cautiously. I made my way down a few more yards when, CRA-A-A-A-C-C-C-K. This time, the lightning hit the frame of the Ferris wheel and I could feel the steel become warm under my hands. The storm wasn't dissipating, it was intensifying and I needed to move even faster.

Hand, under hand, step, below step, I moved until the ground was about twenty feet below my feet. CRACK! The rain became heavier again, turning into a torrential downpour. The metal that I was gripping was becoming almost too slippery to grip. If I dropped now, could I safely reach the ground? Angry thunder continued to explode overhead as it pushed steady streams of water into my eyes. It really wasn't *that* far of a drop. As I wondered whether or not I could really manage it, a flash of light streamed right past my face causing my entire body to pull away. I lost my balance, lost my footing, and lost my place on the girder. Suddenly I was in the air, drenched and falling until everything became dark.

23

I could hear someone calling my name from a million miles away, "Doug?", "Doug! Can you hear me?" Who was trying to wake me from the most delicious sleep I had ever felt? I would just ignore them. "Doug!" came the unrelenting, urgent cry. Was something wrong? Now someone was gently shaking me, clutching the tops of my shoulders, "Doug!" I gave up and decided to open my eyes.

Chief Morreale was hunching over me, his face only a few inches from mine. *Why was the Chief in my bedroom?* I wondered. "Doug?" he spoke more softly now, "Are you alright?"

"I'm fine," I said, pulling myself up onto my elbows, "What are you doing here?"

"Doug?" The Chief asked inquisitively, "Do you know where you are?"

"I'm home in my bed," I said, annoyed, "And I'd like to know why you're here!" He looked concerned, which made me nervous. What was wrong? As I sat-up, my head began to pound and my back felt heavy. Everything came flooding back to me. The Ferris wheel, the lightning, the dead man, Jessica, even the thong. I had made it down alive.

"Easy, easy," calmed the Chief, "We've called an ambulance to come look at you."

"What about Jessica?" I asked urgently, "I saw Jessica Philmore. She was with some man who was holding her, did you see them?"

"Yes, yes, she's fine. We have her. She's just fine, Doug. Don't worry about her, she's just fine. You can talk to her soon enough." The Chief pushed my shoulders back on the ground. I wondered why I could still hear the rain, but I wasn't getting rained-on, and saw that Chief Morreale was holding an umbrella over my face. Jessica was fine. We got her. Soaking wet and achy all over, I suddenly felt relaxed. The soggy grass felt like the most expensive down pillow. I closed my eyes, and allowed unconsciousness to overtake my body.

I was only in the Jersey Shore Medical Center overnight, mostly for observation. Since I had passed out a couple of times, the doctors wanted to make sure that I was fine, which for the most part, I was. Other than a slight concussion from the fall, a few cuts on my hands, bruises all over and a sprained ankle, I was just fine. That night in the hospital, Barbara brought in take out from Moonstruck, honoring our dinner date and leaving Ethan with Polly as planned. Although Moonstruck doesn't do take-out, they honored Barbara's request once they heard that I was in the hospital. We ate rosemary chicken and garlic mashed potatoes like it was our first solid food, as I replayed the afternoon's events for Barbara.

Although I told her everything that happened, I still didn't know any of the details or how the mystery of Jessica Philmore's disappearance got resolved. "So you really climbed down from the top of the Ferris Wheel?" Barbara asked, "Doug! What were you thinking?"

"I was thinking that I didn't want to be crispy-fried like the dead guy in the car eventually was." I replied, "Barbara, you know that at those heights, it must have been my last resort."

"So who was that guy?"

"I still don't know," I answered, shoveling-in a mouthful of potatoes, "He was dead. I'm just sorry that I barfed on him."

"You *barfed* on the dead guy?"

"Not on purpose, but when I looked down for the first time, I heaved all over his back." Barbara tried to hide a chuckle, "It's not funny," she said leaning into me, "You could have been killed." With that, she gave me the sweetest rosemary kiss that I've ever felt.

"Knock, knock?" came a voice from behind the door, and I saw Chief Morreale's big beak emerge in the room, "Are you up for some visitors?"

"Sure," I said, "Barbara was just asking me questions that I don't have the answers to. C'mon in and fill us in on what happened."

"I can do that, but I have someone else who can probably do it better than me," the Chief said opening the door wider. Standing behind him, was Jessica Philmore.

I straightened myself in the bed, trying to conceal a wince. We stared at each other for a moment, until I broke the silence, "Jessica," I said, surprised that my eyes were welling with tears, "It's nice to meet you." The sentiment vibrated in the air like a crescendo. Finally, after what seemed to be a long pause, I broke my own uncomfortable silence with, "Are you OK?"

Jessica moved closer to me with an air of maturity uncommon to most college students, "I'm fine, Dean Doug. I'm sorry for everything. I'm so, so sorry." She looked down and began to cry softly, before quickly wiping her eyes and composing herself, "I never meant to involve so many people. I was trying to help, I didn't know that it'd be dangerous."

"What happened?" I asked, jumping right in, "Did you run away?"

"No, not really." She began, as Barbara gave Jessica her seat next to the bed, "Actually, I was working... I've been trying to help the underrepresented forever," she said, relaxing in the chair. She looked exhausted and I knew the feeling. Jessica continued, "I've always been active in social issues, ever since I can remember. That's why when I came to Westmire, I started STOPP."

"Students Opposing Oppression," I interjected.

"Right," Jessica responded, surprised, "Well, there are a million causes to help with and as I started to think about graduation, I knew that I wanted an internship. I wanted something that would give me some experience so that I could get a job. Last semester, before the summer, I started to talk to Dr. Andrews, he's my advisor." I knew the name, Ron Andrews as a bright, young sociology professor that we had hired a year ago straight from Berkeley's doctoral program. Jessica continued, "He encouraged me to pursue something close to school so that I could do a semester-long internship."

I nodded, encouraging Jessica to tell me more, "Over the summer is when my father really started to complain about his workers... he owns the amusements along the shore, I don't know if you know that." I nodded again without saying anything.

"Well," said Jessica, "I live with my mom, my parents are divorced, and when I found out about the complaints that Daddy's employees have, I did some research and began to see their side of things. Daddy and I don't really get along, but that wasn't the reason I went, I just wanted to help. Being a 'carnie' isn't easy," Jessica looked down at the floor, embarrassed, probably for them, "Daddy's employees are mostly migrant workers who are people that deserve the same benefits as anyone else: healthcare, unemployment insurance, a decent wage, respect. So I decided that I would go to the Prospect Point boardwalk, get a job, and help them organize their cause."

"So you left school and didn't tell anybody?" I asked.

"Well, I didn't want the workers to know who I was, because I wanted them to trust me. That's what Professor Andrews says is important when working with people, getting their trust. So I figured that I would take the semester, follow the workers as they moved south in the fall, and be back home by Christmas and get twelve credits for it." Although she acted mature, she also exhibited the naive innocence of many people her age.

"So, did Professor Andrews know about this?"

"No!" Jessica responded emphatically, "He didn't know anything about it."

"You realize that that's not the typical way to do it, right?" I said, unconsciously taking on the tone of a dean, "Internships are usually approved by the department, especially for credit."

"I know, but I knew that the experience would probably be better than any internship offered at school, and I figured that I'd work out the credits later." She had the mindset of a bohemian, which I found both refreshing and unnerving. "So you did this all on your own?" I asked. Jessica looked sheepish, "For the most part," she said, "Until my mother found out."

"Your mother knew?"

"Not at first. She told me that she came to see you to tell you that I was missing and that you were really nice and put her up in a hotel."

"So how did she find out where you were?"

"It was by accident. The day after she saw you, she went to Prospect Point Beach in the morning. We used to go there when I was a kid, so I guess it reminded her of me. She went there just to walk around, I guess, clear her head. I ran right into her on the boardwalk."

"So she saw you? Why didn't she tell us?" Again, Jessica looked embarrassed, this time for her mother, "I thought that she had, she told me she did..."

"But?" I asked anxiously.

"But, she took it as an opportunity to torture my dad. She went back to the hotel and took all of her stuff. She wanted my dad to think that something had happened to her, too. She knew that it would kill him. I'm so sorry; she didn't mean it, it's just the way she is... after the divorce. I didn't know any of this until a few hours ago, she even said that she spoke to Dr. Andrews about my credits."

"So where was your mother all this time?" I asked, eliciting a perplexed face from Jessica, clearly her mother failed to tell her that she went "missing" too. Jessica tried to answer my question, "What do you mean? My mom was at home." I didn't pursue it.

"So what was happening at the boardwalk today?" I asked.

"One of the men who worked at the boardwalk befriended me... it wasn't funny or anything, he befriended me and watched over me like an uncle or something. After my first couple of nights there, I slipped and told him who my father was... so, he said that he would help me."

"Did he have lots of tattoos?" I asked.

"Yes," Jessica said, "Charlie. Charlie had lots of tattoos." Not only was he the dead man in the Ferris wheel car, but I suspected him to be the tattooed man who paid Cruzer to take the missing person flyers.

"So he helped you?" I asked.

"Yes, he protected me... until today." Jessica's eyes suddenly became full of tears again, and Chief Morreale interrupted, "Let me finish the story," he said.

"Apparently another carnival worker, a guy named Jake Robeville, found out about Jessica's identity and figured that he could get some easy money." The Chief continued, "So earlier today, he grabbed Jessica, and called her dad asking for a ransom."

I shifted my body to get more comfortable and listened intently to the Chief as he glanced over at Barbara, "Apparently," he went on, "this all happened right after your wife left the psychic booth." Barbara's eyes widened, "Yes," she said curiously pointing to Jessica, "Because I was *there* this morning."

"I know, I snuck out the back when I saw you. That's when I ran into Jake." Barbara and I shot each other a glance, apparently, our attempt to help made the situation worse. "He grabbed me as I was leaving the booth," Jessica replied, "and locked me in his trailer." The Chief cleared his throat and carried on the story, "Evidently Robeville was trying to move Jessica just before we arrived, Doug. Before we got there, there was a struggle between Robeville and Charlie," the Chief looked down at Jessica, "Apparently they had quite a struggle; he tried to protect her right to the end." The Chief shook his head, clearly not wanting to discuss the particular of Charlie's death in front of Jessica.

"While I was in the booth," continued the Chief, "you saw the end of the struggle in the amusement area, and like a bonehead, you went to investigate. Robeville's the one who turned on the power to the Ferris Wheel with you in it, and stopped it in mid air so that he could get away with Jessica and wait for the ransom."

"But you got him?" I asked.

"Yup, we got him trying to put Jessica into my cruiser near the boardwalk," the Chief raised an eyebrow in my direction, "You didn't lock it when you left."

"Sorry, but the keys weren't in it." I responded.

"No, but I bet he could have hot-wired it. Anyway, no harm done. I had already called the County Sheriff's department, so they took him, which is when I saw you hanging."

"You could see me?"

"Even in a thunderstorm it's hard to miss a man hanging off of a Ferris wheel in the middle of the day." We all chuckled and made small talk, until Barbara asked another question, "Jessica, did you know it was me that day on the boardwalk?"

"I'm sorry, yes. I'm sorry that I was so mean, but I didn't want Dean Doug to see me, so I told you a story that would scare you away."

"But you and I had never met," I chimed-in, "I didn't even know you."

"No, but I knew you, and I didn't want to take any

chances. So when your wife rushed out that day, I ran out the back of the booth and told Madame Wanda that I was sick. She took over for me. Later on, she said that she spoke to you afterward."

"Yes," I replied.

"And that's who I saw this morning, Madame Wanda?" Barbara asked.

"Right. She's a nice lady."

"A nice lady who needed a new crystal ball?" Barbara asked, using her reporter's voice. Again, Jessica looked embarrassed, "Yes. Madame Wanda said that we needed an extra one."

"Did you take it from Sarah?" I asked.

"No," she hesitated, "I had Chris do it, he still had a key." So... Dirt Fagan was in on it all along.

"So Chris knew, also?" I asked.

"Again, not at first, but I missed him and called him and told him." Jessica said. I decided not to pursue it, and figured that I would deal with Dirt's misconduct when I got back to the office. My head was spinning. I took a breath and said, "Jessica, I'm just glad that you're fine."

"I'm sorry," she said, "I really didn't think anything like this would happen, especially the crazy stuff at school."

"Like what?" I asked.

"Like the vending machine and all of the protests."

"You were involved with those?" I asked, surprised that I could still be surprised at anything. Jessica nodded, "It was all part of STOPP. We had planned the vending machine a few days before I left. We were protesting the animal testing that takes place on campus. We discussed the other protests too, the student protest for academic rights and the save the environment protest. But, according to Chris, they became a little disorganized after I left." She paused, "I'm the President of STOPP, my other officers didn't really have the guidance that they needed to carry everything off when I was gone. I thought they'd be OK."

"How'd you get a key to the vending machine?" I asked.

"We paid the vending worker, I think he was a substitute, $20 to leave it open for us one night." I asked a few follow-up questions, and another knock came at the door.

"Come in," I called as Mr. Philmore slowly walked in.

"They're here for Jessica," the Chief said.

"They?" I asked. Mr. Philmore looked behind him, "Jessica's mom is in the hallway. We want to thank you, Dean, for all of your help." Mr. Philmore walked over to my bedside and reached for my hand, "I'm sorry you had to go through all this. But thank you; from what the Chief tells us, you were instrumental in bringing Jessica back to us." I smiled and shook his hand.

"Well, Jessica, you must be tired," I said, becoming a bit weary myself, "You should go with your parents... I'm sure you have a lot to talk about." Jessica looked sheepishly at her father and then back at me, "Will I get into trouble at school?"

"I'm not sure, we have a lot to talk about. Sarah, your roommate, has been moved out of your room... she didn't want to stay after it was broken into and her stuff was taken." Jessica simply looked down at the floor as I went-on, "Your whole floor is pretty torn-up about your disappearance. We'll have to figure out a way to reintroduce you... let's do this: Let's both take a couple of days. Then call me, and we'll figure things out. Fair?"

"Fair," she smiled, and then leaned down to give me a hug. I was touched, even though it hurt my bruised body like hell. "Thank you," I coughed. Jessica turned to her father, grabbing his hand softly, and they walked out of the room. *Maybe this ordeal will bring them closer together?*, I thought. A minute or so later, another knock came at the door, this time extremely tentative.

"Yes?" I called, and Mrs. Philmore peeked inside.

"May I come in?" she asked, her entire body still

standing in the hallway. I have to admit that I bristled at the sight of her. *She knew!* She knew that Jessica was fine and never said a word. What a nerve.

"Sure." I said flatly. She came in, looked at the Chief and Barbara uncomfortably and we all stayed in silence for what seemed like years. Mrs. Philmore was standing in a designer, navy blue pantsuit and pearls, looking the perfect mix of haughty and pretty. Finally, she spoke, "I just want to thank you for your help. You saved her life." I simply nodded and let the silence remain in the air. She looked at me uncomfortably, and then finally said, "I'm sorry. I never meant to involve you in this way." I continued my blank stare. It was a tactic that I learned a long time ago by working with students, as long as I didn't fill the uncomfortable silence, ultimately *they* would.

"I'm sure that you must have questions," she said, breathing in an air of pompous pride.

"A couple," I said. It was sarcastic, and I couldn't help it. Let's see *her* hanging a hundred feet from her pearls and Liz Claibornes, "Jessica says that you knew."

"Not when I came to see you," she said, acquiring an almost defiant air, "It wasn't until after...the next morning I had my driver take me to Jensen's. I ran into her on the boardwalk." So that explained how she got there without a car.

"Why didn't you tell me? Us?" I said looking over at the Chief. She paused briefly and then said, "You don't know what hell he has put me through," she was referring to Mr. Philmore, I assumed.

"So this was a plot against your ex-husband?" I asked, surprised at my own moxy. It was bold to ask such a personal question.

"It wasn't planned, it just played out that way. Again, I'm sorry."

This time, the Chief interjected, "If it wasn't planned, why was your room at the inn torn-up?" *Good one, Chief! I never liked this woman!*

"I was in a hurry, that's all," she said.

"And it would be more traumatic for your husband if he thought that you were abducted, too." The Chief pursued, with a knowing grin.

"Did I break any laws?" Mrs. Philmore responded coldly.

"Hampering an investigation, for one. But we'll deal with that later. Don't worry, I'll be in touch." With that, Mrs. Philmore nodded and proceeded out of the room.

"Susan," I called, using her first name that she only begrudgingly ever gave me in the first place, "I have one more question. Where were you all this time?" She stopped, turning back toward me but not looking at any of us, "I'd rather not say," she said, "Again, thank you." And she closed the door behind her. I looked at the Chief, "I thought it was a good question."

"It is," he responded, "I'll bet she was at home all the time. It's easy to pay a staff to lie for you." He paused and then said, "But Doug, I think you've had enough detective work for one day. I'm gonna give you a break and leave, too. I think visiting hours are almost over, anyway. I'll call you tomorrow at home so I can finish my final report. You will be at home, right?"

"Yeah," I responded, "I think I'll take it easy for a few days." The Chief winked and walked out of the room. After he left, Barbara kissed me again, and said goodnight as well, "I'm so glad that you're OK," she said.

"So, what do you think now?" I asked, "Did I overstep my boundaries?" Barbara paused thoughtfully, "I think that you're a caring man who wanted to help a troubled student. And *that's* what you did. I could have done without the hanging from the Ferris wheel and the hospital visit, but that's what you did."

"You didn't answer my question."

"There's a fine line between overstepping and

dedication, let's leave it at that." Barbara then leaned down and kissed me again.

Although I hated to see her go, I was exhausted. She kissed me gently and left for the night. I turned off the light with the button on my bedside and drifted off to sleep, thinking of all of the questions I had started with at the beginning of the day. Pretty much, everything had been answered. The psychic, the tattooed man (rest his soul), even my suspicions about Dirt.

I guess Sarah Borden was correct; she didn't have anything to do with Jessica's disappearance after all. I was satisfied with my deductive abilities and impressed with the fact that I had solved the "Jessica Philmore" case. Except for one thing, the anonymous e-mail. Who had sent that? I thought for a minute and ran a list of suspects through my head. Dirt? No. After some thought, I surmised that it was probably Dr. Andrews, Jessica's advisor. Although Jessica assured us that he didn't know any details, she said that they had discussed her "internship" options many times before. My bet was on him. Maybe I would approach him when I went back to campus. Campus. My crazy campus. I couldn't wait to get back.

The next morning, I was released by 11 and Barbara came to pick me up. She brought me some toiletries and some clothes and she packed up my few belongings in a couple of plastic grocery bags while I showered. Since my ankle was still tender, I enjoyed sitting in a geriatric shower chair and letting the hot water sooth my aching body. Although I was still sore, I was just fine and by 11:05, my release papers had been signed, and Barbara was wheeling me down the hospital's corridor in a wheelchair. As we waited for the elevator, a nurse who had helped me during the morning hours called after us, "Mr. Carter?" she called, not realizing my real name, "Mr. Carter?"

Barbara turned me around to face her, "Yes?" I said. She looked a bit embarrassed, and grabbed my hand, "I think you forgot something," she said smiling. She then closed my fingers around something as she turned and walked away. As I realized what it was, I burst out laughing. I was sitting in the middle of the Jersey Shore Medical Center holding my black thong in the palm of my hand. The thing had actually motivated me to get down from the Ferris wheel and had saved my life, but it hadn't saved me from the embarrassment after all.

THE END

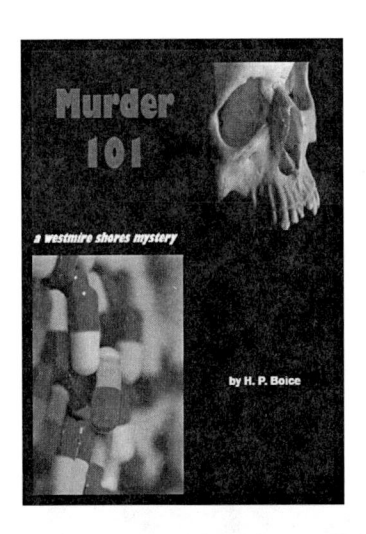

Don't miss Dean Doug's next lesson
Murder 101
Book 2 in *The Mystery 101 Series*

When a skull is dug-up on the Westmire College campus, Dean Doug investigates its origin. A mysterious clue leads him to the college's secret society, "Skull and Cross" and the discovery of a half-century-old secret. Meanwhile, the true identity of the body found on the beach in *Missing Persons 101* is revealed and Dean Doug uncovers a dangerous plot threatening the campus. Can he solve both mysteries before someone else is murdered?

A college administrator for over ten years, Heath P. Boice knows about college life. Heath received both regional and national recognition for his professional work in college administration, boasting over 50 publications and convention presentations. Heath holds a BA in Public Communications and a MS Ed in College Student Personnel and Counseling from the College of Saint Rose in Albany, NY, and a Doctorate in Education from Rutgers University, New Brunswick, NJ. This led him to a successful career as a college dean and instructor at both private and public schools, most recently as the Associate Vice President for Student Affairs at the Rochester Institute of Technology (RIT).

Before working in education, Heath worked as a news anchor, writer, producer, and feature talk show host in radio and television. When not working with college students or writing, Heath enjoys spending time with his wife and daughters. He also enjoys gardening, cooking, and reading... mostly mysteries. Visit his website at www.101mysteries.com

About Windstorm Creative
and our Readers' Club

Windstorm Creative was founded in 1989 to create a publishing house with author-centric ethics and cutting-edge, risk-taking innovation. Windstorm is now a company of more than ten divisions with international distribution channels that allow us to sell our books both inside the traditional systems and outside these paradigms, capitalizing on more direct delivery and non-traditional markets. As a result, our books can be found in grocery superstores as well as your favorite neighborhood bookstore, and dozens of other outlets on and off the Internet.

Windstorm is an independent press with the synergy and branding of a corporate publisher and an author royalty that's easily twice their best offer. We have continued to minimize returns without decreasing sales by publishing books that are timeless, as opposed to timely, and never back-listing.

Windstorm is constantly changing, improving, and growing. We are driven by the needs of our authors – hailing from ten different countries – and the vision of our critically-acclaimed staff. All of our books are created with the strictest of environmental protections in mind. Our approach to no-waste, no-hazard, in-house production, and stringent out-source scrutiny, assures that our goals are met whether books are printed at our own facility or an outside press.

Because of these precautions, our books cost more. And though we know that our readers support our efforts, we also understand that a few dollars can add up. This is why we began our Readers' Club. Visit our webcenter and take 20% off every title, every day. No strings. No fine print.

While you're at our site, preview or request the first chapter of any of our titles, free of charge.

Thank you for supporting an independent press.

Visit
www.WindstormCreative.com
for other excellent mystery titles